What Revenge Would He Extract for Her Moment of Resistance?

Laure stopped her struggle and stared at the bandit who held her prisoner until she had memorized every detail of his appearance. Perhaps he was interested only in ransom. She hoped desperately that this was the case.

To her amazement, the stranger burst out laughing. He raised her hand to his lips and ceremoniously saluted her. "You have nothing to fear from us, lady. Tell me, have I stolen anything from you yet?"

"I have nothing worth stealing," Laure replied sullenly.

"Oh, but you do," he contradicted her softly and lifted a fold of her riding habit between his fingers. "To a desperate man, this good velvet cloth is warmth." His hand went to the cameo pendant at her throat. "To a hungry man, this jewel is food." His fingers moved higher, and traced the curve of her lips. "And to a man who has been alone too long," he said, so softly that she could barely hear him, "these are warmth, and love, and all the joy that is forbidden him."

Laure could not make herself pull away from his touch. She felt as though she had been drawn into a new world where ordinary laws did not apply. This man might let her go without a word, or he might throw her across his saddle and carry her into the forest. But of one thing she was certain, this was no common robber.

Dear Reader,

We, the editors of Tapestry Romances, are committed to bringing you two outstanding original romantic historical novels each and every month.

From Kentucky in the 1850s to the court of Louis XIII, from the deck of a pirate ship within sight of Gibraltar to a mining camp high in the Sierra Nevadas, our heroines experience life and love, romance and adventure.

Our aim is to give you the kind of historical romances that you want to read. We would enjoy hearing your thoughts about this book and all future Tapestry Romances. Please write to us at the address below.

The Editors
Tapestry Romances
POCKET BOOKS
1230 Avenue of the Americas
Box TAP
New York, N.Y. 10020

Alliance of Love

Catherine Lyndell

A TAPESTRY BOOK
PUBLISHED BY POCKET BOOKS NEW YORK

An *Original* publication of TAPESTRY BOOKS

A Tapestry Book published by
POCKET BOOKS, a division of Simon & Schuster, Inc.
1230 Avenue of the Americas, New York, N.Y. 10020

ISBN: 0-671-49514-3

First Tapestry Books printing January, 1984

10 9 8 7 6 5 4 3 2 1

POCKET and colophon are registered trademarks of Simon & Schuster, Inc.

TAPESTRY is a trademark of Simon & Schuster, Inc.

Printed in the U.S.A.

Alliance
of
Love

Chapter One

At the summit of the hill Laure reined in her horse and turned to look back at the city. From this vantage point high in the forest she could look back down the main road, past terraced slopes of vineyards and the huddled buildings of the suburbs, to the roofs and spires of Vienna rising within the great wall that encircled the city. There had been a slight sprinkling of rain that morning, which cleared the air, and the city seemed to sparkle like a miniature toy city, newly washed and polished and set out for display.

In many ways, Laure thought, Vienna in 1825 was like a toy city. While people at home in England were building factories and arguing about the poor laws, the lighthearted Viennese seemed to think of nothing

1

but the latest waltz. She'd enjoyed the gaiety when she first came to visit her Austrian cousins, but lately it seemed rather cloying. The fresh, pine-scented breeze was a relief after the hothouse atmosphere of the city.

Laure turned away from the sight and let her horse amble on at its own, slow pace. She took a deep breath of the cool forest air and tugged her hat off. The hairpins came with it, and half of her pile of long, tawny gold hair floated free around her shoulders. She laughed and shook her head until she was surrounded by a golden cloud. The sense of freedom was wonderful! Josef would be angry with her for riding out without even a groom, but after the surprise of his proposal, she had needed to be alone to think.

Back in England, when she first met her Austrian cousins Josef and Julie, she had never dreamed matters would go so far. She had enjoyed showing them the sights of London, and their invitation to return to Vienna with them for a visit had seemed a heaven-sent way out of a situation that had grown daily more intolerable.

Laure urged the mare into a faster pace, as though riding faster could blow away the unhappy memories of that damp and dreary London spring. She reveled in the feeling of the breeze blowing through her hair and the sight of the tall pine trees stretching away from the road on both sides. This forest, on the very outskirts of Vienna, was so empty that she could fancy herself being in one of the enchanted woods of her old nurse's tales. If she were a silly, imaginative girl, like her cousin Julie, she could easily have thought that the furtive movements she glimpsed from time to time behind the trees were robbers or goblins, instead of forest birds and other little animals.

The mare was nervous about being so deep in the forest. Laure patted her neck and soothed her. They really should turn back soon. But it was so pleasant here! Laure let the mare amble on, choosing her own pace, and drifted back into a reverie in which she was hardly conscious of the subtle noises deep in the woods.

She had to admit that she had been at fault where Josef was concerned. She liked the dashing young officer and enjoyed the waltzes and galops, the hand kissing and the extravagant compliments that he lavished upon her. But her own heart had not been touched, and for a while she had honestly thought that he was being nice to her only because she was his cousin and a guest in his house. Even when his hints grew somewhat stronger, she had pretended not to understand them. The pretense of obliviousness had worked well enough for a while, but his impatience was growing clear. Soon she would have to make a decision: should she marry Josef, or go back to living with her sister's family in London? Neither alternative seemed tolerable.

A rustling sound behind her startled Laure. The horse jumped forward with a nervous start, and by the time Laure had calmed her, there was nothing to be seen in the bushes that lined the side of the road. They must have started a hare from its hiding place.

But the road itself had become narrower, was now hardly more than a bridle path. Laure frowned again. While she had been daydreaming, her horse must have wandered off the main road. There was scarcely room to turn on this thickly overgrown path. She decided to ride forward in the hope of finding a wide place where she could turn the nervous mare without the risk of backing her into thorny bushes. The poor beast was skittish enough already, and her nervousness was infecting Laure. Laure patted the horse's neck and urged her forward along the narrow path.

Once the mare was ambling along again, Laure's thoughts returned to Josef. The trouble was that she could not think of any good reason for refusing him. She liked him well enough, and she certainly had nothing to go back to in England. All the same, she had dreamed that love would be something more than the tepid friendship that she felt for Josef—some powerful, all-encompassing feeling that would sweep her away with an irresistible force.

Laure laughed aloud at her own fancies, startling two gray squirrels chattering in the branches. She had never felt anything like what she imagined. Few enough men had courted her, and before Josef, there'd been no one she even liked. Perhaps what she was looking for didn't even exist.

Suddenly Laure felt impatient with all the clinging restrictions of her life, from the trailing skirts she wore for riding to the trailing branches that impeded her progress along the path. Would they never come to a clear space? The woods seemed to be closing in round her with their slyly moving shadows and soft, unexplained noises. She glanced at the sky and realized that the increasing darkness was only partly due to the thick stand of trees. Evening was approaching, and if she continued to let the mare amble along this path, she would be benighted in the woods.

Laure gave a click of her tongue and touched the mare on the right shoulder with her whip. The horse broke into a canter and rounded the next curve in the path at a satisfying speed.

A crouching figure rose out of the underbrush, almost beneath the horse's legs. Laure caught sight of a soot-blackened face from which white teeth shone out in a terrifying grin. There was a flash of metal in the hand coming up from the man's waist.

The mare neighed and reared. Laure felt an instant of sick terror as images rose and fell before her—the black face, pine-tree tops silhouetted against the sky, the knife in the robber's hand, the trees again. She felt herself slipping backward and threw her weight forward onto the horse's neck. The mare sidestepped and floundered momentarily in the soft dirt by the side of the path. Laure brought her whip down with all her strength and simultaneously kicked hard with her left leg. The mare collected herself and bounded forward with a tremendous burst of speed. Branches whipped Laure's face in passing and she had all she could do to keep her seat and hold on to the reins. She clung awkwardly to the horse's neck and ducked her head, expecting every minute to feel the robber's knife buried in her back. Every shadow along the path became another crouching figure in her imagination.

Around the next curve the path widened, and within moments Laure saw with surprise that they were on the main road again, having followed a winding circle through the woods. She dared not risk a glance behind her to see whether there were other robbers on her trail. The terrified mare needed no more urging to fly up the hill toward the safety of the city walls. Were those hoofbeats behind them?

She looked back and saw that the road was clear behind them. But she was afraid to stop now. She raised her whip and urged the exhausted horse into one last burst of speed. Once over the hill, they would be in sight of Vienna.

There was a rustling of branches, and like a nightmare two mounted men appeared in front of her.

Their horses blocked Laure's path, and for a moment she was in danger of riding full tilt into them. She tried desperately to turn the mare, but the thick stands of trees on either side gave her no way around these new bandits. The mare neighed and reared up in the air, pawing with her forefeet and almost losing her balance at the sudden change of direction.

"It's the wrong one, you fool!" shouted one of the masked men to the other in German. He reached for her horse's bridle and forced the terrified creature down with a cruel twist of his hand.

"Take your hand from my reins!" Laure shouted. She brought her riding crop down in a stinging slash aimed at the bandit's face, but he dodged and the blow fell across his shoulders. Before she could deliver a second blow, he caught her hand and forced her to drop the whip.

It was over in a matter of seconds. Laure's horse stood with her head down, panting and covered with dust. Laure felt sick and dizzy. Her wrist ached where the bandit grasped it. Her own heartbeat sounded loud in the sudden silence.

One of the masked men sat on his horse at a distance of several yards. The other was beside her, keeping firm hold on her bridle with one hand and on her wrist with the other. Laure sat as straight as she could and gave him a defiant stare. Inwardly, she was terrified of what they might do to her. Julie had whispered stories of the masterless men who turned bandits. . . .

No. They wanted money—that was all. Laure shut her mind to any other possibility.

The silence stretched on till she thought she would scream from the tension. She stared at the bandit who held her prisoner until she had memorized every detail of his appearance.

The upper half of his face was obscured by a black silk mask with slits for eyeholes, and the lower part by a full, honey-colored beard. His clothes were of a cut she had never seen before. A long black velvet tunic that reached to the hips was decorated with silver embroidery and ornate silver buttons. Below that, he wore dark knitted pantaloons, which were tucked into boots of soft black leather.

The velvet tunic was slashed where her blow had struck him. Laure saw him look down at the damage and shivered in fear. What revenge would he extract for her moment of resistance?

Perhaps they were interested in only ransom. She hoped desperately that this was the case.

"Herren," she addressed them in careful German, "as you see, I am a poor woman, with no jewels to give you. Would it not be better to let me go on my way?"

To her amazement, the bandit burst out laughing. He raised her hand to his lips and ceremoniously saluted her. "You have nothing to fear from us, m'lady," he said. "We do not wage war on women, or take their . . . jewels."

Laure suppressed a start of amazement at his voice. She had been expecting the rough dialect of a peasant, but this man spoke as well as any of the emperor's courtiers.

His lips just grazed the back of her hand and left her shivering with new sensations. She felt as though she had been pitchforked into a new world where ordinary laws did not apply. This man might let her go without a word, or he might throw her across his

7

saddle and carry her into the forest. Either outcome seemed equally likely. The one thing she was certain of was that he was not a common robber.

The other rider drew near, and there was a muttered colloquy, which Laure strained her ears to hear. She caught the words "emperor's messenger . . . papers . . . dusk . . . ," and then the other man gave an emphatic warning that she could not hear, though she judged from his lowered tones and his gestures that it had something to do with herself. She was relieved when her captor threw up his free hand and laughed as if in acquiescence.

He turned back to Laure with a courtly bow. "Your pardon, m'lady. I apologize for the necessity to detain you. Will you wait in the forest with me?"

The dark woods surrounding the road seemed to have crept closer and grown even murkier, and Laure felt new terror at the thought of losing herself in their shadows.

"My—my relatives are expecting me," she told him. "If I am not back soon, they will send search parties." He could not know that it was a vain threat. No one knew where she had gone.

He bowed again, apparently unmoved by the threat. "A thousand apologies," he murmured. "It will only be for a very short while, m'lady, and—." The pause was significant. His hand lightly encircled her wrist, and his fingers caressed the bruises he had given her only minutes earlier. "It would grieve me excessively to employ force." He dropped her hand, and Laure felt colder without that touch. "Do me the honor of accompanying me of your own will?"

As he spoke, he handed the reins of her horse to the other rider and dismounted. He stood at her stirrup and joined his hands to make a step for her. "It will be necessary to lead the horses . . . ," he murmured, so softly that she had to bend down to hear.

To dismount, Laure had to rest one hand on his shoulder to steady herself. Although she stepped from his joined hands to the road in one swift motion, the second of intimate contact set her cheeks flaming. A touch from this—this nobody, this bandit—had the power to disturb her more than Josef's embraces. The thought itself was disturbing. She put it away from her.

Standing in the dusty road, she realized that they were almost of a height. The superb black horse he rode, a full eighteen hands high, had disguised the fact from her. Now that they stood facing one another, his eyes behind the black mask level with hers—and his lips with hers—Laure felt herself mesmerized by those smiling lips above the full, corn-colored beard. She could look at nothing else.

He reached out to grasp her arm and Laure jerked away as though she had been struck. An ironical smile flitted across the bandit's lips.

"Forgive me, m'lady. I meant only to guide you." With a gesture he indicated a narrow passage between the trees at the side of the road, half-disguised by overhanging branches. He lifted the largest branch and indicated that she should precede him into the wood.

The path was even narrower than the one she'd been on before, and the branches were so low overhead that she had to duck from time to time. Stinging wisps of green needles passed across her face, and her feet sank deep in the brown carpet of dead pine needles underneath. But the trail was clearly marked and she had no difficulty in following it to a small clearing.

9

The clearing was little more than an open circle around the fallen log of a gigantic tree. Soft needles carpeted the ground, and hundreds of tall pine trees grew all around the circle, forming a mysterious curtain of shadows and silences. The sky seemed as far away as if they were at a bottom of a well.

Laure knew that they were only a few hundred yards from the road, but they seemed to have entered into another world. She could not even glimpse the road from here, and if a branch fell across the narrow path, she might never find her way out.

The bandit came up softly behind her and took the reins of her horse from her hand. He tethered both horses to a convenient tree at the edge of the clearing. While he was busy, Laure sat down on the log and spread the skirts of her riding habit about her with an internal sigh of relief. It was a tricky business to walk in one of these trailing habits, and it had not been made easier by the necessity to guide her horse and keep the overhanging branches out of her face. She pushed the tangled strands of hair away from her face with one hand.

The bandit threw himself down on the carpet of pine needles with every appearance of ease. "Ah, now we can be comfortable!" he remarked, exactly as if he were a gentleman who had just escorted her to a picnic spot. The impudence tickled Laure's fancy, and she tried hard not to laugh.

His eyes assessed the smile tugging at the corner of her lips. "Ah, that's better!" he exclaimed. "You are beginning to forgive me." He rolled over and propped his back against the log. His pose was so relaxed that Laure began to wonder if she might run away. She made a stealthy movement to get her feet under her and measured the distance to her horse.

"I wouldn't try it," remarked the bandit. Laure was startled. Did the man have eyes in the back of his head? "I have tied your horse with a special knot known only to me. You would never get her loose in time." His hands fiddled with a branch of pine needles, plaiting and unplaiting it in intricate patterns. Laure watched his hands and the back of his head, and listened to the hypnotically slow voice with its trace of an accent. "Do you treasure your freedom? You are free now to walk about the clearing. If you behave foolishly, we would both regret the necessity of tying you up with the same knot that I used on your horse."

Laure swallowed and sat back. For all his courtly speech, she did not doubt for a moment that the bandit would carry out his threat.

"Besides," he added, "there is not the least reason for you to put yourself to the trouble of escaping. It is only to detain you for a little, little hour. One hour in the woods, m'lady—is that so terrible?"

He looked up at her with a knowing smile. "Come now! We shall entertain each other with stories for an hour, and then you shall go free—you have my word on it."

"The word of a common thief!" Laure exclaimed.

"The word of a gentleman of the road," her companion corrected her.

"Oh, I see," Laure said sarcastically. "That makes all the difference. I can't tell you how reassured I feel." But she did, however illogically, feel better for the promise. She drew the skirts of her riding habit about her and sat clutching her knees, staring into the green depths of the wood.

After a few moments of silence the bandit laughed again. "Well, if you will not talk, m'lady, I must, or I

11

will go to sleep. I shall tell you the story of my life. I was born of poor but honest parents—."

"They must be deeply ashamed of your present career," Laure interrupted.

The bandit appeared to consider this for a moment. "No, I don't think so," he said at last. "After all, it is not as if I had chosen to work for a living. My people count that disgrace indeed!"

The note of irony in his voice distracted Laure from her private fears. She propped her chin in her hand and studied the reclining figure of the bandit. "I don't understand!" she exclaimed. "You talk like an educated man. You are strong and healthy. Why are you leading this shameful life?"

"Perhaps there is a price on my head?" The bandit laughed and began another story. "I was tilling my fields one day when the unprincipled duke rode me down on his horse. Animated by a manly desire for revenge, I leaped at his throat and savagely killed him with my—with my—what the devil do peasants carry, anyway? With my flail, or hoe, or something of the sort. Thereafter I fled into the woods and adopted the miserable existence in which you see me now."

"You don't look very miserable," Laure pointed out. "Where did you steal those buttons? They must be worth a lot."

The bandit sighed. "You persist in seeing me as a common thief. Tell me, m'lady, have I stolen anything from you?"

"I don't have anything worth stealing."

"Oh, but you do," the bandit contradicted her softly. He sat beside her on the log and lifted a fold of her riding habit between his fingers. "To a desperate man, this good velvet habit is warmth." His hand went to the cameo pendant at her throat. "To a hungry man, this jewel is food." But it was the line of her throat he caressed. Laure could not make herself pull away from the delicate touch. What use was it, anyway? She was his prisoner.

His fingers moved higher, and traced the curve of her lips. "And to a man who has been alone too long," he said, so softly that she could barely hear him, "these are warmth, and love, and all the joy that is forbidden him."

His face was so near hers that she could count the gold hairs in his beard and mustache. He slipped one hand behind her neck and tilted her head forward to meet his.

The warm touch of his lips sent tremors of excitement through her whole body. He caressed her cheek with one hand and pressed her to him with the other. She could feel his hand through the heavy velvet of her habit, molding her body to his. Nothing existed but the moment.

The sound of drumming hooves, a horseman riding fast on the main road, echoed through the trees. She opened her eyes again and saw the black silk of his mask. Reality struck her like a deluge of cold water. While this common robber kept her prisoner in the woods, what would his men do to the next unfortunate traveler?

She twisted her head away from his and drew in breath to shout a warning. "Ah, no!" he said in an undertone. Inexorable fingers clamped on the back of her neck and forced her back to him. He stopped her mouth with his own.

The second kiss was as ferocious as the first had been gentle, tinged with the power of the battlefield. Through the blood drumming in her ears, she could hear sounds of struggle, a horse neighing wildly, shots fired. His lips roved over her face and left her no breath or strength to fight. He did not release her until she ceased her struggles and lay limp in his arms, eyes half-closed, surrendered to him.

Heavy footsteps crashed through the trees. Laure felt herself released. She fell back against the log and sat up quickly. The bodice of her habit had become disarranged. She lowered her head and busied herself with tucking her scarf back into place.

Something heavy was dropped in the leaves at her feet. "Here you are, master!" said a rough voice.

Laure steeled herself to look up, expecting to see the blood-stained body of the poor soul who had been stopped on the road. Instead, there was only a shapeless leather mass. It took her a moment to recognize it as a pair of saddlebags, all tangled in their straps.

Two men stood at a respectful distance behind the saddlebags, waiting for their master's orders. One was the rider who had first stopped her horse; the other, the man with the soot-blackened face who had frightened her in the woods.

The bandit leader was watching her face. "Ah, I see you know Jansci!" he remarked at her recoil from this apparition. He studied the men through the eye slits of his mask. "I have a strange feeling, Jansci, that you and this lady have met before. Could it have been your carelessness that frightened her into galloping down the main road at such a pace that we took her for the emperor's courier?"

Jansci's response was in a language that Laure could not understand.

"Speak German!" the leader rapped out. "It is discourteous to our guest—and to the other member of our party," he added, with a bow to the third man.

Laure's brain, temporarily paralysed by fear and uncertainty, clicked back on. One of the band was Austrian, then. But the other two—what were they? Slavs? She had never heard anything like this language.

Jansci pulled off his cap and mumbled that the lady had near ridden him down; so she had, and scared him worse than he'd scared her!

"Good!" said the bandit. "You deserve worse than a fright for your carelessness. Apologize to the lady."

Jansci came forward and bowed to the ground, muttering apologies in a rough German so heavily accented that Laure could barely understand him. She saw that under the mask of soot, he was only a boy whose beard had not even started yet.

Only when the formal apology was over did the bandit turn his attention to the prize that lay before him. He and the Austrian went through the saddlebags quickly, examining the papers one by one and thrusting them back. He stopped when he came to a thick envelope bordered in red and black scrollwork and stamped with gold seals.

"Here we are!" He slipped a sharp knife under the gold seal and lifted it from the paper. The large hands showed an astonishing delicacy as he unfolded the crackling paper and spread it out on his knees. After a few moments' perusal of the document, he nodded with satisfaction and folded it up again. Before resealing it, he drew another paper from the recesses of his black velvet tunic and inserted that into the package. The completed package was then slipped into the saddlebags between other papers. He stood up and stretched, showing the relief of a man who has just completed a delicate operation, and motioned to the Austrian to take up the saddlebags again.

"Good!" The masked man stooped and slung the bags across his shoulder. "Our friend has hardly been tied up long enough to give him the cramp. He should ride all the faster for this little rest."

Both men laughed at this joke. Laure felt a wave of relief at the news that the courier was not dead. The bandit leader saw her relieved expression and laughed even more uproariously. "The lady thinks we are murderers!" He bowed in her direction. "No, m'lady. We leave killing to our opponents. Our ends can be achieved by peaceful means."

"I suppose you call it peaceful to kidnap innocent travelers!" Laure exclaimed before she could stop herself.

The bandit turned to his men. "Go on, set the courier on his road!" he commanded. "What are you standing around here for? Do you need me to hold your hands?"

The two men slunk off toward the road with hangdog looks, and the bandit turned back to Laure. "Now, m'lady. Can you truly say you have been harmed by us?"

As he spoke, he held out his hand to assist her to rise from the log. The gesture was as courtly as if he had been inviting her to dance with him.

"Not yet." Laure knew she sounded like a sulky child. She gathered her trailing skirts and stood up without taking his hand.

A smile creased the bandit's lips. "You sound disappointed! What sort of harm did you anticipate?"

"Oh, you are intolerable!" Laure could feel herself blushing. She turned her back on him and marched across the clearing to where her horse was tethered. The dignity of her move was somewhat hampered by the fact that her skirt caught on a snag at the edge of the wood and she had to tug herself loose.

"Allow me." The bandit was on his knees beside her. With patient fingers he worked the velvet skirt free of the thorns that had captured it.

From the road there came the sound of a wild halloo and a rope thwacking against a horse's rump. Clattering hoofbeats echoed down the main road and faded away. The bandit gave a rueful laugh. "I am afraid Jansci was a little overenthusiastic in speeding our other guest on his way." With a last tug on a recalcitrant branch, Laure's skirt came free. "There now, you see? No harm done." His mocking smile challenged her to read the double meaning in his statement.

"I'm going now!" Laure announced defiantly, as soon as she was free. She fumbled with the knot in her horse's harness and looked sidewise over her shoulder, challenging him to stop her.

"Of course you are," he agreed. "Allow me to assist you?" His fingers made nothing of the knot that had baffled her. The harness fell away, and he gathered up the horse's reins in one hand and offered them to her.

Laure stared at his face for a long minute. The black face mask effectively concealed all expression. Finally she took the proffered reins and started down the path to the road without a word. A crackling sound behind her warned her that he was following.

She was startled to realize how the shadows had lengthened while they sat in the clearing. Her eyes had gradually accustomed themselves to the twilight. Now she raised her eyes to the sky and saw that the first stars were twinkling. The main road was visible only as a pale blur through the trees. Soon it would be quite dark.

At the edge of the road, she stopped and looked about for a log or stump from which she could mount her horse. The bandit moved forward. "May I help you?"

She nodded and waited for him to form a stirrup with his hands. Instead, he grasped her about the waist and lifted her into the saddle as lightly as if she had been a feather. His hands lingered for a moment in just the shadow of a caress; then he stepped back and swung himself into the saddle of his own horse.

"I shall ride with you as far as the outskirts." He announced.

"There's no need for that," she said in an ungrateful tone. "I can find my way quite well."

"My apologies, m'lady." The bandit's voice was suspiciously meek. "I was well brought up, you see. I cannot possibly allow a lady to go home alone in the dark."

He waved his hand and the other two men mounted behind them. They rode down the hill and turned aside at the bottom, into a winding road that Laure had never explored.

"This also is a way to the city," he explained before she could question him, with a flash of white teeth in the darkness. "You will understand that a gentleman of my profession does not generally travel by the main road."

They rode on in silence until the first scattered dwellings of the *faubourgs* that surrounded the city were within view. There were a thousand questions Laure wanted to ask, but the consciousness of their silent followers kept her quiet.

At the first sight of the houses she reined in her

horse and held out one hand. "I—thank you for your escort," she said. "Farewell."

The bandit kissed her hand, and Laure felt a tremor of pleasure run through her at the pressure of those warm, firm lips on the back of her hand. "In Austria," he corrected her, "we say, 'Auf Wiedersehen'—'until we meet again.'"

"We're hardly likely to do that!" Laure could not keep a trace of regret from creeping into her voice.

The bandit laughed. "Who knows? Fate is mysterious. You may meet me when you least expect it. Until then, you may tell your friends that you have passed an afternoon with the famous Csikos. I assure you they will be impressed."

The confidence in his tone irritated Laure beyond all bearing. "You sound as though you had done me a great favor by kidnapping me for half a day!" she said. "I assure you, I am hardly likely to boast of such an encounter!" She kicked her horse into a trot and rode away without a backward look.

Chapter Two

By the time Laure reached the stone-faced town-house that was the Schulenbergs' city residence, it was quite dark. The groom whose services she had refused stood on the front steps, arms folded, in a patient attitude that suggested he had been standing just so since she rode away that afternoon. Laure felt a pang of guilt at the sight of the white-haired, stolid figure. Old Hansl had been a favored servant of the Schulenbergs' since his boyhood. He would regard it as an affront to the family's honor and his own that a young lady guest of the house had been allowed to ride out alone.

"Don't scold, Hansl," Laure begged, as she accepted his aid in slipping down from the saddle. "I needed to be alone a little while."

An unwilling smile tugged at the old groom's lips. "For an *Engländerin*, Miss Laure, you've got the true Vienna accent for sure! One sees that your blessed mother was a true Schulenberg. Never let you forget her homeland, did she?"

For a moment Laure thought wistfully of her mother, who had died two years earlier, and then replied, "No, Hansl, and I am only sorry that I waited so long to make this visit. She would have loved to come with me."

Hansl spoke with the freedom allowed an old and valued servant. "But it was not good to go alone, Miss Laure. Do you know there are bandits in the woods outside the city wall?"

Laure turned away, but not swiftly enough to conceal the light in her eyes. "Yes, Hansl, I know. I am sorry—I will tell Josef not to be angry with you, for it was all my fault. Anyway, you see I have come to no harm, so there is nothing to worry about."

Hansl took the reins of the horse from her hands and plodded off toward the stables, grumbling and mumbling to himself in his practiced undertone, just loud enough to let the master and mistress know he was displeased, and just low enough that they could not catch his actual words and punish him for insolence. "No harm done, English missy, says. Huh! That's to be seen. Old Hansl isn't so old that he doesn't know what it means when a girl slips out alone and comes back with her eyes shining and her lips bruised red. Been slipping out to meet a lover, Miss Laure has—her that's meant to be young master's lady. Huh! Modern goings-on."

Laure caught enough of the mutterings that they produced the desired effect. She frowned after Hansl's retreating figure and caught her lower lip between her teeth. She couldn't quite catch the words, but it was clear he was still upset by her mild adventure. Would Josef be equally minded to scold? Well, so much the better, if it made him see she was no wife for him.

Laure straightened her back and looped the long folds of her riding habit over her wrist, unaware that a decision had been made in the last few minutes.

"Cousin Laure!" Josef came down the stairs as soon as her step sounded in the hall. "You're unhurt? We have been so worried!" He took her two hands in his and smiled down at her. A straight, slim, dark-haired young man, he was the very figure of romance in his close-fitting dress uniform of dark blue with loops of gold braid.

Laure felt disloyal for noticing that Josef had to stand on the step to smile down at her like that. Unbidden, her mind returned to the image of a gold-bearded man whose eyes, behind his black silk mask, were exactly on a level with her own. She pulled her hands free and answered more sharply than she had meant to do.

"As you see, Josef, I am quite well—only somewhat travel stained!" She forced a smile. "I—I rode farther than I meant to, and lost my way in the woods when I tried to take a shorter road back to the city."

"You should not ride alone," Josef said, "and particularly not out beyond the city gate, Laure! There are still bandits in the woods, you know—this is not a tame country, like your England." He laid a hand on her arm as Laure attempted to sidle up the stairs past him. "Laure, dearest, you must not put me through such agony as I have known this last hour, imagining you slain—or worse."

"I don't think there is much worse than being

slain!" Laure snapped, and regretted her flash of ill temper the next instant. But Josef's compliments and caresses were irritating her as they'd never done before. She suppressed her irritation with an act of will. "I suffered nothing worse than getting some twigs in my hair and dust on my habit, as you can see, and now I should like very much to wash the dirt off me! Can a maid be found to bring a can of hot water to my room, do you think?"

Her deliberately prosaic tone brought Josef's dramatic flights back to earth, as she had hoped. "Of course, dearest. But do make haste, will you not? We are invited to the Mecklenburgs' tonight."

Laure smiled and nodded and finally slipped past Josef to ascend the narrow stairs that led to her bedchamber on the fourth floor. She was almost at the top when Josef called after her.

"Wear your blue velvet gown! We will make a fine pair!"

Josef's sister, Julie, was hanging out at the door of the room she and Laure shared, insecurely covered in a floating negligee of finely embroidered white muslin decorated with knots of pink satin ribbons. She giggled at these words.

"I never know whether Josef's impulses are aesthetic or romantic," Laure remarked as she entered the room, hoping to stave off another discussion on the folly of riding out alone. "In any case, it is too hot for blue velvet, don't you think? I see no reason why I should swelter just because Josef must wear his dress uniform."

She stood in the middle of the room, arms raised, while a maid unhooked the tight bodice of her riding habit. The ties at the waist were loosened and she stepped out of the skirt, leaving the heavy folds of fabric to rustle to the floor. "Ah, that's better!" She dropped her undergarments on top of the skirt and unpinned the heavy loops of her hair while she waited for the maids to carry up the cans of hot water to fill the bath. Julie curled up on a corner of the tester bed, arms wrapped around her knees, and watched Laure with the bright-eyed curiosity of a small forest animal.

"How did you get so dusty?" she asked. "Did you fall off your horse?"

In counterpoint to her question, the maid who had undressed Laure picked up her riding skirt and shook it out before folding it. A cloud of white dust rose from the folds of fabric, and the astringent scent of pine trees floated through the room, recalling to Laure's mind for an instant the cool forest hills.

"Yes, I—." Too late Laure realized that if she admitted dismounting from her horse, she would have to explain who had helped her remount. "No, but I took a path through the woods for a little while, thinking I could get home faster, and then I caught my hair on some branches and had to stop to put it up again."

"You were lucky," Julie observed. "Do you know—."

"Don't tell me," Laure sighed. "There are bandits in the woods."

Julie regarded her with surprise. "Tell me about the bandits. Are they very handsome? As handsome as Josef? But then they can't be, can they? For I suppose bandits wear rags and tatters, and Josef and his friends look so fine in uniform. I'm thinking of having my next riding habit cut *à la hussarde*, with gold soutache and three rows of braid round the skirt—so—and a line of little, little gold buttons all the way from my waist to the neck." In her excitement at describing this

dream creation, Julie jumped off the bed and pirouetted around the room, gesturing around her slim
body until Laure could almost see the coveted riding
habit. She laughed at Julie's antics and stepped into
the tub, now full of steaming water, and sighed with
delight as the hot water soothed aching muscles. She
closed her eyes and leaned against the wooden rim of
the tub, but Julie's voice chattered on.

"How many of them were there?"

"Oh, do stop romancing, Julie. Do you really think
I met bandits a mile from the gates of Vienna?" Laure
was glad she could phrase her denial as a question.

"N-o," Julie admitted, and Laure gave a sigh of
relief. "But you could have! Some of them are very
daring—especially Csikos." Her voice dropped to a
whisper on the last word.

Laure looked up sharply. Csikos! That had been the
name mentioned by the stranger.

"Who is this Csikos?" she asked.

Julie giggled. "Why, Laure, have you been with us
for two months and not heard of Csikos? He is the
Hungarian bandit who has been stopping the emper-
or's couriers, slipping broadsides for Hungarian
freedom into the diplomatic bag—oh, all sorts of
mischief!" She lowered her voice again. "They say he
is very handsome—and very gallant! Imagine, Laure;
how romantic if he had captured you!"

Laure scrubbed so vigorously that her skin turned a
bright pink. "I don't see that there would be anything
romantic in being captured by a smelly peasant who
probably had fleas and hadn't washed in half a year."

Julie gave an irritated sigh. "Laure, you English are
so dull! Don't you have any sense of adventure?"

"No," Laure lied. She stood up in the bath and let a
maid wrap her in a linen towel. The chilly air raised

bumps of gooseflesh on her bare skin. It had been cool like this under the pines. She shivered involuntarily at the memory of a cool, caressing touch along the line of her throat, and rubbed herself with the coarse linen as though to rub away the touch of Csikos's hands.

Julie had given up on the topic of romantic bandits. She went on chattering, retailing the latest gossip about the guests they were to meet that night at the Mecklenburgs'. Laure answered at random whenever Julie paused for breath, and wandered off into her own thoughts while her clothes were put on her. The light silk chemise rustled over her head and molded itself to her form like a lover's caress. The stays that her maid laced tight hugged her slender waist like the hard strength of Csikos's hands when he had lifted her to her saddle. She stared into the greenish, cracked oval mirror on the dressing table while her hair was braided and coiled, and did not recognize the wide-eyed, dreamy girl who stared back at her. Large dark eyes, lips full and red and bruise-ripe, pale cheeks and a floating crown of gold hair, and a faraway stare, as though she were looking at something invisible to normal sight. She looked, Laure thought, like a medieval lady out of some dim legend—not like a sensible English girl on a visit to her cousins.

The dress Julie chose for her reinforced that feeling. Of dark gold satin, very severely cut, with wide flowing sleeves and a square neckline, it could have been worn by a medieval lady staring from her castle walls. The heavy satin rustled when she moved, and the folds of the skirts rippled like water with the sun on it. When she walked, she felt as though she were moving through water, slow and graceful as a dream.

Still wrapped in that dream, she hardly heard Julie's chatter, or noticed Josef's start of displeasure when

26

they descended the narrow stairs and he saw that she had not dressed to please him, after all. The short carriage ride to the Mecklenburgs' grand house seemed like an extension of the dream.

The long ballroom, specially constructed to accommodate the dizzying revolutions of waltzing couples, was brilliant with clusters of candles and torcheres down both long sides. The walls were mirrored, so that the candles were reflected back on themselves in an infinity of reflected rooms, making the ballroom seem as big as the Prater deer park. The ladies' dresses and their brilliant jewels, the men's bright officers' uniforms and the occasional counterpoint of black evening dress made a symphony of color that rivaled the best productions of the orchestra the Mecklenburgs had hired for the evening.

Always before, Laure had been stiff and unsure of herself, very aware of her height and of her reputation for English reserve. But this evening everything seemed to have been made easy for her. She laughed at the young men who clustered around her and Julie—how could she ever have been shy of these popinjays? She laughed at them, and they loved it; and quite half a dozen transferred their attentions from the little, black-haired Schulenberg to her English cousin. Laure waltzed from one end of the ballroom to the other, royally sent her courtiers for champagne and cakes, ruthlessly sent them off to dance with other girls when she was tired of them.

"The English duckling has become a swan," remarked Frau Mecklenburg, watching Laure's triumphant progress. "Is she so happy to be courted by Josef Schulenberg?"

The Princess Melnikoff waved a fan composed in equal parts of feathers and rubies, to match her parure of the Melnikoff rubies. "They say she rides alone in the woods," she answered obliquely. It did not take long for gossip to spread in Vienna.

"Ah, so she has a lover. I wonder who?"

But Laure did not seem to be favoring any of her partners with special attention, and the ladies were frustrated in their desire for further gossip.

After some hours of waltzes and galops, polkas and lancers, Laure began to grow bored with her dream. The air of glittering unreality that hung over the evening was as insubstantial—and as unsatisfying—as the spun-sugar creations that graced Frau Mecklenburg's supper table. Laure nibbled at a sugar rose when the company sat down to supper, and listened with half an ear to the boy beside her, who compared her eyes to topazes and her hair to golden silk. There was something missing from the evening—and the worst of it was that she couldn't say what.

When they returned to the ballroom, the French windows had been opened, and beyond them could be seen a paved stone terrace decorated with tubs of flowers from the Mecklenburgs' forcing houses. The heavy, sweet odor of lilies and tuberoses stole through the room, carrying with it a suggestion of moonlight and dew on the grass. Laure felt restless, charged with energy, yet tired of dancing with these overpolished young nobles. She glanced around the room, seeking for she knew not what.

He stood in the doorway that led from the supper room, also glancing about the room as if in search of something. As tall as she was herself, he had glittering blue eyes and a tawny beard. Recognizing him, Laure noticed that he had changed his black mask and tunic for the green coat and cream-colored pantaloons of an officer in the Imperial Guard.

What a disguise! Laure laughed softly to herself. All evening her partners had been filling her ears with stories of the daring bandit Csikos. But who would suspect that he was so daring as to appear at Frau Mecklenburg's ball, dressed like an officer in the service of the emperor he defied?

The Gypsy violinist who led the orchestra began a plaintive, throbbing melody designed to steal into the ears of the chattering crowd returning from supper and remind them of the pleasures of the dance. He fixed his eyes on the tall English girl with the crown of gold braids and was pleased to see her face light up as his music began. Concentrating furiously on her expression, he swayed in time to his own music and spun a seductive tune that sang of moonlit nights in the forests, of deep, cold rivers and shaded grassy banks, of wild dancing about the leaping flames of a Gypsy fire. The English girl's parted lips and starry eyes inspired him to new heights of melody.

Laure never knew he played for her. As couples around the ballroom hushed their gossip and touched hands for the after-supper waltz, she rose from her seat and walked toward the man she knew as Csikos. The vast, glittering room seemed to have dimmed to the half-light of a dusky forest glade. Somewhere there was a bird singing, and the scent of lilies was strong on the night air.

He moved toward her through the dancing crowd. His hands were firm and warm about her waist, and his eyes were level with hers. She stepped backward to match his step and found herself turning in a slow, sweet waltz.

They were by the opened French windows. He led her through and they danced on the terrace. The night breezes caressed her cheek and lifted a stray tendril of hair along her neck. Their steps matched so perfectly that she felt as though she was floating in his arms.

"You're mad to come here," she whispered.

A deep chuckle was her only answer.

"What if someone else recognizes you?" But she knew that could not happen. This night was magic, and it was right that he should have come to claim her. Nothing would interfere with that magic.

The Gypsy violin's sweet, sobbing melody was lost in a crash of sound as the rest of the orchestra swung into the galop that followed the first waltz. The slow, enchanted turning ceased and they stood still on the terrace. He did not drop his arms to release her at the end of the dance. She could feel his chest rising and falling against hers, as though he had just run a race. Her own blood was pounding in her ears so loudly that she thought he must hear the drumbeat in her veins. His arms slid around her and pulled her so close to him that her breasts were scratched by the gold braid on his coat.

Laure sank into his embrace as if this moment was what she'd been waiting for since they stepped out into the garden. Perhaps it was. His hands roved over her body at will, and she did nothing to stop them. A detached corner of her mind wondered at her passivity. But she didn't want to stop him. She wanted him to touch her all over. His hands were molding her into a new shape, a being all fire and quicksilver, wonderfully alive. If he stopped touching her, she would no longer be so alive. She lifted her lips to meet his in a long kiss that took her breath away. Disjointed images flashed through her mind. The Gypsy women she'd seen encamped outside the city, lying down under the hedges with their men. The hedge behind them. His hands caressing the curve of her hips. The women again, whose shamelessness she'd never understood. His lips tracing fire down the line of her throat. His head bending lower as he traced the firm curve of her breasts, revealed by the low square neck of her bodice. His tongue flickering out and tantalizing the soft swells above the bodice.

In a corner of her mind Laure wondered what he would do next. Perhaps he would take her behind the hedge. Perhaps he would throw her over his black horse and ride away into the mountains. She clasped her arms about his neck and leaned against him, completely boneless, fluid, melting.

"So, Andrassy!"

The booming laugh was accompanied by a handclap on Csikos's shoulder that caused him to stumble against Laure. Swearing under his breath, he released her. Laure stared in wide-eyed exasperation at the man who had interrupted them. It was Baron von Staunitz, a German nobleman who was friendly with Metternich and, therefore, in high favor at the Austrian court.

Laure had never liked or felt comfortable around the baron. A tall, well-built man growing paunchy with middle age, he was popular with a certain segment of Viennese society and enjoyed an amazing success with ladies. But, behind his jovial smiles and hearty laugh, she was always uncomfortably aware of his keen, small eyes darting about the room, as if to assess the effect of his act. Once, he had taken her hand at a ridotto and flirted with her in an overfamiliar manner, which made the Viennese ladies squeal and slap at him with their fans. Laure had been revolted, and showed it. She sensed that he had never forgiven her, though his manner when they met was unfailingly polite.

Now he was laughing and exchanging gossip of the court with Csikos, whom he called Count Andrassy, and all but ignoring her. Under the circumstances, that, too, could have been considered polite. Laure knew she should take the chance to slip back into the ballroom and mingle with the other guests. But curiosity, and a dawning sense of betrayal, kept her rooted to the ground where she stood.

"So, Andrassy," the baron repeated. "Only today returned to the capital, and already you steal away the flower of all our ladies! No, no, my young friend, we cannot allow such acts of banditry within the emperor's own city!" As he spoke, his small eyes remained fixed on Andrassy's face with disquieting intensity.

The younger man laughed and threw up his hand, as if acknowledging a hit. "You dare speak of banditry, baron, when by such bold-faced means you attempt to separate me from this lady before I have properly met her?" He turned away from von Staunitz and bowed to Laure. "Allow me to introduce myself. Count Andrassy Istvan—you would say, 'Stephen Andrassy.' My rude companion here I do not introduce—he does not deserve it!" His voice was higher and lighter than Csikos's had been.

"No need," the baron interrupted, with a rumbling laugh. "Miss Standish and I are already acquainted. You must not think that time stands still when you are away, Andrassy! We who serve here at court have been busy with our own work." Again that measuring, sidelong glance, as if he expected Andrassy to make more than the surface meaning out of his words. But Laure was too confused and distressed to interpret the byplay between the two men. Count Andrassy! And it could be no pretense; the baron recognized him. Her fantasy that Csikos had dared to seek her out in the heart of the city died for the foolish girl's dream it was. Why should he risk his neck to follow up a chance encounter? And why should she care what a common bandit did? She ought to be glad that this young man was not an outlaw. She pressed suddenly cold hands to her burning cheeks. What must he think of her?

"Miss Standish." Count Andrassy grasped her reluctant fingers in a firm, warm grip and raised her hand to his lips. "You will favor me with the knowledge of your *Vorname?*"

"It seems Miss Laure has favored you with more than that already!" interrupted Baron van Staunitz with a guffaw. "Pretty fast going, my dear count, with a young lady whose name you did not even trouble to learn!"

"Laure." The count ignored von Staunitz, and Laure found it easy to do likewise. His voice lingered over the liquid syllables of her name, turning it into a caress. "A lovely name—for a lovely lady. And for how long do you mean to honor our city with your presence, Miss Laure Standish?"

Laure could have cried with vexation. To be wakened from a dream of being in Csikos's arms again, only to find herself subjected to the banal chitchat of yet another young nobleman, while the baron leered and winked at them both—it was too much! But this man's voice was definitely too high; and—now she looked carefully—wasn't he an inch or so shorter than Csikos? If she and Csikos had been of a height when she was wearing riding boots, she should be shorter than he now that she had put on her heelless gold satin slippers for the ball. But Stephen Andrassy's eyes gazed into hers at the same level.

She realized that the silence between them had

stretched out too far for any pretense of light social conversation. The baron, evidently tiring of his game, had moved off to pluck a flower from one of the tubs at the edge of the terrace.

"I—am sorry, sir," she stammered at last, "for my seeming inattention." Yet she could not forbear one last flicker of hope. "You are—your name is really Stephen Andrassy?"

"If it displeases you," the young man promised, "it shall be changed! What shall I be? Jakob, or Karl, or Hans, or Josef—no, not Josef; that is a name I could never abide!" He dropped to one knee before her with a theatrical flourish. "Come, lady, rechristen me. Wilhelm, or Friedrich, or Franz—no, better not to take the emperor's name, do you think? It might be thought of as unbecoming pride."

Laure could not help but laugh at his foolery. "Please rise," she begged him. "We are already conspicuous enough. It is only that—." She sought words to hedge about the truth and save her pride. "For a moment, when you came in, you reminded me of someone I knew once. Do you understand?" Her eyes pleaded with him to understand all she dared not put into words.

Stephen Andrassy scrambled to his feet and stood looking at her with a suddenly grave expression in his eyes. "He was a lucky man, then, this 'someone' you once knew," he said in an undertone. Then he laughed, and all the grave lines fell away from his face. "And a fool—since he is not here with you! Do you think that I can take his place, Miss Laure?"

Laure looked away. There was too much in Stephen that reminded her of Csikos. It would be a sweet agony to relax in his arms again, pretending it was Csikos who held her. "I don't think you would want to do that," she said, evading the question. "The last time I saw him, he was—in a very good position."

Stephen laughed again and offered her his arm. "I see that you think no one can take the place of this so-mysterious friend of yours," he conceded. "But he is not here, Miss Laure, and I am—a very good dancer and an excellent horseman and—oh, the deuce of a charming fellow all round!" He listened for a moment to the strains of a new dance inside the ballroom. "Come, they are forming sets for the lancers. Will you dance with me?"

Laure placed her hand on his arm and they passed inside, back to the overheated, brilliant, feverishly gay world of Vienna in the waltz season.

Chapter Three

IN THE WEEKS THAT FOLLOWED, LAURE TRIED TO SUP-
press her memory of that strange, bittersweet meeting
with the bandit called Csikos. It was difficult when
Stephen Andrassy was constantly at her side, reminding her by his sheer physical good looks of that other
man.

In character they were miles apart. It seemed to
Laure that the young Count Andrassy represented
everything she most disliked about the artificial, hothouse existence of Vienna. Frivolous, extravagant, a
known womanizer—she counted his faults in her
mind, but none of them kept her from looking forward to his presence to enliven an otherwise dull
party or ball. He might be unforgivably flippant about
the weighty social and political concerns that Josef

addressed in his mysterious job at the Hofkanzlerei, but he could always make Laure laugh. He might be the greatest flirt in Vienna, but there was something intoxicating in the steady gaze of his intense blue eyes, even when she warned herself they might be turned on another woman the next day. But they weren't. For that one giddy season in Vienna, Count Andrassy was at the feet of a tall English girl—and she learned to laugh and be giddy with him.

She was warned about him.

"He is never serious about any girl for too long," Julie told her. "Last season it was Clementine Willensdorff. *And* Doris Petrovka."

"He makes me laugh," Laure said, brushing out her long golden hair with steady sweeping strokes, "and he's a good dancer." She did not mention, even to Julie, the thrill that ran through her whenever she was in Stephen's arms. The memory of that one passionate embrace on the terrace, when she took him for Csikos, was always between them. Laure did not know whether to be annoyed or relieved that he did not attempt to kiss her that way again.

Stephen's courtship could hardly be described as assiduous; for days on end he would be absent from all the balls and entertainments she attended, only to turn up one moonlit night and serenade her under her bedroom window. Unfortunately, given the cramped design of Vienna townhouses, Laure's window was directly over Josef's. Josef was annoyed at being awakened and scandalized to see his sister and her cousin hanging over the balcony in their nightgowns.

Laure suppressed a pang of desire at the sight of Stephen's gold hair and moustache shining in the moonlight, of his broad-shouldered figure. At moments like these he might have been Csikos himself, riding into the city to carry her away into some misty dreamland where social rites and customs no longer mattered.

But a moment later the mood of the longing song changed, and Laure was clinging to the balcony railings, helpless with laughter as Stephen brilliantly improvised verses describing the irate brother and the confrontation he sensed was coming. The servants Josef sent to drive him away moved slowly enough, having no desire to lay violent hands on a count. "Farewell, beloved, farewell," Stephen sang, waving his hands to the Gypsy violinist to produce a last, despairing crescendo of melody. "We part but to meet again. Your cruel relatives forbid me the door," he improvised to the tune of an old Austrian folksong, "but tomorrow we shall dance in the meadows of—the Rennweg." And with a last flourish of his cloak, he vanished into the blackness of the narrow streets just moments before Hansl and his fellow grooms arrived.

Josef was left to express his opinion to the two girls in the morning, which he did in no uncertain terms.

They were sitting at the breakfast table, enjoying a late-morning snack of pastries and coffee, when Josef marched in. He was already correctly attired for the day in a close-fitting dark coat and trousers, with a frill of immaculate linen at his neck, and he looked disapprovingly at the two women trailing the lace and ruffles of their dishabille over the breakfast room. He was used to seeing Julie perched on a Biedermeyer chair, her dark curly head peeking out of a lacy froth of ruffles, but there was something subtly disturbing in the sight of Laure attired similarly. He glared at her and was both gratified and disappointed to see that a warm flush spread over her high cheekbones and that

38

she pulled her *robe de matin* together at the neck, covering up the shadowy cleft between her breasts, half-revealed by the ruffles of point lace, that had so disturbed him. If she showed such glimpses to her Hungarian lover—the thought infuriated him, and he launched into a lecture on the impropriety of her behavior.

"You, Julie, are too young and innocent to know better," he announced, "but I should have thought you would have too much sense to be taken in by his antics, Laure!" Unaware that he had offended both women at once, he put his hands on his hips and surveyed them with a disapproving glare that reminded Laure of nothing so much as a banty rooster in a farmyard. His immaculately disarranged crop of dark hair framed snapping dark eyes and closed lips that she had once thought firm, and now found only pettish. Fortunate, she thought, that Josef had not the inches to match that air of confidence; she might once have been taken in by him. Now he seemed as swaggering and silly as the rest of the young men who flocked around her and Julie. She did not ask herself what new insight prompted this comparison.

"He's wild, reckless, not a fit man for either of you to associate with, for all he stands so high in the emperor's favor," Josef announced. "Why, do you know what the Baron von Staunitz was telling me about him only the other night?"

Julie's half-parted lips and smile of anticipation warned him just in time. "Well, never mind. It's not a story fit for young women to hear."

Julie pouted and soon made an excuse to leave the breakfast table, as Josef showed no signs of ending his lecture.

Josef poured out a cup of steaming black coffee

from the exquisite Meissen coffeepot and seated himself beside Laure. The delicate porcelain cup, fluted and gold-rimmed and painted with a riot of improbably bright flowers, should have looked incongruous in a man's hand. Instead it made Laure aware of how slender Josef's fingers were, the nails perfectly manicured, the skin softened with daily application of scented creams. She could not help comparing it with another hand, large, with gold hairs on the backs of the strong fingers, that had seized her wrist with an inexorable command once on the road through the Vienna woods. What would Josef have done if it had been he she slashed at with her riding crop? She doubted very much that he would laugh and kiss her.

"Von Staunitz was telling me," Josef murmured confidentially in her ear, "that whenever Stephen visits his sister in Budapest, she has to send all the pretty servant girls to her farm in the country. Last time, he asked her if there had been an epidemic of the smallpox in Buda, for every chambermaid he saw was marked with the pox!" He laughed. "Now you see why I do not wish you to associate with such a man." He laid his smooth, overmanicured hand on Laure's long brown fingers, and she converted her involuntary movement of distaste into a withdrawal from the table.

"I can cap that story," she countered. "Baron von Staunitz told me the end of it—perhaps he thought you were too innocent to hear it!" And she retailed with relish the closing lines of the story. "His sister said that when Stephen dies and goes to heaven, he will have to wait a long time at the gate while Saint Peter hides away Saint Ursula and her eleven thousand virgins."

Satisfied with the shock she saw on Josef's face, she drew the trailing skirts of her lace-trimmed morning robe about her and swept from the room.

"Laure!" Josef breathed as she paused at the door. "Have you no delicacy of mind?"

Laure pretended to think this over. "Why, no, cousin, I don't think I do. I find Count Andrassy a delightful companion, and am only sorry you find it necessary to repeat such scandal broth, as though you thought I could have my head turned as easily as one of his sister's maids!"

But the wicked little story disturbed her more than she chose to admit. Once safely in her room, Laure pushed back the long honey-colored plaits from her face and examined her own eyes for a long time in the mirror. Was she really in danger of losing her heart to a practiced seducer, the sort of man she despised above all else? Had this dangerous flirtation turned into more than a game?"

The wide, amber-colored eyes in the mirror were unable to answer her. They stared gravely back, charged with a nameless warning. "You know what he is, and you know what you are," they seemed to say. "What has a Hungarian nobleman to do with a dowerless English girl? Keep away from the fire before you are burned."

With a little laugh, Laure arose from the dressing table. A little late for those warnings! And of course she knew better than to take Stephen's courtship seriously. She told herself that she encouraged him only because he was amusing, and because Josef would not take the risk of proposing in form until he felt sure he had cleared this rival from the field. Once Josef actually proposed, she would have to refuse him, and then propriety would dictate that she return to England. And Laure did not wish to leave Vienna —not yet.

She did not choose to examine her reasons for wanting to stay on in Vienna. Nor did she examine the eager pulse beating in her throat when she considered the broad hint in Stephen's verses that he expected to see her at Prince Metternich's ball in the Rennweg that night. She had already thought out her reasons for encouraging Stephen's courtship. It was a safe-enough game, as long as neither of them took it seriously. The bittersweet torment of being around a man who reminded her of Csikos—well, that had nothing to do with it. She was hardly such a fool as to moon over that encounter in the woods! Just because the man had more polished manners than his fellow banditti, there was no reason to think he was, at heart, anything but a common out-law.

Nonetheless, she had become an eager collector of the stories about Csikos. She wondered that she had not heard of him when she first came to Vienna, but evidently there had been a hiatus in his activities just then. Now, hardly a week passed without his being named the author of some new and daring exploit. The episode in the midst of which she met·him—when he stopped the emperor's courier—had been but the first of a new wave of stories. By the time it was retold to Laure, Viennese gossip had it that Csikos, with a band of forty desperados, had stopped an imperial coach guarded by twelve outriders, despoiled the mails and tied a placard for Hungarian independence to the back of the unfortunate coachman. Laure remembered the three men hiding in the forest shadows, the one mailbag and the single letter that Csikos had inserted. She smiled and reminded herself to discount future stories by at least 150 percent.

Even with that rule in force, the tales of Csikos's exploits were amazing enough. It was said that he was the one responsible for covering over the posters for the opera with boldly lettered demands for a reopened parliament in Hungary; he who had replaced the Austrian flag on top of the Karlskirche with a Hungarian banner.

"Boring," Julie said with a pout when Laure recounted this latest tale to her, in the carriage on their way to the Rennweg. "Political."

"I thought you found him romantic," Laure teased. Privately, she thought the political bent of Csikos's exploits made him more, not less, interesting. "At least there is some point to what he is doing! Do any of us have as much reason for our lives?"

"The waltz," Julie teased. "That is reason enough for living—if you are true Viennese." The carriage drew up outside the broad flight of steps leading to Klemens Metternich's summer villa; Julie sprang lightly down the folding steps and pirouetted between the blazing torches that lighted the carriageway, humming one of the ever-popular waltz tunes as she danced. "And I thought you found it reason enough, dear cousin—when you dance with a certain Hungarian count—hmm?" She laughed and pirouetted away, up the broad stone steps to the lighted ballroom.

"Little minx," said Josef indulgently. He took Laure's hand and placed it over his arm. "We need not imitate her madcap pace."

Laure was forced to accommodate her step to his, and they walked slowly up to the villa. Halfway up the stairs, when they were alone and in shadow, he broke the silence.

"You should not speak so approvingly of this robber," he warned her.

Laure laughed. "Why, do you think the emperor's secret police will take me away? I am English, Josef, not Austrian—they cannot arrest me for saying what I think!"

"I hope you will soon be Austrian," Josef said simply. "Laure—."

"This is hardly the way to persuade me," she interrupted. "First the threat of the secret police— now, do you hint that if I marry an Austrian, they will forgive me?"

"If I could report that you were to be married to me," Josef said, "it might make all our lives simpler."

Laure drew away from him in astonishment. "You, Josef—report? Report to whom, pray?" A cold suspicion grew in her. Josef had never explained his official duties in any detail, but she had thought that was just because he believed women were not interested in such matters.

Josef chuckled and tucked her hand back into the crook of his arm. "Ah, *Liebchen,* you English are so naive! Did you truly not know that I've been reassigned to the offices of the *Geheimpolizei* for just this matter of Csikos? Already some of your careless speeches have been noted. Think how it must pain me to report that my own intended wife has spoken so treasonably!"

"Then you had best not do so," Laure said, in a voice made clear and carrying by the pitch of her anger. "Stick to the literal truth, Josef—that your mad English cousin has an unfortunate partiality for the side of freedom!"

They had reached the top of the stairs. Laure stalked down the red-carpeted entryway ahead of

Josef. She was too angry to take in the fairyland sight of the Rennweg ballroom, too angry even to enjoy the effect of her new ball gown of greenish bronze gauze with gold spangles. The gown was very simply cut, for Vienna taste, with no ornament but an extra draping of the rich gauze around the low neckline and a fold of the same gauze caught in her hair. She had designed it herself, with pleasure, picturing herself dancing with Stephen Andrassy in it. Now she felt like an idiot for allowing her mind to be so taken up with courtship and dances that she had not even noticed that her own cousin was an informer for the secret police.

And Stephen was not there, after all. So what was the point of the gold-spangled ball gown and the gilt sequins adding luster to her hair?

Laure was surprised at how insipid the ball seemed to her, once she had circulated through the busy rooms and satisfied herself that Stephen was not there. What was the matter with her? Surely she had not started to take him seriously! If so, then it was time to go back to England, indeed.

Still, she found it so boring to exchange polite inanities with one partner after another that she was positively relieved when the Baron von Staunitz approached and invited her to sit out the lancers with him and share his amusing gossip.

"Frankly, I am no longer so young as I used to be," he confessed, sitting down with a relieved sigh. "The cardroom is more to my taste, or a good old-fashioned minuet or quadrille, rather than all this prancing and galloping about." And he launched into a slightly improper story that had Laure simultaneously laughing and wondering where on earth he had learned the wealth of detail with which he embellished the story. How, for instance, could he have known the exact

words with which Prince Ratisborsitz had refused
Madame Vignee-Lebrun's extremely improper invitation?

The baron smiled when she asked this. "How does
Csikos know the day and the hour when the emperor's
courier will pass through a lonely stretch of woods?"
he countered. "You know we are all gossips in Vienna, my dear. You might as well ask how I know the
words of the song that Stephen Andrassy serenaded
you with last night."

Laure turned uncomfortably from the mention of
Stephen. She was still hurt that he had not come to
the Rennweg ball, after his hints the previous night.
She would much rather have heard another story
about Csikos. The baron had fallen into the habit of
collecting such stories and retelling them to her; that
was how she had grown to tolerate his company.

"So what is the latest tale?" she asked. "The
courier stopped again? I should like to meet this
Csikos. He seems an amusing fellow."

The baron's eyes seemed to sharpen and brighten,
until they were like two sword points aimed at her
face. "You have not encountered him, then? You
seem so interested in him."

Laure widened her eyes and gave the baron her
prettiest, most innocent stare. "I? But what should I
know of him, my dear baron, but the stories you are
so kind as to bring me? It is you who seems so
fascinated by the fellow!"

"Call me Friedrich," the Baron advised, patting her
hand. Laure restrained the desire to wipe off the feel
of his sweaty palms. From the sudden seriousness of
his expression, Laure guessed that she was about to be
subjected to some good advice. "But seriously, my
dear—do not be misled by romantic tales of this

outlaw. When all's said and done, he is nothing but a common brigand. Oh, he may play at politics, but he also stops coaches for gold and jewels, like any common highwayman. Yes, and more—." His beady eyes roved over Laure's slim body, assessing the trim waist and the long shapely legs outlined by her thin skirts. "He stops ladies, too, and some of them have all too good cause to regret the encounter. You heard that only last week he robbed the Princess Bagration's coach just outside the city gates, and took—certain liberties with her person?"

Laure nodded. It had been that very episode that had put to rest her lingering doubts as to whether Stephen Andrassy and Csikos could possibly be one and the same. She had been dancing with Stephen in the hour when the princess's coach was being held up.

"Impossible," said a cool voice behind her. Laure looked up and discovered the Duchess of Sagan, elegant as ever in green silk with a parure of the Sagan emeralds. "Nothing one could do to the person of Katharina Bagration would be a liberty." She tapped von Staunitz on the shoulder with her fan. "Give me your seat, friend. Miss Laure is tired of hearing your horror tales, and I am tired of dancing." She slipped into the chair vacated by the baron and glanced up in some irritation when he remained standing. "Have you not been away from the cardrooms too long, baron? I am sure the game is not complete without you."

Von Staunitz's face reddened above his tight collar, and he moved off without another word.

"Tiresome man!" said the duchess. "I cannot see why he has been accepted so long—unless it is for the money he loses at the card tables. He did not like my reminding him of his gaming habit, did he? It is beyond me how his estates can support the debts he mounts up at the tables. Prussian land is poor and thin—he must starve his peasants to pay for his life in Vienna. Ah, well, it is no concern of mine. They say he always pays promptly, and what does it matter where he gets the gold?" She fanned herself and glanced around the room with an expectant look. "This Csikos will not be troubling us much longer, either, so the baron will have to find some other stories to tell."

"No?" Laure leaned forward, betraying her eagerness in the tense lines of her body. "Why do you say that?"

"Why, his star is on the wane," the duchess replied carelessly. "Did you not hear the gossip of the night? One of his daring tricks has finally failed. This very evening he tried to stop the emperor's courier again, but this time there was a trap laid; two men with pistols followed close on the heels of the courier. They did not catch Csikos himself, but they think a ball went through his shoulder—and, better yet, one of his confederates was unmasked; so they will know him again."

Laure felt sick and dizzy. Csikos wounded, possibly dead! She controlled her feelings with an effort of will and forced herself to speak lightly. "You say they will know him again? But I do not see what good that will do, for I am sure he would not be so foolish as to come into the city."

"Ah, that is the best part!" the Duchess of Sagan said. "These dispatches that he tried to seize are very important, for they contain the archduke's recommendations on how to treat these absurd Hungarian demands for a parliament of their own. If Csikos really cares about freedom for his people, he will try to recapture the dispatches—and will be captured himself. If not, he will be unmasked as a common robber using politics to cloak his robberies, and no one will take him seriously any more."

"I don't understand," said Laure. "How can you be so sure he will be caught this time?"

"The dispatches are here!" the duchess whispered. She nodded at Laure's look of amazement. "Yes, in Prince Metternich's own private study. Klemens has long suspected that "Csikos" is the pseudonym of someone in our own circles, someone very close to the emperor—how else could he know exactly when and where to strike? Tonight he is letting it be known that the dispatches are in his study—unguarded, of course, for who would have the temerity to rob Metternich's own house? It is only necessary to watch and see who slips into the study now, and we have our man. I had the entire plan from Klemens himself," she added with an air of self-satisfaction. The duchess and Klemens Metternich were said to have been lovers some ten years previously, and she still plumed herself on the political tidbits he dropped in her ear when they met.

Immediately following this revelation, the duchess looked worried. "You won't tell anybody, will you? Oh, you can tell about the dispatches being in Klemens's study. He wants that piece of information spread as widely as possible. But don't hint that it is a trap. Klemens would never forgive me. Of course, I knew it was safe to tell you. You could hardly be our bandit in disguise!" Wilhelmine de Sagan laughed, and Laure joined her.

After a moment, Wilhelmine's somewhat forced laughter broke off, and Laure followed her gaze. Stephen Andrassy was standing only a few feet from them, very pale and erect in his Imperial Guardsman's coat of dark green. Wilhelmine stretched out her hand to him, and he clicked his heels and bent to kiss it with a sort of mechanical propriety.

"Ah, I know it's not my hand you want to kiss, but you need not be so obvious!" the duchess chided him. "Here is Miss Standish, who is tired of sitting with old people like Baron von Staunitz and myself. You have come to dance with her, and it's about time, too!"

To Laure's surprise, Stephen looked as dismayed as she at this sudden invitation. "I—I have but newly arrived," he stammered.

"I'm still tired," Laure put in quickly. Ten minutes ago she would have liked nothing better than to dance and flirt with Stephen. Now she could think of nothing but the danger Csikos would be in if he responded to Metternich's trap. She must slip to the study and warn him! "It is really too hot and crowded in here for dancing," she improvised.

At the same moment Stephen excused himself politely, but firmly. "I must make my apologies to Prince Metternich for my lateness."

"Nonsense!" exclaimed Wilhelmine. She rose and placed Laure's hand firmly in Stephen's. "Miss Standish, you are being too polite. I am sure you would rather dance with a handsome young guardsman than hear more of my gossip."

Laure forced a smile at Stephen and raised her free hand to his shoulder as the waltz began. She was surprised to get no answering smile. His face was whiter than before, and he held himself so rigidly that she could scarcely believe this was the man she'd danced the night away with the previous week.

It was an awkward, uncomfortable waltz. Stephen moved with military precision instead of leading with his accustomed dash and vigor. Laure stumbled once and thereafter concentrated on matching her steps precisely to his.

It was a relief when the music finally came to an end. Laure curtsied and began framing an excuse about the heat in the ballroom and her desire for a breath of air. But she had not finished the sentence when Stephen gave a stiff bow and reiterated that he really must go and make his apologies to his host.

Laure noticed, though, that when he turned away from her, he strode off in quite the opposite direction from the corner where Prince Metternich was chatting with a few close friends. Instead, he seemed to be heading straight for Doris Petrovka, his flame of the previous season.

She felt unaccountably hurt at this sudden dismissal. Hadn't she always known that their courtship was only a game to while away the spring evenings? Something to be forgotten as easily as it had begun? Enough people had warned her about Stephen Andrassy! But she would have expected him to be more mannerly in breaking off with his flirts.

That was all, she told herself as she slipped between dancers and sought her own exit from the ballroom. She was surprised at his bad manners—nothing more.

But the strange little ache in her heart remained and would not go away, even with the expectation of seeing Csikos again.

Laure had not visited the villa on the Rennweg before, and she wasted precious minutes exploring a wing that led only to the family's sleeping quarters before she stumbled on the study. Every minute she was tense, expecting to hear an outcry as Metternich's guards captured Csikos or caught sight of her. But they would hardly accuse her of being the bandit!

Laure paused with her hand on the study door, turning over a dozen stories in her mind to explain her presence there if she were caught and questioned. Should she pretend to know nothing of the plan? No, that was hardly safe; the Duchess of Sagan might betray her. She would pretend to be a scatterbrained English girl who thought to seize this opportunity of seeing the famous bandit. Yes, that would work. If Josef was any example, these Viennese thought all women fools.

The half-formed story vanished from her mind when she pushed the door open and saw the man standing behind Prince Metternich's leather-covered desk. A single candle on the desk cast a pool of light down on the papers that were scattered across the desk top, and it reflected enough of a glow into the room to outline the tall figure in an imperial uniform of green coat and cream-colored trousers.

Chapter Four

STEPHEN ANDRASSY FLUNG UP ONE HAND AT THE CREAK-
ing of the door. The reflected candlelight winked and
glimmered on all the tracery of gold braid and gilt lace
that decorated his coat. His face was half-hidden in
the shadows above the desk.

"You!" Laure breathed. So Stephen was the agent
set to entrap Csikos! She was infuriated beyond
reason. Was everyone in this town of spies a spy or an
informer? First Josef, now Stephen. "How could you
sink so low?"

Stephen lowered his upraised hand and stood wari-
ly, regarding her over the candle flame. "It is a matter
of definition, is it not? Some people would consider
my calling an honorable one."

"Some people," Laure declared, "think nothing of betraying their own countrymen." No, that was the wrong tack. If she let him see how thoroughly she sympathized with Csikos, she would never get him out of there before Csikos came. She swallowed her sense of betrayal and outrage. Time enough for pain later. Now she must get Stephen to leave. She put a hand to her head and swayed toward the desk. "The shock—I feel faint," she murmured.

In two steps Stephen was around the desk and supporting her. "Then get out of here!" he hissed in her ear. "This is no business for a woman."

No business for any decent person! Laure bit back the reply. This was no time to stand here quarreling. If only she could get Stephen out of the room! She let her knees buckle under her. She fell heavily against Stephen's shoulder. He gasped and dropped her onto a chair.

"If you could bring me a glass of water?" Laure looked up under her lids.

Stephen knelt beside her. "It would be better if you went back to your cousins."

"I'm too weak to move," Laure lied. "Please, Stephen, some water?"

A footstep sounded in the hall. Laure caught her breath. That could be Csikos now, walking straight into a trap! She opened her mouth to cry out, to warn him.

Stephen glanced over his shoulder at the turning doorknob, swore under his breath in Magyar and grabbed Laure in an awkward, left-handed embrace. Before she could cry out, his mouth covered hers in a punishing kiss. His body lay half across hers, pinning her down on the leather chair. Laure could not have pushed him away from her if she had fought, and she felt no inclination to fight. A deceitful languor was spreading through her limbs, leaving her limp and open to his touch. Her lips parted under the insistent pressure of his probing tongue, and she surrendered herself totally to his desire. A wealth of sensations coalesced into one shimmering desire that drove her to arch her body against his, mutely begging to prolong the contact of his arm encircling her waist, the hard muscles of his thigh pressing against her own legs.

The door was thrown open with a crash that briefly restored Laure's senses. A host of new, unrelated sensations came crowding in upon her. She was aware simultaneously of the salt taste of blood on her lower lip, of voices and laughter and lights behind her, of the crackling sound when Stephen hugged her to his chest. He was still using his left arm only. Laure gasped in surprise as the full meaning of that awkward embrace became clear to her. What a fool she'd been!

"Andrassy, you fool!" It was Captain Genzler, Metternich's policeman. He swore and turned to the men beside him. "Would you believe it? Our pretty trap ruined, because this young ass must needs choose the chancellor's own study to lift his lady love's skirts."

Stephen scrambled to his feet and pulled Laure up after him. The pressure of his left hand on her wrist forced her to stand a little behind him, so that her face was hidden in shadow.

"My apologies, gentlemen!" His voice was light and gay as ever. Laure felt the pressure of his hand increase, with an implied warning. There was no way, now, to tell him that he had nothing to fear from her.

The men standing behind Captain Genzler were dressed in cream-colored trousers and green coats that matched Stephen's own, but only the first had an officer's gold braid. This man lowered his drawn sword and nodded to Stephen. "Genzler, I know this man. Shall I vouch for him?"

"No need," said Captain Genzler with genial contempt. "All Vienna knows Andrassy is harmless—except to the ladies!" He laughed heartily at his own jest, then scowled at Andrassy.

"Take your skirt into the rose gardens, Andrassy. *Himmel,* one would think Prince Metternich had designed this villa for dalliance—why must you pick the one spot of all others that we wished undisturbed tonight?"

"My apologies again," Stephen said, with a hint of laughter in his voice. "Believe me, captain, I am as disappointed in this interruption as you were!"

"Out," growled Genzler. "By the windows. We have work to do here."

Stephen kept his body between Laure and the soldiers as they moved toward the window, so that they could not see her face. Neither could they see the cruel twist of her arm with which he compelled obedience. "Don't," she whispered. "I'll help you."

The study windows opened onto the grounds of the villa on the opposite side from the ballroom. Laure had assumed that Stephen would lead her around the house by the stone path that wound in and out of the shubbery; but instead, he set off at a breakneck pace down a slope where the bushes grew thickest, directly away from the villa. He was still grasping Laure's wrist, and she was forced to hurry to keep up with him, stumbling on the uneven ground and feeling her face whipped by twigs and leaves. Were those footsteps behind them, or the sound of their own progress? The back of Laure's neck prickled with anticipation and fear. Every second she expected to hear a shout from the study.

He finally stopped when they had put what seemed like half a mile of landscaped gardens, rose bushes and terraced walkways between them and the villa. They were standing on a gravel path, which ran between high hedges on either side. Laure could feel the dampness from the wet gravel soaking into her little kid slippers. A light breeze caressed her bare arms and she shivered. She looked uncertainly up at Stephen.

He dropped her wrist and gave her a little push away from him. "Far enough, I think," he said cryptically. "Go on now—go back to your Josef, and tell him what you will of this night's work!"

Laure stood in the middle of the graveled path, staring at Stephen in the moonlight that filtered down through the branches of the trees. His hair and beard seemed tipped with silver in the clear, pale light, and his eyes were an unreadable shadow. Her wrist ached where he had tugged her along at his merciless pace, and her lips stung from his bruising kiss. Those were the real things that she knew. Everything else was a chaotic tumble of guesswork and questions.

"You are Csikos." The words sounded flatly unreal, hanging between them. Her head was aching. "I thought you were part of the trap, but you are Csikos, aren't you? Because they didn't know you were going to be there." She raised one hand to brush away the strands of hair that had fallen across her face in their hurried flight, as though that would help her to understand. "But how—." She seized on the one fact that had seemed clear until a moment ago. "How can you be in two places at once? Or are there two of you? Because I was dancing with you when the Princess Bagration's coach was robbed."

Stephen's lips hardened into a thin line. "Csikos has become quite famous," he said. "He gets credit for far more than he has done. Laure—I don't know who has started to assume my character for these jewel robberies; perhaps it is one of the emperor's own men. A move to discredit me. I swear to you, Csikos has never harmed anyone or stolen anything of value. Only papers—worthless papers!"

Laure nodded. "Yes. You have the dispatches in your coat."

Stephen jumped as if he had been stung. "You saw me take them?"

Laure shook her head. "No, but you—ah—." She sought for delicate words, could find none. "You crackled when you kissed me. I guessed then. And you're not using your right arm very much. Is that where they shot you?"

Stephen laughed under his breath and caught her about the waist with one hand, drawing her to him. She did not fight the movement. "Ah, Laure, Laure, did you truly not guess before?" He bent his head to kiss her lightly, brushing her lips. Laure's blood tingled with the touch. Csikos—or Stephen? Did it matter? "Did you think Stephen Andrassy the rapid fellow he pretends to be, and never connect him with Csikos?"

Laure felt as if she had been drugged. She couldn't think when every nerve was so aware of his body beside hers, his arm resting lightly about her waist. Why did he keep touching her so lightly, and never kiss her properly? Now his hand was teasing the delicate soft tendrils at the back of her neck, sending shivers of delight down her spine. It was almost impossible to control her voice. "That first night—but then you acted so differently! Your voice was higher, too. And—." She gazed levelly into his eyes, which were shadowed and unreadable in the moonlight. "I thought Csikos was taller."

"Csikos," said Stephen, "is a very good actor. So is Stephen Andrassy! As for the height—I am afraid, Laure, that your memory has been improving upon the original portrait." There was an undercurrent of laughter in his voice. "I shouldn't laugh at your romantic images. They may have saved me from premature discovery."

Laure felt chilled by his tone. A romantic girl, playing games and easily fooled—was that what he thought of her? But it didn't matter now. She would never see him again. These few minutes under the hedge were all she would ever have. "All right," she said unsteadily. "I'm a romantic fool. And you'd better go now. How long do you think it will be before Captain Genzler notices the papers are missing?"

"I copied the papers." Stephen caressed her high-piled braids and traced the path of one errant curl down her neck. "There's no hurry. Say good-bye to me properly, Laure. You have all the rest of your life to spend with Josef. You can spare five minutes for a poor bandit, before you go back to your worthy cousin."

The sneer in his voice stung Laure. "You must have thought it very amusing to make love to a girl whose cousin is a police spy." She slipped from his grasp and stood just out of reach on the gravel path, straining to make out his features in the cool light.

Stephen's voice was low and strained. "I did not. I thought it a damnable situation!"

"You could have kept away from me altogether!"

"No."

The single negative hung between them on the soft spring air. Stephen took one deliberate step toward her and put his hands round her waist again. His left hand slid upward from her waist, caressing the ripe curves partially concealed by her gauze-draped bodice and coming to rest over the pulse beating in her throat. "Laure? I did not mean to hurt you."

But she must have been convenient for him. His courtship of her would account for his lingering in the city this spring, would explain the time he spent at balls and parties where he picked up the right sort of gossip. And there must have been an additional fillip in courting the girl who had actually seen him as Csikos, and been persuaded out of the evidence of her own eyes later.

"No." The touch of his hand burned her. Laure stepped back, away from the caress. "You must have been mightily concerned that I would see through your playacting!"

"Believe it or not," said Stephen in a low voice, "I was also concerned for your feelings. But I see I need not have troubled with that. May I congratulate you on your engagement to Josef Schulenberg? He announced it to me as I came through the ballroom. It is the greatest relief to me to know that I was not trifling with the feelings of a girl who might take me seriously."

This time Laure felt genuinely faint. So Josef had announced their engagement! Did he think to force her with a fait accompli? And Stephen believed it. Chose to believe it. Of course. "Yes, of course," she murmured. "It's very convenient."

She meant that it was convenient for Stephen to

believe she'd never really cared for him. But he took it differently.

"There may, of course, be some slight awkwardness attached to your next meeting with Josef. I should fancy he will not be pleased to hear that you helped the great Csikos escape. But you should be able to buy your way back into his good graces by announcing my identity."

Every word of the low-pitched, savage speech was like a blow to Laure. "You cannot think I would betray you!"

"Why not? By your engagement to Josef you have clearly announced your side in this matter. You, my dear Laure, are on the side of the police—the informers—the empire and all its power."

Laure shook her head. "No. I won't tell anyone who you are. That is between you and me—it has nothing to do with Josef." She gave an unsteady laugh. "If you can really escape from this mess, Stephen Andrassy may return to Vienna and go on with his life of pleasure. Only—don't bring any more girls into your political games. It's not fair to them."

Stephen raised his hand to her face and traced the line of her lips with one finger. "Laure—."

Whatever he had been going to say was lost when the bushes rustled behind them. A low voice called out some words in a language Laure did not understand.

"The devil!" Stephen turned and replied briefly in the same language.

"That was Jansci." He turned back to Laure. "Laure, there is so much to say. Jansci is waiting with the carriage." He paused and stroked her cheek with one hand. "I must be gone before they suspect the trick I've played on them. Laure, I dare not return to

Vienna before the fall. Stephen Andrassy has put it about that he is going to his estates, and he must remain there until Csikos's wound has healed. Do you understand?"

Laure nodded, her eyes fixed on his face. This was all the farewell she would have—these hurried moments in the garden, with his carriage waiting, and he thinking her betrothal to another man! Better that way, she told herself. Hadn't he admitted it was only sport for him?

There was a rustle and another urgent, low-pitched call from the bushes. Still Stephen did not tear himself away. "Laure—."

She waited. When he finally spoke, the words came rushing out, as though he dared not think them over. "You have said you will not betray me. Do one thing more for me. Please, don't rush into this marriage with Josef just because you are angry with me."

He put one arm round her waist and bent to kiss her. Laure spun out of his grasp, cheeks flaming. How dare he insinuate that she was running to Josef out of pique! Hadn't she been at pains to show him that the courting game they had played had meant as little to her as it had to him? All right, let him think that she meant to marry Josef, if it bothered him. It was high time something bothered him.

"Don't treat me so!" she cried. "Do you think I'm a child, to be cozened with a few kisses and a soft word? It's nothing to you whom I marry!" Her voice rose in her anger.

"Laure, hush! Someone will hear you." He looked over his shoulder and snapped out a few words in his strange language.

"Then run away," she taunted him. Something moved behind her—a hare running into the bushes, or a cloud across the moon. "That's what you are best at, isn't it? Go on! Run—"

Her breath was cut off by a hard, evil-smelling hand over her mouth. She was jerked backward, off her feet, and an arm about her waist crushed her against the body of the man behind her. Laure kicked backward, but her soft kid slippers made no impression against the masses of billowing material she encountered. She stared in horror at Stephen. Would they kill him now?

He was laughing.

"Jansci is very devoted to my interests," he told her. "You force this upon me. Will you be quiet now?"

Laure was unable to answer, imprisoned as she was by Jansci's hard, encircling arms.

Stephen stroked his beard, and his eyes crinkled with amusement, as though he had just hit on the answer to all his problems.

"I really cannot afford to have you screaming and attracting people's attention just now," he went on. "Perhaps it would be best if you accompanied us on the first stages of our journey. In fact, you could be some help to me at the police boundaries. And—the journey will give you some time to reconsider this engagement to Schulenberg."

Chapter Five

THE HEDGE THAT SHIELDED THE BACK OF METTERNICH'S lands was not impenetrable after all. Not quite. Laure stumbled along, half-carried by Jansci. One of his hands was still over her mouth and the other arm went around her waist, holding her arms down so that she could not raise her hands to protect herself from the stinging branches. She squeezed her eyes shut and ducked her head to protect herself as best she could. A leafy branch slapped her in the face. Something tugged at her hair, causing exquisite pain; then there was a sharp jerk and the pain was gone, but she no longer felt the gauze scarf fluttering about her head. A sharp branch trailed along her cheek and left a stinging pain behind. Other branches caught in her gown and were snapped free.

They broke through the last barrier of branches, and Jansci let Laure stand on her own feet in the coarse grass of the meadow. A dirt road, little more than two ruts and a puddle, ran alongside the hedge. A boxlike shape loomed against the sky, dark in the moonlight: an old-fashioned traveling carriage. Jansci wrenched the door open and pushed Laure in with a hand on the small of her back. She bruised her shins on the high ledge and landed ridiculously, half-across the musty leather-covered seat. Jansci pushed his way in beside her and covered her mouth again, forcing her back against the seat. Bitterly, Laure recognized that she had lost her one chance to scream.

Stephen's head at the window. "Laure—I will explain later. For now, you must be a young lady of good family, going on a visit to your relatives in Baden, and Jansci is your maid. Do you understand?"

"She'll understand," Jansci muttered in heavily accented German. "Or I'll break her neck."

"You will not lay one hand on the lady," Stephen said, also in German so that Laure could understand. "She has promised not to betray us." He reached into the coach and touched Laure's shoulder. "Laure? We have to get through the police boundary. If you make an outcry, Jansci will swing at the rope's end, and I will end my days in the emperor's prisons."

"Don't tempt me," Laure said between her teeth.

Stephen sighed, started to say something, thought better of it and checked himself. "No matter. You will be cold. Wear this." He thrust a rolled-up cape in at the window. Laure felt soft, warm velvet spread out across her lap. She wrapped the cape around her and discovered that the front was stiff with scratchy metallic braid and clasps of heavy metal, intricately worked.

He disappeared into the darkness, and she heard him clucking to the patient horses. A moment later the coach gave a lurch and a shudder, and they were off down the rutted lane.

Laure found that her heart was beating unpleasantly fast. She could sense Jansci beside her in the darkness of the coach and knew that he was aware of her every move.

"Where is Stephen taking me?" she asked in slow, careful German, so that he would be sure to understand.

"None of your business," Jansci growled. "Not for the likes of you to question the count."

"He is being very foolish," Laure said.

"Huh! Not for the likes of me to question the count, either. Now shut up. This isn't women's business." Laure felt the leather cushions sigh as Jansci leaned back in the corner. There was a strange rustling noise, too. She remembered the soft fabric that had stopped her when she kicked at him, and Stephen's comment that he was to pose as her maid. She reached forward and passed her hand through the blackness before the seat, some twelve inches above the floor. She was rewarded with a handful of ruffles. She grabbed hold and tugged.

"Here! Cut that out." It was Jansci's voice.

Laure sat up again, smiling to herself in the darkness. "How quaint," she said. "Do you like dressing up as a girl, Jansci? I bet you look really cute with worked muslin flounces on your petticoat. Do you have one of those little gold caps the serving maids wear?"

"Huh! You shut up," Jansci growled. "And don't get any ideas about making trouble at the boundary. See this?"

"Of course I don't see whatever it is, you idiot," Laure snapped back. "How could I? It's pitch dark in here."

Jansci's hand encircled her throat, and she felt a pinprick in the side of her neck. "It's my knife," he told her unnecessarily, "and it's what you'll get in your ribs if you make any trouble for the master."

Laure sat rigid, hardly daring to breathe. Any bounce of the coach as it swayed over the rutted road could drive the knife blade into her. She could hear her heart thudding in the silence.

"Thought that 'ud shut you up." Jansci's arm released its pressure and he moved the knife away from her neck.

"Very thoughtful," Laure said. She found release from her fear in sarcasm. "How helpful it will be to Stephen if the police find a dead body in his coach! Do you want to get your master in more trouble than he's in already? You can trust me to help you get out of Vienna—not that you deserve it."

There was a chuckle in the darkness from Jansci, but he left her alone. Laure leaned back in the opposite corner of the coach and preserved a rigid silence. If only Stephen were in the coach! She could have talked him out of this wild plan. As it was, there was nothing to do but wait till they crossed the *Polizeilinie,* where all travelers leaving Vienna were stopped and questioned. And perhaps, she reflected, it was not such a mad plan after all. The police would be looking for two men, one wounded. A young lady traveling with her maid would hardly arouse their interest.

Laure discovered her mistake at the city boundary.

A single lamp lit the hut where a police officer dozed over his book of exits and entrances. The light fell in a wavering half-circle over the empty road, creating menacing inky shadows from innocent bushes. For a moment it seemed that they might drive by without question; but as the coach was just level with the hut, a half-dressed man ran out, shouting and tucking his shirttail back into his trousers as he ran.

"Where bound?" he shouted at the coachman.

Stephen gave an unintelligible grunt, and the police officer turned his attention to the passengers in the coach. By the time he approached the coach window, his shirt was completely tucked in and he had buttoned up his uniform jacket again. He picked up a swinging lantern that sent rays of light dancing across the road and in and out of the coach.

"Pardon, *gnädiger Herr*—." he began, thrusting his head in at the coach window, and then stopped in some confusion. "*Fräulein.* A thousand apologies, gracious lady. It is but to record the names and stations of all parties leaving the city, and their destinations. By order of the emperor."

"How is this?" Laure asked. "I have never been questioned so before." The prick of Jansci's knife in her side, hidden under his voluminous petticoats, warned her not to say anything that he might consider a betrayal.

"A special order," the man insisted. He was sweating, and the black locks of hair that fell over his forehead were damp with grease and sweat. "It came down only tonight. By special order of the emperor!" He repeated his catchphrase as if sure that it would command obedience.

In a bored and haughty tone, Laure gave her name as Countess Eleonore Bernstorff, saying that she was traveling with her maid, Anna, and her coachman, Hansl, to Baden.

"A pretty place, Baden." The police officer rested his elbows on the window frame and looked Laure over. "But soon to be improved by the presence of so lovely a lady. But why——."

"My good man, you are impertinent," Laure said. "Drive on, Hansl!"

"Not so fast!" The police officer's warning shout stopped them. He stood in the roadway, legs spread and boots solidly planted in the white dust, hands on his hips, rocking back and forth. "There are still some questions to be answered."

He enjoys this, Laure thought. *Petty power. I don't think I care for this fellow.*

"It is not the custom for lovely ladies to leave town so late at night to take the waters at Baden," he began, with a leer. "Perhaps the gracious lady is meeting a friend—eh? Why does the Count Bernstorff not travel with the lady—eh?"

"Who?"

"The gracious lady's husband. Has she forgotten him already?"

As a matter of fact, Laure had completely forgotten her made-up name.

"My family affairs have nothing to do with you, my man," she said in glacial tones worthy of a princess of the blood. "You are impertinent. I come from Metternich's ball at the Rennweg, and can very well return there should you detain me further. I should regret to tell Klemens how ill the emperor is served."

The casual use of Metternich's first name impressed the police officer. He stepped back and waved them on.

"Disgusting toady," Laure muttered under her breath in English.

She let out a sigh of relief as the coach rolled on

beyond the circle of lamplight at the police station. Now they were safe, in open country.

For the first time she seriously considered the question of how she was to get back to the Schulenbergs' residence in the city. She supposed that soon Stephen would stop the coach and let her go. But she could not very well walk back past that same police station, nor could she go cutting across the fields in her impractical gauzy evening dress. Perhaps he would circle the city to let her return by some other gate. But where would she find a carriage so late in the evening? Would he have arranged for one? No, he hadn't meant to take her along at all, until she made him angry. And now they were well beyond the police station, and still the coach had not slowed or turned.

Just as Laure felt panic rising in her, the horses were pulled almost to a halt and the ponderous coach made a sharp turn to the right. She sighed with relief. Yes, he must be planning to circle round to another gate to let her off.

This new road was significantly worse than the Baden highway, though better than the rutted cart track on which they had begun. Stephen lashed the horses into a gallop, and for some minutes Laure was fully occupied with holding onto the leather-covered seat with both hands so as not to be thrown about the inside of the coach. When they pulled onto a smooth stretch again, she stuck her head out the window to see if she could guess how near they were to the next gate.

The city of Vienna had been reduced to a few lights twinkling on the horizon behind them.

"Where are we?" Laure pushed Jansci out of her way and clambered over his petticoats to look out the other window. No, it was the same story. Behind them, a cluster of lights rising up the city wall; before them, nothing but blackness and the stars. "Stephen!" She pounded on the front of the coach with her fists, until Jansci seized her arms and dragged her back into her seat.

"Stop making such a fuss," he growled. "What's the matter with you, anyway? Took it quiet enough when the count told you you had to come with us, didn't you? Why fuss now?"

"I thought," Laure said, "that he would let me go once he had passed the city boundaries."

"So did I," Jansci agreed. "But he didn't; so he must have thought of some other use for you." He chuckled, and Laure was grateful for the darkness that covered her blush. "Don't worry," Jansci advised her. "You're too skinny for my taste. And don't start nothing, either. I've still got my knife." There were rustling sounds, followed by a gusty sigh, as he made himself comfortable in the corner of the coach.

Laure sat upright, clutching at the frame of the coach as it swayed from side to side. Where was Stephen taking her? What madness was this?

In the darkness she could not even see the road to judge how fast they were going. Perhaps she should risk throwing herself out now, before they were too far from Vienna. She felt stealthily along the coach door for a handle.

"Don't try nothing," warned Jansci. "You jump, could break a leg. We stop and pick you up again. You don't like traveling with a broken leg!"

With a sigh, Laure sat back in her own corner of the seat. There was nothing to do but wait. And besides, wasn't that the wisest course? After all, she knew Stephen. He would never hurt her . . . would he?

The hours of the night dragged by with tortuous

slowness. There was a change of horses at some wayside posting house, where Stephen had to waken the sleeping hostler with a shout. Once the sleepy man had staggered out of the stables, yawning and scratching, he poled up the new team with the efficiency of years of practice. Jansci's knife was out and held at Laure's waist, in case she should be so foolish as to call for help. She could make out nothing of the inn beyond the circle of light cast by the hostler's lantern, which showed a filthy stable yard where chickens and pigs wandered underfoot looking for scraps to eat. Within three minutes, the new team was ready to go and they were on their way again.

Laure actually dozed off for a few minutes before dawn, huddled in her corner of the coach under Stephen's warm, soft cloak. When she awoke, the first streaks of dawn were lightening the sky, showing a flat featureless plain whose monotony was broken only by a line of hills along the eastern horizon.

Jansci informed her with a grin that she had slept through the passing of the customs post. "Customs! But where are we, then? Where is Stephen taking me?"

Jansci turned his head to the window and spat into the dust of the road. "Where else but the count's own country? We are in Hungary."

Laure clenched her hands till the nails bit into the palms. How could she have been so stupid as to fall asleep! Surely at the customs post there would have been somebody to help her.

Jansci shook his head when she voiced this thought. "Who should question the count in his own land? Not you. The count's woman? Nobody will worry about what happens to you."

"My cousin is in the secret police," Laure said. Perhaps if she spelled it out very clearly, this Jansci would help her reason with Stephen. "There will be a search. Your master could be in a great deal of trouble for taking me away. If you want to help him, you should let me go."

Jansci spat again into the dusty road. "The police are in Austria. You think they come over the border?"

Laure folded her hands together, tightly, to stop their shaking. She had been in Vienna long enough to understand that most Austrians thought of Hungary as a land of barbarians, removed from Vienna by forty miles and several hundred years of civilization. She was not even sure how the internal affairs of Hungary were regulated. Maybe the Austrian police had no jurisdiction here. Jansci's complete confidence was daunting in itself.

"You like the count well enough," Jansci went on. "Think I didn't see you in the bushes? And riding out in the woods alone—huh! You were askin' for it."

Intolerable to listen to this. Laure descended to schoolgirl insults. "You look just as silly as I thought you would in that dress, Jansci. You're ugly enough without tilting a lace cap over one ear and wrapping yourself in petticoats."

Jansci folded his arms and sat back in offended silence, and Laure stared out the window on the opposite side of the coach. There was nothing much to stare at. The sun rose higher and the featureless gray plain became green, and here and there in the distance she could see little clumps of brown and green; villages, hardly more than a dozen huts, with a few trees and a well, and maybe a great onion-domed church rising out of the middle of the cluster of poor little houses. The air in the coach grew oppressively warm. She folded up Stephen's cloak and used it as a headrest.

Suddenly the jolting of the coach grew much worse. Laure stuck her head out the window and saw that the horses were wandering back and forth in wavering zigzags across the road, as if nobody were directing them. A clump of green weeds in a ditch caught the eye of the near wheel; it headed for them, dragging its companions along, and the coach lumbered up to the ditch and settled one wheel into a deep rut with awful finality.

"You stay put," Jansci warned, and scrambled out of the coach. Laure followed on his heels.

Stephen's unconscious body had fallen across the coachman's box. It was a miracle that he had not fallen off the box completely. Jansci scrambled up and lifted his master down as tenderly as a woman nursing her sick child, and laid him in the shade of the ditch with his back against the bank. He opened the heavy sheepskin cloak, scooped water out of a stagnant, slimy pool with his hands and sprinkled Stephen's face and chest with the greenish stuff.

Stephen opened his eyes and said, "Hell! My best shirt." His head fell sideways and his eyes closed again. Jansci shuffled his feet.

"Hey, master! What do you want us to do?"

Laure knelt beside Stephen's prostrate body and put her hand to his head. "He's burning up with fever," she said. "Jansci, go and see if you can lead the horses out of this ditch. We must get him to an inn. Wait—give me your petticoats."

"Take the whole outfit!" Thankfully Jansci stripped off the peasant skirt and shawl that Stephen had provided as a disguise, revealing a brawny young man in loose-fitting shirt and black breeches. He dumped the bundle of clothing in Laure's arms and shambled off to see to the horses.

Laure tore off a flounce of the muslin petticoat and dipped it in the slimy ditch water, then squeezed it out over Stephen's face. With two more applications, his eyelids flickered open.

"Not—sick," he whispered. "Shoulder. Hurts."

Laure laid his shirt back with trembling fingers and exposed a very inexpertly bound-up wad of stained linen around his right shoulder. The old brown stains were overlaid by fresh blotches of red, which grew larger even as she watched. Stephen twitched and mumbled something, and flung up a hand to shade his eyes.

Above her, the heavy coach creaked and groaned as Jansci coaxed it out of the rut. He stood at the horses' heads, encouraging them with soft words and gestures to pull a little more, give it one more effort. A cry of triumph announced that the coach wheels were back on the main road again.

Once that was done, Jansci stood beside the horses, shuffling his feet and glancing down at Laure. She realized that he was waiting for her to tell him what to do.

"Help me lift your master," she said. "Is there an inn nearby?"

"Dunno," Jansci muttered.

"Which way is the nearest village? Is there a surgeon?"

"No surgeon."

"Well, how far is it to the village?"

"Dunno."

"Then how do you know there's no surgeon?" Laure almost shrieked. Stephen lay so white and still—she didn't have time to play games with this stupid peasant!

"No surgeons in these parts. Might find a priest."

"Well, he doesn't need a priest," Laure said, "and he's not going to if I have anything to say about it! Help me get him into the coach." Laure looked indecisively up and down the dusty road. She knew they had not passed a village for a good hour. They were bound to come on one soon. "We'll drive on the way we were going."

The leather-covered seat of the coach was too narrow and too short to support the full length of Stephen's body. With some difficulty they propped him on the seat, with his legs trailing over the edge. Laure perched on the folding seat opposite Stephen, where she could support him with her knees and keep him from rolling off.

Before they had progressed a mile down the road, she knew that would not work. The entire road was so deeply rutted that they might as well have been in the ditch still. The coach lurched from side to side continuously, and with each motion Stephen's unconscious body threatened to slide off the seat. Laure slipped to her knees on the floor, bracing her back against the folding seat, and put both arms round him to keep him on the coach seat. She could just keep her balance and support him if she held on to the back of the seat with one hand and leaned her head against his chest, but it required a constant muscular effort to keep him there. Before they had gone another mile, her arms were aching intolerably. But Stephen was still propped on the seat, and it did not seem that his wound was bleeding any worse.

The enforced intimacy with his half-naked body was something she had never experienced before. Her arm lay across his chest, and she could feel the powerful muscles moving with the slow rise and fall of his breath. The short golden hairs that covered his chest tickled her arm and cheek. To keep away from his injured shoulder, she had to turn away from his face and lean her head against his flat, taut stomach. She was surprised by the temptation to turn and brush her lips against his golden skin. She gripped the back of the seat and stared ahead, willing herself to think of other things. But all she could see from this position was the thickening line of hair running down his belly and disappearing into the waistband of his knitted trousers, the hard lines of his muscular thighs and the masculine bulge where his thighs met. She found herself wondering how it would feel to run her hands down that flat stomach and under the band of his trousers. The clinging knit material left nothing to the imagination.

The coach pitched forward into a deep pothole and Stephen's whole body rolled toward her. Laure threw up the arm she had braced against the floor to catch him and felt the hard edge of the folding seat digging into her back, as it took her full weight and most of his. As soon as she had pushed his legs back onto the seat, the coach lurched backward with equal force and threw her across his prostrate body. She lay across him with both arms outflung protectively, her face buried against one hard muscular thigh. Every line of her body was intimately aware of his touch. The hot sun, the smell of the leather upholstery, the creaking of the coach wheels, the smooth bronzed skin under her hand and the powerful thigh muscles against her cheek blended together into one moment of total and irrational happiness.

This time she gave in to the temptation, brushing

her lips up the line of his thighs, lingering over the bronzed skin at the waistband of his trousers. She pressed her lips to the line of golden hair running down his flat stomach and trailed kisses up along his chest, pausing at one nipple and teasing it to a peak with her tongue.

The coach came to a lurching halt and Laure scrambled back onto her seat, blushing furiously. What had come over her? It must have been a moment of insanity. Thank goodness no one would ever know.

Voices outside in the inn yard, hurrying steps. The coach door was wrenched open and Jansci hauled Laure out unceremoniously. He and the innkeeper gently eased Stephen's body from the coach onto a flat door, on which they carried him into the inn. Several times during the process, Stephen groaned aloud, but his eyes did not open until the two men were ready to lift the door and begin carrying him. At once Jansci dropped to his knees beside the improvised stretcher, babbling in the same strange tongue that he had been using with the innkeeper.

Stephen's eyes traveled up from Jansci's face until he found Laure, standing by the stretcher and looking down at him. "Don't apologize for jolting me, Jansci," he said slowly and deliberately, in German, looking directly at Laure. "It was a delightful ride. I would not have missed it for the world."

His eyes closed again and his body relaxed into unconsciousness.

Chapter Six

STEPHEN LAY PERFECTLY WHITE AND STILL ON THE GREEN door. Laure knelt over him and made an ineffectual effort to shade his face with her hand, while a confusing babble of strange languages went on about her. The innkeeper's wife, his daughter, the stable groom and half a dozen geese had all come crowding into the yard, and all of them had to comment at length on the amazing sight. Laure couldn't translate their words, but the gist of them was perfectly clear: look, the count with a wound in his shoulder, and a foreign girl in an indecent dress! What is the world coming to? What shall we do?

Laure looked up and found Jansci standing over the stretcher and looking as bewildered as the rest of the peasants. "Help me get him inside!" she said, more sharply.

There was a renewed babble from the two women. "They will ready the best bedchamber for him," Jansci translated. "Will you come and see that all is prepared?"

The innkeeper's wife led Laure inside to show her the best bedroom—a small, airless chamber opening directly off the taproom. Laure suspected it was the only other room in the house. At least it was clean. The walls were newly whitewashed and the massive box that served as the family bed was piled high with down quilts and pillows. The top layers, of both quilts and pillows, were covered with deep red embroidery in an intricate pattern of flowers and vines. She threw back a corner of the quilts to check the sheets and discovered bare, rustling straw underneath.

One high, arched window opening in the outer wall let in light and a grudging whisper of a breeze. The innkeeper's lady bustled around the tiny room, lighting oil lamps that, set into the wall at intervals, illuminated a tiny painting of the Virgin, an arrangement of dried flowers and weeds and a gilt belt buckle set in some kind of wooden frame. Her full skirts and voluminous petticoats almost filled the space between bed and door. No wonder they had no other furniture!

Laure wiped the sweat from her forehead with the back of her hand and gazed around her in dismay. Stephen could not be left in this airless hole, or he would surely die! She went to the door and called for Jansci, who was already seated in the taproom with a flask of wine before him.

"Is there no other place where Stephen can rest?" she asked. "He needs fresh air and to be out of the sun—but this heat will do him no good." She forbore mentioning her suspicion that the straw under the brilliantly embroidered coverlets was already inhabited.

"Count won't be any better for you keeping him waiting," grumbled Jansci. "Huh! Foreign notions." But he exchanged a few words with the innkeeper, who nodded and beckoned for them to follow him outside.

Stephen was lying in the shade provided by two barrels with a quilt draped over them. The heat in this improvised tent was stifling. Beads of sweat rolled down his face and darkened the fresh gold of his hair and beard. His body lay totally limp, as though he were asleep or unconscious, but his eyes opened when the quilt was moved aside.

"Come to nurse me again?" he asked. Laure bit back an impatient exclamation and contented herself with fanning his face. The movement when the two men picked up the door wrenched an involuntary groan from him. Laure walked behind them as they shuffled around the side of the inn, praying that they had not put him through this only to move him to a worse place.

Her fears were relieved when they rounded the side of the inn. Here, posts had been set into the ground at intervals and branches laid across the top to support a grape arbor. The mass of green leaves overhead shaded them, and the breeze blew unimpeded between the rows of vine-covered posts.

"Oh, how delightful!" Laure exclaimed. She turned to Jansci. "Bring me straw from the stables and a sheet to cover it. Oh, and water, and fresh linen for bandages, and—." She paused. What would be needed? She cursed her impractical education. She was better fitted to paint watercolors or sing a ballad than to nurse a wounded man.

"Knife," Jansci suggested. "To cut the bullet out of him."

Laure swayed where she stood and felt nausea rising inside her.

Jansci took over the task of making a bed for Stephen in the arbor, and Laure found a chair gently pushed up behind her and a round-bottomed flask of wine in her hand. The innkeeper's wife and daughter, two round-faced, smiling presences in identical gay costumes of many skirts, stood in front of her smiling and chattering. The older woman took Laure's hand and patted it while uttering what must have been reassuring promises, while the younger urged the wine upon her. Laure shook her head politely and tried to think of some universal sign language for explaining that she could not take wine so early in the day. And without having eaten anything, too! "I would be as drunk as a lord," she told the women in English. They smiled and patted her hand.

"Erdekosi Kati." The older woman pointed at herself, then at her daughter. "Erdekosi Maria."

"Kati, Maria." Laure pointed in turn at herself. "Laure Standish."

"Stan-dish?"

"Standish Laure," Stephen interjected. To Laure he added, "Last names come first—as in the census accounts. Hungarian is—a very logical language." He stopped and bit his lip as Jansci gently eased his body from the door to the pile of straw covered with a leather sheet.

Laure clenched one hand and bit her knuckles when Jansci began his ministrations. Stephen was so white;

and now that he was conscious, she could almost feel the tension running through every line of his powerful body, the anticipation of pain to come.

Jansci knelt over his master and cut the stained shirt away from his body with swift but surprisingly gentle strokes of his knife. When Stephen's upper body was bare except for the blood-soaked wad of bandages, Jansci sat back on his heels and stared helplessly at the dressing. "You better look at it, miss," he called.

Jansci and the innkeeper's family stood back from Stephen and stared at Laure. The message was clear. Only gentry should meddle with the wounds of gentry.

Laure took one look at the fresh blood seeping around the edges of the bandage and recklessly downed her wine.

The next few moments were some of the longest and most unpleasant of her life. The clumsy bandages, when unwrapped, proved to have slipped, so that they were exerting next to no pressure on the wound. The bullet wound itself was pronounced by Jansci, who hung over Laure's shoulder, to be a nice clean cut. It looked terrible to her, that jagged tear in the flesh from which fresh blood continually welled.

Laure laid her fingertips on his chest for the reassurance of feeling the strong heartbeat. Stephen's eyes flickered open. "Very—reviving," he teased, "but your lips would be better still."

Laure flushed and snatched her hand away. What was it about this man! Half-naked, wounded, in pain—still, he dominated the scene.

She cried out in horror as Jansci lifted him by the shoulders, causing a fresh seeping of blood from his wound. Jansci pointed to a matching, though smaller, wound in Stephen's back.

"Good," Jansci said. Laure looked at him in astonishment. What was so good about having two wounds instead of one to tend? "Means the bullet passed through," he explained. "You won't have to cut it out." He sounded almost regretful.

Laure knew nothing to do except sponge the wound clean and bind it up again, this time pressing folded wads of linen against the bullet holes in the hope of stopping the continuous slow bleeding. By the end of the process Stephen was fully conscious, white and close-lipped, and Laure had to retire to her chair for a moment to hang her head between her knees until the world stopped spinning.

She was back beside him in a minute, though, to hold to his lips the flask of wine the innkeeper brought out. "Says the count's lost blood," Jansci translated. "Wine will put strength back into him."

"Won't it raise his fever?" Laure asked.

"Don't argue with the prescription," said a somewhat unsteady voice from the pallet on the floor. "We Hungarians—have red wine for blood." Stephen raised himself on his left elbow to take the wine, but the effort forced a grunt of pain from him. In an instant Laure was on her knees behind him, supporting his weight in her lap.

Stephen drained the flask and thrust it back at Jansci. "Better." He snapped some orders to Jansci and at once the peasants and Jansci vanished from the shaded arbor.

"What did you tell them?"

Stephen leaned his head back in Laure's lap and looked up at her with a sardonic gleam in his eye. He was relaxed again, the long legs in his tight knit trousers sprawled out over the straw, as though he were merely taking a few minutes' rest. Laure was intensely conscious of his naked back lying across her thighs, the rise and fall of his chest, the sprinkling of golden hairs that caught the sun. He had no right, she thought, to look so intensely masculine, even when he was weak and in pain.

"To look to the horses," he answered her after a long, measuring silence. "We've a few leagues to travel yet."

"You've a few days to rest yet," Laure contradicted him. "Do you want to kill yourself?"

"No," Stephen said, "I want to frustrate the efforts of other people toward that end. We're going to the Bakony."

Laure frowned, and Stephen jerked his head toward the range of hills to the east. "The Bakony. Forest, rocks, hills—and the old castle of the Andrassys. Perhaps not so fancy as a modern manor house—but impregnable. No one has ever taken Fekete Var—the Black Castle—by storm in four hundred years of wars and invasions. Few have dared enter the Bakony." There was a note of pride in his voice.

"The Black Castle," Laure repeated. It had an ominous sound. She tried out the strange name Stephen had used. "Fekete Var?"

Stephen nodded. "That is its name in Magyar—what you call Hungarian." He reached up with his good hand and stroked her arm. When she withdrew, the fingers closed round her wrist with surprising strength. "You may as well start learning Magyar." He spoke with quiet deliberation.

Laure's arm tingled where he had stroked along the soft underside, from elbow to wrist. His head lay heavy in her lap, a dead weight that could at any moment become disconcertingly alive. "I don't expect to be here long enough to make that worthwhile," she said. "In fact, I think you should send me back from here. You have used me to help you escape—isn't that enough?"

Stephen laughed deep in his throat, and the caressing hand slid up her arm again until the backs of his fingers just touched the soft curve of her breast. "I think not. Perhaps I can make you want to stay."

Laure rose to her feet and dumped his head unceremoniously back on the straw pallet. "You're spoiled, Stephen Andrassy," she said in a low voice. "Just because the peasants here toady to you, you think you can have anything you want on a whim. Well, you can't have me! I helped you get out of Vienna because I wouldn't hand over a dog I liked to those slimy police spies, and the least you can do in return is help me get home again."

Stephen raised himself on one elbow and stared at her with his curiously intent blue gaze. "What—send you back to marry one of those 'slimy police spies'?"

Laure had temporarily forgotten that she was supposed to be engaged to Josef. She stood mute in the center of the grape arbor, searching for words. Stephen turned his head to look at her, and she stepped back out of his range of vision.

"I wonder if dear Josef would like to hear about that little coach ride we took?" Stephen went on. "You have some unusual methods of treating a wounded man, my dear. Not that I have any complaint to make. Feel free to be my nurse any time you like!"

Laure put both hands to her cheeks to still the fires that burned there. Oh, how could she have been such a fool as to succumb to that mad impulse! "You're no gentleman," she said at last, "to remind me of that."

"True," Stephen replied, too promptly. "I'm not a gentleman. I'm a noble. That's better."

"And you can't keep me here against my will!" Laure marched out of the grape arbor and around the corner of the inn, fuming. She would find the innkeeper and make him understand that he was helping a criminal, and that if he would provide her with transport back to Austria, he would be richly rewarded.

She tried very slow, clear German on the innkeeper, with no result but a grin of incomprehension. Italian and her schoolroom French worked no better. The man kept grinning and repeating a single sentence, which Laure found totally incomprehensible. Jansci lounged against the wall of the taproom, paring his nails with that omnipresent knife and grinning in a manner that suggested he had no fear at all that Laure would achieve her objective.

Eventually, when she threw her hands up in exasperation, he stepped forward and interpreted the innkeeper's one sentence. "He's telling you that he only speaks 'Deutsch, Slavisch and Ungarisch'," Jansci translated.

"Impossible," Laure protested. "I've already tried German."

Jansci gave her an unpleasant sideways grin. "Then you'd better start learning Magyar—Hungarian national tongue—like count suggests."

Laure sank into a rickety wooden chair balanced in front of the one table.

"Wouldn't do any good if he did understand you," Jansci advised. "He's the count's man. All here—his arm encompassed the horizon of the wide, flat plain outside the inn—is count's land."

"You mean he's a serf?" Laure said. "He belongs to your precious count—like a thing? That's disgusting!"

"It doesn't work quite like that."

Stephen stood in the doorway, supporting himself with his left hand on the roughly cut timber of the doorpost. He was somewhat white about the lips, but his voice was deep and strong as ever—the voice of Csikos, not of the man she had known as Stephen Andrassy. "You might with equal truth say," Stephen went on, "that I belong to him." He turned his head and asked a question of the innkeeper's wife. She nodded and smiled and responded with a torrent of Magyar. Stephen turned back to Laure. "Go with Kati."

"What for?"

Stephen sighed. "Will you stop asking so many questions!" He took a step forward, and Laure picked up her skirts and retreated to the inner room. Ridiculous to feel menaced by the man who had just risen from his pallet and who shouldn't be on his feet yet. But she found herself in the bedroom with Kati without ever knowing how it came about.

She could just see Stephen's shiny hussar boots if she peeped round the door. Then Kati pulled a curtain of some coarse wool stuff across the doorway, and she could only hear. There was a creak of a chair in the taproom; she heard Jansci asking a question, and a burst of laughter from both men at Stephen's reply.

Kati raised the lid of an intricately carved wooden chest at the foot of the bed and lifted out a bright blue silk skirt. She held the garment up against Laure's slim waist, gave a cluck of disapproval and delved into the chest for more clothes. The rest of the chest proved to be filled with linen petticoats and shifts. All were cut very full, and the hems of the petticoats and sleeves of the shifts were covered with painstaking cross-stitch designs in black and red. At the very bottom there was a bodice of velvet embroidered with gold thread, and a stack of triangular silk shawls with soft fringe.

Kati indicated by gestures that Laure should discard her ball gown and replace it with the clothes she had laid out on top of the feather beds. Laure was relieved to get out of the impractical gauze dress at last. The clothes Kati offered her were at least clean, even if they had been creased by lying so long in the chest. But she felt some misgivings. The silks and embroidered linens were so much finer than Kati's own everyday wear of a blue cotton skirt and bodice, with a coarse linen shift underneath. She pointed at herself, at Kati and at the new clothes several times over, until at last Kati laughed and held up one of the skirts to show that it was far too small for her ample waist.

Laure had thought Kati expected her to wear the chemise and skirt, with perhaps one petticoat underneath. But as Laure stood in the embroidered chemise with arms raised high, Kati slipped not one but a dozen gathered white skirts over her head. When the blue overskirt was finally laced on, it stood out like a bell from the many petticoats swaying underneath. Only then did Kati proceed to fit the velvet bodice on over the skirt and chemise. She tucked two of the flowered shawls around Laure's shoulders and, as a final touch, produced a pair of knitted white stockings and high red boots from a wall cupboard.

Laure was perspiring with the heat in the tiny room and the many layers of clothing, but Kati was not finished yet. She made Laure sit down while she combed out her hair and fastened it in braids wrapped around her head with a white ribbon. Then, and only then, did she throw the woolen curtain aside and usher Laure out into the taproom.

Jansci and Stephen had evidently been drinking steadily since Laure left the room. Jansci applauded with handclaps and a piercing yell, while Stephen pounded on the table with his good hand.

Laure flounced into the one free chair—any other movement was impossible in those swaying skirts. "I feel like a pig brought to market," she announced crossly, to no one in particular.

Stephen snapped out a curt order in Magyar. Both Jansci and Kati hurriedly left the room.

"You look beautiful to me," he told her. He left his chair and came around to her side of the table. Laure stood up and backed away from him, until she was standing against the wall.

Stephen followed her with patient, inexorable steps. "So vulnerable," he murmured. "Are you really afraid of me, *Laurica?*" He ran one hand around the neckline of her chemise and gently tugged at the drawstring until it spilled open, revealing the shadow of her breasts as they were pushed up and confined by the tight-laced bodice.

"Beautiful—and tempting," he went on. "Like a peasant girl working in the fields."

His hand slipped inside the loosened neckline of her chemise and caressed the firm ripe curves partially revealed under the thin material. The warm pressure of his hand was hypnotic. Laure felt unfamiliar waves

90

of pleasure spread through her body. Stephen gently tugged the chemise entirely open and slipped the thin embroidered garment over her shoulders. He held one bare shoulder with his good hand and lowered his lips to the soft places he had caressed into arousal with his fingertips. His lips and tongue teased her nipples to throbbing peaks of ecstasy. Laure moaned and her head fell back against the wall. The only points of reality were his hand pinning her to the wall and his mouth rousing her to undreamed-of pleasures.

"Don't fight me," Stephen whispered.

Fight him? She couldn't even remember the meaning of the word. Blindly, she reached out to caress the thick lion-colored mane of hair.

"That's right. Laure—*Laurica*—you belong to me now!" His hand gripped her shoulder in triumph until she thought the bones were grinding together. The sudden shaft of pain cleared her head for a moment.

"Belong to you? You mean like one of your serfs?" she spat at him. "Take your hands off, Stephen Andrassy! I told you that I'm no man's possession!" Reckless anger, with fear underlying it, spurred her to new invective. "You may be able to order the serf girls to your bed, but I'll not come so easily."

Stephen stepped back a pace, his face a mask of pain and bewilderment.

"I did not think it was a matter of orders," he said.

"No." Laure was calmer now. "You own these people so completely that you have only to express a desire and they come running to serve the count. Tell me, what do you do to them if they don't serve well enough? I should like to know what is in store for me. After all, you've got me on your land now and even dressed me like one of your peasants. What comes next? I've heard the great lords here still have the power of the lash. Will you have me stripped and flogged if I don't perform well enough in your bed, like a poor peasant who dared refuse you his last few grains of corn?"

Stephen's face darkened and he seemed to tower over her. Laure shrank back, half-expecting him to strike her. But after a moment, the anger left his eyes, to be replaced by a cold control more chilling than any blaze of passion. "Don't talk of what you know nothing about," he advised her. Then, disconcertingly, he laughed. "You will have time enough to learn the duties of a serf to her lord, and the obligations of the lord. I shall make it my special pleasure to teach you—once we are in the Bakony—in Fekete Var."

His mention of the Black Castle sent a wave of pure terror through Laure. "I won't go with you!" she spat out like a cornered cat. As Stephen moved closer, she struck out in blind panic. Her fist caught his injured shoulder, and he staggered back with a groan of pain. Laure seized the moment to twist past him and race out the door of the inn.

By some miracle there was no one in the yard. Laure dodged around the great traveling carriage and glanced up and down the road. To her left rose the hills of the Bakony, a black shadowy presence breaking the monotonous lines of fields and vineyards. To her right was the road they had come from.

The midday sun dazzled down on the road and the fields outside. Little waves of heat shimmered in the distance. Laure ran down the road, away from those mountains where the Black Castle stood. Still there was no pursuit from the inn. She ran on, and when the road rounded a corner and she was out of sight of the inn, her aching side and burning lungs forced her to slow to a walk.

She trudged along the road, between green ditches holding puddles of stagnant water. On either side the fields stretched out, flat and featureless, with new crops that grew no higher than her knee and offered no concealment. She knew that she should turn off the road and seek a hiding place, but where could she go that she would not be instantly visible? She walked on.

A pain in her right heel warned her that a blister was forming. She walked gingerly, trying not to let the boot rub up and down on the painful spot. How much farther? It must have been all of ten miles to that village they had passed. She could stop at the church and beg for help. She discounted Jansci's wild tale that all the land she saw belonged to the count. One man couldn't own whole villages, dozens of them, and all these miles and miles of land. Jansci had been exaggerating. The priest would speak a civilized language. He would be able to help her.

Soon her boots and the hem of her skirt were covered with thick white dust. Thirst tormented her, but she would not drink the ditch water with its green scum on top. Surely it could be only a little farther to the village! But the green plain stretched out before her, featureless, shimmering with heat at the horizon. Laure lowered her eyes and plodded on, promising herself that she would not look up until she had gone another hundred steps—two hundred—a thousand.

She lost count of the steps and the number of times she looked up, hoping to see the outline of a church surrounded by peasant huts. There was never anything but the tantalizing shimmer of heat rising from the road where it stretched to the horizon. Presently, she lowered her eyes to watch the toes of her boots moving forward. Left, right, left, right—she stumbled and giggled. "Can't keep rhythm," she admonished her boots. "Never learn to dance that way."

Talking made her realize how dry her mouth was. And the sun beating down on her unprotected head made it ache. She remembered the cool green arbor behind the inn as a long-ago haven of peace and security. Now it seemed as though there was nothing in the world but heat and dust and this endless road.

At least Stephen had not sent anyone after her. A man on horseback could have caught up with her long ago. So his whim to take her with him must have passed. Laure knew she ought to be relieved at that thought, but her head ached so that all she could feel was a dull and stupid depression.

"If I'm not being followed," she said aloud, "there's no reason to keep hurrying." She knelt beside the ditch and looked with more interest at the stagnant water in it. She still could not bring herself to drink it, but she dabbled her fingers in the puddle and trailed cool water across her forehead. How hot it was! If only there were some shade, she could rest until it was cooler before she went on. But it would be foolish to go on sitting here in the full sun.

She was still telling herself how foolish it was, and that she would rise and trudge on in just a minute, when hoofbeats sounded behind her.

It was not a peasant on one of those scrubby little Magyar ponies. Nor even Jansci. It was Stephen, as she'd known all along it would be, coming for her.

With a sigh that might have been relief, Laure rose from the edge of the ditch and stood facing him in the road. She knew she must make a pathetic figure, her skirt and apron soiled by the white dust of the road and her braids darkened with sweat, but that did not seem to matter any more.

He reined in his horse at the side of the road and sat looking down at her. He was still somewhat white about the lips, and he held his right arm close to his side. He was dressed in a flowing peasant shirt that he must have borrowed from the innkeeper. And he was smiling.

Without a word spoken, he leaned down and extended his left hand to Laure. She took the proffered grasp, placed one foot on his stirrup, and was lifted to the back of the horse in an undignified scrambling leap, petticoats and colored skirts flying about her. She straddled the horse behind him and smoothed down the full skirts of her costume as far as they would go.

"You'll have to hold on for yourself," Stephen warned her. "I can't spare a hand to help you." He turned the horse about and they proceeded back to the inn at a walking pace.

Laure wrapped her arms around Stephen's waist and laid her head against his back. She could feel the muscles in his back and sense the spicy male smell of his body under the sun-warmed linen. His whole body was lean, muscled, perfectly formed, like a machine tuned to one purpose. She wondered dreamily what it would be like to touch him like this without the barrier of clothes between them.

"What took you so long?" she asked. Her voice seemed to come from somewhere far away.

Stephen turned his head and kissed the sweat-dampened curls on her forehead. "I thought I should let you find out for yourself." She no longer resented the hint of laughter in his voice. "Did you plan to walk back to Vienna?"

"I had a plan." It was hard to remember now. The rhythmic motion of the horse under her, the comforting warm feel of Stephen's back, were lulling her into sleep. "I was going to the village. I thought the priest would speak something besides Magyar, and he would help me."

Stephen laughed outright. "I should have let you get all the way to the village. But I doubt you would have made it that far. The priest speaks Magyar—and Latin. And the village is mine. Do you know what they would do with a stranger? They would have kept you there and sent to me for orders. So you see, my little spitfire, you may as well come with me. Wouldn't you rather come back to the inn and ride in my carriage than walk in the dusty roads?"

"Mm." Laure couldn't give up without a fight. "Your carriage was going in the wrong direction. We're riding the wrong way now."

"I hardly thought you wished to stay at Erdekosi Marton's inn for the rest of your life," countered Stephen. "And you will be better off staying with me at Fekete Var than in the priest's house."

"I don't know." Laure traced the crisp curls at the back of Stephen's neck with one finger. He was all golden and brown from the sun. Would she become like that if she stayed in this land? But there was some reason why she must not stay with him. Slowly, she dredged it up out of memory. "The priest has no designs on my virtue."

"Precisely. Think how boring that would be." They were back at the inn. Stephen turned in the saddle and gave Laure his hand for balance as she slid down. The petticoats billowed over her head again and caused shrieks of dismay from Marton's wife. When Laure got her skirts under control again, Stephen had dismounted. He smiled at her with a familiar wicked gleam in his eyes. He put out his hand to touch Laure's cheek. Was he going to kiss her? Even as her eyes half-closed in anticipation, the caressing fingers were withdrawn and she heard him shouting at Jansci to put the horses to again. "We've lost enough time here!"

There was a momentary bustle and confusion in the stable yard as Jansci, Marton and the stableboy ran in different directions to do the count's bidding. Laure was left standing by the well.

A gentle hand on her shoulder urged her to sit on the well curb. Marton's wife brought up a bucket of cold water from the depths of the well and handed Laure the hand-carved wooden dipper. She drank gratefully, taking great thirsty gulps of the clear cold water, until the woman laid a hand on the dipper and said something, shaking her head.

"Not too much at one time." Laure grinned and wiped the stray wisps of sweat-dampened hair out of her face. "All right—I understand."

The coach wheels turned and creaked in the narrow space. Stephen came striding over to the well and offered Laure his hand.

When she stood up, every muscle protested. She was sore from the long walk, and the insides of her thighs had sore patches where they had rubbed against the horse on the way back.

"I am sorry, *galambom*." Stephen's good arm cradled her protectively against his chest. "You can sleep in the carriage."

Almost too tired and dazed to think, Laure stumbled passively toward the traveling carriage that was taking her the wrong way, away from everything that was familiar to her. She should have fought him still—she knew that—but what did it matter? She was defeated before she began. She accepted her defeat as Stephen pillowed her against his good shoulder inside the coach, and a moment later slid easily into the lesser defeat of sleep.

Chapter Seven

Fekete Var!

The Black Castle!

They had been riding for what seemed an eternity through the mysterious rustling woods and rocky foothills of the Bakony, that range of hills that had once been no more than a mysterious shadow on the horizon of the fertile Hungarian plain. The traveling carriage had been left behind at a farmhouse on the very edge of the hills, and the three of them had mounted fresh horses there to take them over this last and most grueling stretch. The most tiring part of traveling through the forest was not the actual riding, but the necessity of paying constant attention lest one's horse put a hoof into a hole between two rocks or lead one into a thicket of low-lying branches.

Laure rode between the two men, her head down to watch the path. The evening glow had long since faded, and they had to pick their way by moonlight. Every bone in her body ached with exhaustion, and she was kept awake only by the need to watch her horse's steps carefully.

Suddenly Stephen's hand caught the reins of her horse. "I can guide her myself," Laure snapped, and Stephen laughed.

"I know you can. But there is no need. Look!" His upraised arm, pointing, it seemed, into the sky, guided her eyes to where the Black Castle reared like some primitive animal crouched on its rocky crag. In the moonlight its walls of rock seemed not black, but silver, and the pale light picked out old arrow slits and crumbling crenellations in a delicate chiaroscuro.

"My castle," Stephen said. He raised himself in the stirrups and hallooed up the hill with one hand cupped round his mouth. Moments later, the black arrow slits sprang to life with flickering lights, and a cluster of men carrying torches advanced from the main gate of the castle. Laure watched with her mouth half-open, drinking in the beauty and the strangeness of the wild scene. It was like a picture from a medieval romancer's book. She turned uncertainly toward the man at her side. He, too, seemed changed from the young officer she had danced with in Vienna. At one of their posting stages, he had put aside the emperor's uniform for his black and silver tunic and high black boots. Now, in the pale cold light that turned his face into a sharp pattern of boldly etched features, he seemed all Csikos. Laure could scarcely believe that only twenty-four hours earlier they had whispered in the shrubbery outside Prince

Metternich's villa. It seemed, rather, that they had traveled hundreds of years, back in time to some barbarian state where this man ruled like a king. "Count's land—count's men." Jansci's words came back to her, and she shivered.

She was too tired that night to take in more than fleeting impressions of the great keep. Torchlight danced along the rough stone walls and created mysterious patterns of shadows. The men who clustered around Csikos—no, *Stephen* (she must not forget that this was Stephen Andrassy, a civilized man of her own world)—were mustachioed bandits, who laughed and slapped his back familiarly and talked in that harsh language that she could not understand. She understood well enough the curious glances that were cast at her, though, and straightened her back and returned them with a steady gaze that refused to be ashamed. Even when the crowd around Stephen forced her from his side, she did not cry out, but set her back against a wall and waited for what might come. Her eyelids were heavy with fatigue, and to keep them open she stared at a crude mask carved out of the stone at the top of a pillar. In the flickering light the face seemed to move as if it were alive and laughing at her.

"Good." Stephen had slipped away from his men and come up beside her. "You don't show fear. They respect that, you know."

"Why?" Laure countered, her brows raised. "Surely I have nothing to fear from the count's men?"

Jansci, following close behind Stephen, guffawed and translated to the men standing beside him. There was a wave of laughter. Approving laughter, Laure thought. Did it matter? She was lost here, interpreting tones and shadows and expressions. Her ignorance of the land and the language imprisoned her more surely than the stone walls of the keep.

Stephen offered his arm. Laure, her legs stiff from the long hours of riding and from standing still against the wall, stepped forward to take it and almost fell.

He caught her in time, and for a moment she leaned gratefully against the warm strength of his body. At least he was familiar to her—the one link with her old world.

There were steps to be negotiated, a narrow passageway, and then a great, bare, stone-walled room that had been given an incongruous air of luxury by a sprinkling of modern furnishings. The heavy iron torch holders on the walls supported delicate wax tapers that showed Laure a gilt bed with embroidered hangings, a white enameled hip bath and a tile washstand with porcelain dishes. But the floor under her feet was of rough-planed beams, and in place of a carpet there was the great black pelt of a mountain bear, flung down before the elegant bed with its tapestried hangings.

The last thing she remembered before exhaustion overcame her was the round, smiling face of a peasant girl who had been sitting on a carved chest at the foot of the bed.

A thread of sunshine crept up the bed hangings, found a crack in the tapestries and glittered into the interior of the bed, turning the down mattresses and embroidered hangings into an enchanted cave. Laure blinked in the light, bemused for a moment and wondering if she had strayed into some magic world where jeweled birds perched on trees covered with flowers.

Then, with a rush, memory returned and the world came back into focus. She was in a bed piled so thick with feather mattresses that she had almost sunk out of sight. A bar of sunlight was slanting in through the hangings and illuminating the embroidered pictures. And beside her there was a dented pillow and corresponding dent in the feather mattress, as though someone had slept beside her and had gone out while she was still asleep.

Laure sat up as quickly as if the other pillow had housed a poisonous snake. She swung her feet over the side of the bed and jerked the hangings open.

At once there was a click of bootheels from the far side of the room, and the peasant girl she had seen the night before came around the bed and curtsied to greet her. "The water is warm," she said in careful, correct German. "If it please the lady?" She offered her hand to help Laure down from the high bed.

There was warm water for washing, brought up from the kitchens in tin pails. And, at last, there was somebody she could talk to and find out more about this strange place. Laure luxuriated in the lukewarm water that the girl poured into the hip bath, submitted to having her fair hair combed out and her skin massaged with rose water, and listened. There was no need to draw the girl out with questions; she was eager to talk.

Her name was Magda, she told Laure, and her mother was from one of the Saxon towns in the north; that was why she could speak German and why the count had sent for her to wait on Laure. It was a lucky chance for her. She liked to work in the castle; now her hands would be soft and her skin white like a lady's, and she wouldn't be so tired from helping her father in the fields. The count was a good man, too.

He'd sent money, enough so that her parents could hire a field worker to take her place. Everybody admired the count. He was good to his people, and such a fine man—strong and handsome. When he first sent for her, Magda had hoped he meant something else—she wasn't ashamed to confess it, for wouldn't any woman be pleased if the count's eye fell on her? Her parents had warned her that he'd never give up that Gypsy slut, though, even if he did have an eye for every pretty girl in the county, and—.

Magda gave an embarrassed giggle and fell silent. She paid exaggerated attention to combing the last tangles out of Laure's hair.

"What Gypsy?" Laure asked.

"Oh, you know how the peasants gossip!" Already Magda felt some distance between herself—called to wait on a lady in the castle—and the peasants working in their fields. "Besides, they were wrong; for aren't you here now, and in the count's own chamber?"

Laure turned her head so sharply that Magda's wooden comb caught in a tangle and brought tears of pain to her eyes. "The count's room!" It could not be true. He would not dare. But there had been that dent in the pillow beside hers.

"It is a great honor." Magda separated the long tangled strands of hair with her fingers and worried at them with the wooden comb. "There now, you will be beautiful for the count." She spread the clean, shining hair out on Laure's shoulders like a mantle and stepped back to admire her work. "I don't know how to put it up like the great ladies do," she apologized.

"Braids will do." Laure's fingers flew through the heavy mass of her hair, jerking it into two tight braids that she wrapped around her head and skewered into

104

place with the ivory pins she had found in a little tray in the chest. Strange, to find these woman's things in this place. Perhaps they had belonged to the Gypsy. Not that it mattered to her. She had no more to do with Stephen than to make him aware of his presumption and force him to send her back. How dare he! Lying beside her all night and then tiptoeing away, leaving his peasants and his men to snigger over the count's latest conquest.

"Please, lady." Magda had caught just enough of Laure's angry mutterings to know that they boded ill for her master. She stood squarely in front of the oaken door, twisting her fingers in her embroidered apron. "Please. It wasn't like that—the count said you were tired, I was not to wake you. Truly, he meant to honor you, to show all men at once that you are his!"

Laure swept past Magda without a word.

The narrow passageway she had followed the night before split in two directions around a corner. Laure paused for a moment, and then heard a burst of laughter from the right-hand corridor. A few more steps brought her to the head of the stairs going down into the great hall.

Stephen was standing with one booted foot on the stone hearth, drinking from a flask and laughing with two men. One was Jansci. The other was a darkly handsome man of about Stephen's age, with a smile that flashed brightly under the trailing mustache that seemed to be the common trademark of these bandits.

This morning Stephen was dressed like any other of the bandits. His close-fitting dark breeches and linen shirt showed all too clearly the lines of his lean, powerful body. A short white woolen cloak, lavishly ornamented with designs in red and black cloth, was slung across one shoulder, revealing a knife and a pistol stuck into his dark blue sash. Only his neatly trimmed beard and mane of tawny gold hair differentiated him from the two dark-visaged fellows with whom he was talking.

Laure paused involuntarily halfway down the stairs. Here, in his own world, Stephen Andrassy seemed more formidable than the bandit on the run, or the smart young officer she had danced with. An impression of raw power and absolute certainty radiated from every line of his casual pose.

While she still stood there, uncertain whether to go on or retreat, he looked up and saw her. He gave a flashing careless smile and saluted her with his free hand. They might have been at the ball in the Rennweg, instead of this bandit's castle.

She was not conscious of descending the stone stairs and walking across the hall to where he stood. There was a mist of fury surrounding her, through which she saw nothing except Stephen's smiling face. It seemed like the last insult that he should look so happy. It was nothing to him to use her as he saw fit. Pretending to make love to her in Vienna, pretending to be her lover here. And no doubt, as Magda had said, he thought she should feel honored by the pretense. Honored!

His face was very close before her now. The other two men had stepped back before her determined stride. They were alone in an island of silence. Stephen was still smiling. He reached out a hand to draw her to him. He started to say something. She never heard what it was.

There was a crack that echoed through the hall. The smile was gone from Stephen's face, to be replaced by a slowly spreading reddish blotch. Laure's palm stung. He caught her hand at the wrist and forced it backward until she thought she must cry out from the pain.

"Go ahead," she taunted him in a low, breathless voice. "Break my arm. That's what you're good at, isn't it—hurting defenseless girls?"

Stephen dropped her hand and felt the side of his face with his fingertips. "Oh—hardly defenseless, would you say?"

Goaded beyond bearing, Laure snatched at the knife in his belt. This time it was Jansci's hands that restrained her, catching her arms at the elbows and holding her fast. He said something in Hungarian and Stephen laughed.

"He is warning me," he told Laure, "that my kitten has claws."

"Well," Laure said, "perhaps if he holds me very tightly, you can manage to rape me. Or have you had enough fun already, ruining my life and my reputation?"

At a sign from Stephen, Jansci dropped Laure on the cold stone floor. She went down on one knee and struggled to her feet, somewhat hampered by the full, short petticoats of the peasant dress.

"Too much trouble, master." This time Jansci spoke in German so that she could understand. "Why you bring her so far? Plenty girls in Hungary who wouldn't fight the count."

The other man sniggered behind his hand and Stephen rebuked him with an oath. "Shut up, Geza!" He turned back to Laure. "And you—don't interrupt when the men are taking counsel, or I shall be forced to raise my hand to you."

Laure smoothed down her disordered petticoats

and stared back at him. "How brave," she said at last. "Will you have Jansci hold me?"

Stephen cursed all women with a fluency and invective that encompassed all the languages known to Laure and several that were unfamiliar to her.

"Oh, I don't know, master," Jansci said when he ran out of words at last. "This one could be some use. You think Prince Metternich likes her?"

"His taste may even be that bad," Stephen allowed.

"Maybe we trade her for the Diet," Jansci suggested. "Tell him name the day—if he doesn't answer, send him a finger." He spat into the empty fireplace. "Austrians aren't mên; they don't like to see blood. Maybe couple of fingers, an ear—pretty soon they call the parliament, like you want." He grinned at Laure's white face. "I think she won't make so much trouble, either."

Laure felt the sharp taste of fear rising in her throat. These staring, grinning men, with their mustaches and long knives—how could she guess what they might do? And Stephen, now, seemed as much a brigand as any of them. She glanced from face to face. Jansci was openly grinning, the older man stared without comprehension; Stephen's face had a measuring look, as if he were thinking over Jansci's plan and finding it good.

She whirled and ran in a blind panic for the great double oaken doors of the hall. Her boot soles slipped on the smooth stones, and the froth of petticoats at her knees hampered her. Before she had gone a dozen steps, a hand fell on her shoulder. She twisted like a hunted animal to get away from the touch, and fell gracelessly on the stone floor for the second time that morning. This time her hands were up over her head and nothing broke her fall. The breath was knocked out of her and she was half-stunned for a moment.

Two shining leather boots, wrinkled at the ankle and tight at the calves, stood before her, between her and the door. Stephen reached out his hand. "Come now, little one. Don't run from me again."

When she closed her eyes and would not see the proffered hand, he took her arm and hauled her to her feet. "Let me go," Laure spat at him, twisting and fighting in his inexorable grip. "How dare you touch me?"

Stephen's hand on her arm tightened. There would be bruises there. But he was still smiling. "There was a time when you did not object to my—touch. Shall I remind you?"

His face was coming nearer, blotting out the hall and the staring, grinning men behind them. Laure set her teeth and turned her head away from him. She could feel his warm breath on her cheek. She struck out blindly with her free hand and wrenched a gasp of pain from him. The blow had fallen on his injured shoulder. The men laughed out loud, and Jansci called out a suggestion on the taming of tiger kittens.

Stephen swore again in his own tongue. "You should be taught manners!"

The smile was gone now. The lines of his face were cold and stern. Laure felt renewed panic.

"If you dare hurt me," she threatened, "do you think you will get away with it? My cousin is in the secret police—even now he is searching for me. They will bring soldiers and—and burn your castle!"

Unexpectedly, Stephen laughed, throwing his head back. "Burn the Black Castle? I think not." This time his smile was tinged with triumph. "You talk too much, Laurica. Do you really think the arm of the Austrian police can reach into the Bakony for you? Do you think I was such a fool as not to take precautions? You have already written to your cousins, my dear. You apologized for taking such sudden leave, explained that you were embarrassed by Josef's attentions and had accepted Count Andrassy's invitation to visit his country estates for an indefinite period."

Laure felt as though the air in the room were being drained away, leaving nothing but the blackness which threatened to overpower her. What was Stephen talking about? She had written no such letter.

"It was a very well phrased letter," Stephen went on with a smile. "I devoted several hours to composing it. You will be glad to know that your writing style is particularly elegant, although the German is a little awkward, as is only to be expected from an English girl. So you see, you have nothing to fear from Jansci's proposal. I would not compromise my own excellent story by allowing "Csikos" to use you as a hostage. And—Josef will institute no search."

"He won't believe it!" Laure interrupted.

Stephen's smile held a flicker of menace. "You had best pray that he does. As long as he accepts the letter, you are my guest and not a hostage."

"There seems to me to be very little difference! And you will find it out when Josef sends men after you! This is a civilised country—we are not in the Middle Ages! You cannot hope to get away with this!"

But the grim stone walls of the ancient fortress seemed to belie her words and hurl them back, mocking her.

Stephen smiled again. His hand tightened on her

arm and he drew her unresisting body closer to his, until she could feel the raw power emanating from his muscular frame. "Shall I show you just how much your cousin can protect you?"

Suddenly, he released his grip on her arm and Laure made a spring for freedom. She was stopped by two hands that closed around her waist like iron fetters. He lifted her into the air and she remembered the effortless ease with which he had mounted her on her horse once. Not a man to fight. He threw her across his shoulder as if she had been a sack of grain. Her face was buried in the white felt cape, scratched by the rough embroidery. The breath was crushed out of her by the hard angle of his shoulder under the cape. She gasped and pummeled his back with her fists without effect, even when she directed her blows at his wounded shoulder.

A bouncing movement. He was mounting the stairs, bending so as not to crush her against the low beams at the turn of the staircase. Calls of encouragement from the men in the hall. Now the passageway, worn stones and narrow slits of light.

When they reached the room where she had slept the previous night, Stephen jerked his head and Magda scurried out of sight. He pushed back the embroidered hangings that walled around the bed and dropped Laure into the middle of the softly billowing feather mattresses. She felt as though she were drowning in their softness. Before she could struggle free, Stephen had sat down beside her. His weight tilted the mattresses so that she was pressed against him, and his hand on her shoulder, gentle now, exerting no pressure, still kept her from rising.

It was very quiet inside the room. Magda had

slammed the door shut when she left, and the heavy oaken beams and the long passageway filtered out the noises from the great hall. It was so still that Laure could hear as separate sounds the pounding of her own heart, Stephen's ragged breathing and the lazy buzz of a fly that had been enticed inside the castle walls by that one ray of sunlight that lay across the bed.

Stephen lifted his hand and stroked her cheek with one finger. The tenderness of the gesture reminded Laure of the first time they'd met, when the bandit Csikos had lifted a vagrant curl from her face with the same gentle touch. And now Csikos was Count Stephen Andrassy, and Stephen was a brigand, and all her fighting and evasions had led her to this one room at the heart of the castle, where they faced each other in silence. Laure felt tears prickling under her eyelids, and lowered her lashes so that he should not see.

"Why do you hate me, Laure?"

The words were as soft as the breeze that whispered in at the window. The fingertips that brushed her face, hardly touching her, left her skin absurdly, achingly sensitive to the slightest movement of the air. Laure felt her own breathing becoming as ragged as Stephen's.

"I don't—hate you," she managed to say, in a whisper that hardly sounded like her own voice.

The tormenting, feather-light touch moved down along the line of her throat, traced the curve of her gathered peasant blouse. Stephen grasped the tie strings and pulled. The blouse fell open, revealing the soft skin, whiter than the linen blouse, that had never been exposed to daylight. He traced the curves of her breasts with a teasing finger that circled each sensitive peak without touching, then laid his hand again against the side of her face. All the while his eyes, intent and blue, never left hers. His mouth was grave now, not stern, and there was a questioning look in his eyes.

The sunlight fell across the bed and glowed on Laure's body where Stephen had laid back the embroidered blouse. She thought confusedly that that must be why she felt this unfamiliar warmth glowing through her body. Warmest of all was where he'd touched her—no, where he had not touched her, where her nipples were tingling with unsatisfied desire. And the palm of his hand was hard and warm against her face. She turned her head and pressed a kiss into his palm.

Fingers and thumb closed about her jaw and lifted her face to meet his. His eyes closed, Laure was sinking in the softness of the feather bed, pressed down by the weight of Stephen's body upon hers, drowning in the sweetness of his kisses. He took her mouth with a practiced insistence, gently urging her lips to open to him until his tongue invaded her half-open mouth; then he left her with parted lips only to rove farther down her throat and white shoulders with his kisses. His lips traced the swelling curves of her breasts and tormented each nipple in turn to a throbbing peak of desire. Laure's hand moved of its own to caress the back of his tawny gold head and press him closer to her. The sun fell across his hair now, gilding him to the semblance of a young god whose absolute right to her body could not be denied. His hands moved lower, to strip off with impatient haste the skirts and embroidered petticoats that Magda had dressed her in with such care. They slipped to the floor, a little heap of white openwork and bright silk flowers, and Laure opened herself to his demanding caresses like a flower to the sun.

Stephen raised himself, fumbling with his own clothes. A moment later the pile of white flounces was weighted down with a man's dark trousers and the heavy silver-mounted weapons of a mountain brigand.

The length of his body pressed against hers, warm and firm, and she could feel the insistent demand of his maleness rising against her thighs. A moment of fear flashed through her mind—this was the secret part of marriage, which Julie and the other girls whispered about.

As if sensing her momentary withdrawal, Stephen raised himself to take his weight from her. His lips, warm, demanding, urgent, traced a line of passion down from the hollow between her breasts and along her flat stomach. Tiny, nibbling, biting kisses with tongue and teeth nipped at the sensitive inner skin of her thighs and wrested a moan of pure pleasure from her. Laure sank into the embrace of the feather bed and gave herself over to the tides of pure sensation that were sweeping over her. Stephen's fingers stroked between her thighs and she parted her legs for him, feeling the warm, darting touch of his tongue where his fingers had first invaded. She was drunk, she was flying, she was floating on clouds.

This time when his weight settled over her, she clasped him to her eagerly. She wanted to know him—all of him—without even knowing what that meant.

His knees forced hers farther apart, the rough skin, the golden hair on his legs brushing against her inner thighs.

There was a brief stabbing pain between her legs. Laure's eyes widened in shock and she twisted to get away from the source of pain, but her movements only helped him to drive deeper into her. Stephen was stroking her neck and shoulders, coaxing her as he would a favorite mare.

"There, there, little one, it is only once that I shall have to hurt you. Now rest, relax, let me show you pleasure. It will be all right now, you will see; it only hurts for a moment—see, it is over already."

His hypnotic voice and rhythmic rocking movements lulled Laure into quiet again. And it was true; the pain was not repeated. There was only this gentle rocking, his body pressing into hers, this sense of fullness and completion. She put her arms around his shoulders and pulled him down against her, his hard chest crushing her breasts. If only they could lie still like this forever, totally belonging to one another! But Stephen kept up that gently insistent movement, and a strange, warm sensation was replacing the pain she had felt earlier. Her own body moved without conscious command, her hips thrusting up to meet him in the age-old rhythm.

The growing warmth at the core of her body exploded into a shower of light that flooded her veins. Laure cried out in surprise at the waves of delight that rocked her. She was only dimly aware of Stephen's cry of triumph, and of the pulsing of his body inside hers. Everything—the room, Stephen, her own self—was obliterated in this explosion of pleasure. How long the waves rolled through her she did not know; only that, when she was aware of the room again, she lay trembling in Stephen's arms. She felt as if she had returned from a long journey.

His eyes were fixed on her with a look that blended

triumph and tenderness. "Now you know that you are mine," he told her.

The words admitted no reply. It was a statement, not a question. Laure turned her face away from the triumphant blaze of those blue eyes. She buried her face in his shoulder, savoring the warm strength of his body.

Chapter Eight

"PAWN TO KING'S BISHOP FOUR," LAURE ANNOUNCED, more to recall Marton's wandering attention to the game than because she thought it was a particularly good move. It didn't matter. She would win; she always did. In the two weeks since Stephen had brought her to the Black Castle, Laure had had ample time to discover the strengths and weaknesses of Marton's chess game, Magda's gossip and Jansci's malicious pinpricks. Those were the only amusements öpen to her.

Marton was not a very good chess player, but he was kind enough to sit with her for an hour now and then and move the pieces about the board, giving her thoughts somewhere else to go than their regular, frustrating circle. Now, while Marton pondered his next move, Laure leaned back in her rough wooden chair and glanced idly around the great hall. There'd been a flurry of movement around the door while she was moving her piece. She'd resolutely kept her back turned and feigned absorption in the game. If Stephen should have come in, she didn't want him to think she was eagerly awaiting his return—or to give him an excuse to laugh once more at her notion that Josef would rescue her. As the weeks passed, she had gradually acknowledged that the letter Stephen sent under her name had stopped any hope of rescue. Josef's pride, his anger at her refusal, his jealousy of Stephen—all would combine to make him believe the story that Stephen had concocted. More than that—to save his pride he would see to it that the tale was hushed up— No inconvenient questions would be asked in Vienna, and she would receive no help but her own wits and the few friends she'd made in the castle.

But it wasn't Stephen; just one of the hunting party, back early and complaining loudly about his stupid horse, who had lamed herself in a rabbit hole and spoiled his morning's sport. Laure listened to Geza's inventive flow of curses with mild amusement. She could scarcely believe these were the ferocious bandits who had terrified her so, that first night in the castle! Now that she had sorted them out, putting names to the fierce, mustachioed faces, they seemed no more terrible than a group of English soldiers. They were no longer mysterious figures, glittering with armaments and shrouded in their elaborate cloaks, but only Geza, Jansci, Marton and a half-dozen others.

Geza was talkative and boastful, a younger son of a

poor noble. Without land or a career, he'd cherished romantic notions of becoming a bandit in the wooded hills of the Bakony, until Stephen persuaded him to turn his love for adventure to fighting for Hungarian freedom. Jansci was a peasant whose brains had destined him for the priesthood, until his rebellious streak earned him one too many thrashings from the good fathers. At thirteen he had run away with only a crust of bread and a knife from the monastery kitchens to see him through the world. Stephen had taken him on as body servant and had earned himself a slave who looked with a jealous eye on anybody who dared come close to his master. And Marton—.

Laure frowned and looked back at the grizzled man, who knotted his brows over the chessboard of black and white marble. She did not know Marton's story yet. He was older than the rest of Stephen's men, something in his speech and bearing suggesting that he had seen many years of military service. But he never let slip a hint of what his life had been before he joined Stephen, or of how he happened to meet the young count and his band. Even Magda, that fountain of gossip, knew nothing of Marton's past. But he was as absurdly devoted to Stephen as the rest of the band. Laure's hints that a reward awaited the man who would convey her safely to Austria had been met with blank incomprehension. Laure had learned a few Hungarian words by now, enough to make herself understood or to follow the stories the men told; but whenever she raised the subject of escape, suddenly no one understood a word she said.

Marton was still frowning over the board. Laure stood up and paced from the table to the fireplace and back again. At this rate, she might wear a path in the stone floor before she ever got out of the castle, let alone out of Hungary! If only Stephen would talk to her! She could try to explain to him that he was only harming his cause, whatever it was, by keeping her prisoner in this manner. Why did he insist on keeping her? It couldn't be for love. He had hardly spoken two words to her since the day he had swept her off to his room and made furious love to her all day and long into the night.

Laure's angry frown softened as she remembered that night, her initiation into the arts of passion. Stephen had been different then—tender, loving, sensual—the man she had begun to love in Vienna. All night he had caressed her, raising her untried body to new heights of sensation and drugging her with pleasure. And she had surrendered herself totally to him.

The cold light of first morning had brought them back to reality. It had been a cloudy day, and Laure had slept late in Stephen's arms. She woke slowly to find the room filled with a cool gray light that showed impersonally the tangled heap of clothes on the floor, the tumbled bedclothes and the strands of their hair, pale and tawny gold, mixed on the pillow. The room looked like the squalid aftermath of a tavern scene. Laure closed her eyes and snuggled into Stephen's shoulder to blot out the sight. She supposed that what they had been doing was wicked, but she no longer cared very much.

Stephen wouldn't let her sink back into sleep. He teased her by drawing her long strands of hair over her face, whispering in her ear and tickling her with his beard. *"Kedves lányom,"* he whispered. *"Szeretlek.* Come on, Laure, take your first Magyar lesson. Say it after me."

"Don't want lessons," Laure protested. Her voice cracked on a yawn in the middle of the sentence.

But Stephen kept teasing her until she repeated the strange, harsh syllables. *"Szeretlek."*

"Good! Now try this: *'Szeretlek, Istvan.'* That means—."

Laure put her fingers over his mouth. "I think I can guess," she whispered. "I love you, Stephen."

"És én szeretlek, Laure."

But somthing about that cold light made it seem indecent to stay whispering and giggling under the eiderdown. Laure bent over the edge of the bed and fished in the heap of clothing for her bodice and petticoats.

Stephen's hand on her arm stopped her. "Leave that," he said. "Magda will take those things away and wash them. I don't wish you to go about like a peasant."

Something in the calm superiority of his tone stung Laure. "What a pity, my lord, but I omitted to pack my trunks when you abducted me. So if I'm not to go about quite naked, I'm afraid these are the only clothes I have."

Stephen caressed his beard with one hand while a wicked smile danced in his eyes. "Hmm, now that is an interesting possibility. I couldn't let you go about in the castle without clothes, of course. It might distract my men. But here—shall I take those skirts away, and keep you a prisoner in your skin? Such lovely skin, all white and gold, and smooth like ivory." He ran a hand down her side as he spoke. Laure felt like a mare being appraised for sale. She flounced away and fumbled with the laces and fastenings of the peasant dress.

"I told you not to bother with that!" Stephen

snatched the lace-trimmed petticoats from her hand and threw them down on the floor. "Do you think Count Andrassy can't dress his woman in a fitting manner? Look at this!" He stamped across the floor and threw back the lid of the big carved wooden chest that Laure had been using as a dressing table. She gave an involuntary cry of protest as the lovely ivory-backed brush and comb fell to the floor, but Stephen did not heed her. He plunged both hands into the chest, furiously tossing through a jumble of bright silks and velvets. "Here, you can wear this." He drew out a silk lustring sacque, forty years exquisitely out of fashion, and tossed it onto the bed. "Or this." A flowered muslin round dress of more recent vintage followed, and a severely cut riding habit of dark green cloth.

Laure's precariously held temper hit the boiling point. How dare Stephen treat her like this, one minute talking of love, the next ordering her around as if she were a piece of property. "Put that stuff away!" she ordered in a voice grown shrill with strain. "How, how dare you—." Her foot tapped as she sought for words to express her sense of outrage. As always, unluckily, they came. "How dare you treat me like a doll to be dressed in the castoffs of your mistresses—or did those clothes belong to your victims? How many other girls have you dragged to this castle against their will? And do you always save their clothes to pass on to the next prisoner? How economical," she gibed. The words were coming now in a torrent over which she had no control. "My God, that lustring must date from Josef II's reign. Even if you started raping women when you were in leading strings, you're not old enough to have got that one. Is this a family business? Slightly used girls and their old clothes? Are you showing me the Andrassy heirlooms?"

Stephen stood almost at attention, his hands at his sides, until she ran out of words to throw at him. His blue eyes were as cold as ice.

"In a manner of speaking," he said, not disowning her last accusation. "These dresses belonged to my mother. I thought you might do me the honor to make use of some of them. But I see they are not to your taste. I apologize that the village does not boast a Parisian dressmaker."

He bowed once, his hands still at his sides, and went to the door. When his hand was on the latch, he looked back to where Laure stood speechless. "As for your other accusations," he said in a silky tone, "rape has never been a custom of the Andrassy family. I beg your forgiveness for last night. I had the impression you were—not unwilling. I apologize that it is impossible for me to send you back to Vienna at this time. But you have my assurance that I will not again enter this room except at your express invitation."

And he had kept his word. Laure had kept to her room for the rest of that morning, staring unseeing at the tapestries on the walls, while Magda—who had scurried in, in Stephen's wake—clucked around her, setting the bed to rights and airing the dresses from the chest. Late in the day she had finally plucked up the courage to descend to the great hall, wearing the simplest of the dresses Stephen had offered her, the figured muslin. He had favored her with a curt nod and shortly afterward had gone out with two of his men, not returning till long after dark.

That had been the pattern for the subsequent days. Stephen spoke to her only when necessary for politeness and spent as much of his time as possible away from the castle. She had no idea where he slept; he had not returned to his bedchamber since that disastrous quarrel.

Laure was left very much on her own. There were no restrictions on her movements within the castle; only when she tried to leave would a smiling guard turn her back with incomprehensible words. For a few days she amused herself with exploring the crumbling keep, from the malodorous cellars below the kitchen to the roofless cells on the upper story. More than half of what she saw was ruinous; for all its appearance of strength, only the central tower was defensible. But that had been kept up with a care that seemed excessive in these days of modern armies. Missing stones had been replaced, crumbling mortar smoothed over, and the doors were all of new oaken timbers laid across each other in many layers and bound with new-forged iron hinges.

Later, when Laure had a few words of Hungarian, she asked Marton why Stephen took so much care to preserve a castle that could be destroyed in a matter of days by siege engineers and cannon. "And who would be bringing cannon into the Bakony?" Marton asked rhetorically. "How far would a siege train get, before my lads picked 'em off one by one?"

But he left unanswered the question of why Stephen kept the castle's defenses so strong, and Laure had not enough Hungarian to make him go on.

At that time, though, Laure could not talk to anybody except Magda and Jansci; so she had no one to question about the castle. After a few days of exploration, and verifying that she would not be allowed to go outside, she settled to helping Magda unpick and remake the simpler of the clothes in the chest to fit her. Over the long hours of needlework,

Magda chattered away in her mixture of German and Hungarian, and Laure began to learn something of the people in the castle and the village.

The chess set had been an unexpected find, at the very bottom of the chest. Hand-carved of light and dark woods, the pieces were loving representations of a shepherd's life on the plain. The knights were Hungarian nobles with stiffly bristling mustaches and flourishing cloaks, the bishops were real shepherds with their tall crooks, and the pawns were peasant men and women, the men in wide-fringed trousers and the women in full skirts with many petticoats. Laure laughed aloud as the meaning of the little pieces came to her. "He had a sense of humor, whoever made this," she said.

"Please?" Magda still had trouble understanding Laure's quick German. "Old Tomas, he who was the head shepherd for His Excellency the count's grandfather, he made the pieces. They are long days out on the plains, you understand, and sometimes a man will not come back to the manor for weeks together. All shepherds learn to make things with their hands, but Tomas, he was a master."

"He was indeed." Laure felt the satiny texture of the hand-rubbed wood with pleasure. "But why were the pieces buried in this chest? Does no one here play?"

"Please?" It had obviously never occurred to Magda that the chess pieces were anything other than a set of carvings made by Tomas for his amusement. She polished the head of a shepherd with her blue-fringed apron and set the piece reverently back on the top of the chest. "Old Tomas, he was my father's cousin. . . . Perhaps His Excellency knows what you should do with them."

"I'm sure he does," Laure said between her teeth. "His Excellency the count seems to know what everybody should do. Well, I'm not one of his serfs!" Ignoring Magda's cries of protest, she scooped up a knight and a pawn, and marched down to the great hall to inquire in sign language for a chessboard.

It turned out that among Stephen's men, only Marton knew the rudiments of the game. He scratched out an improvised board with charcoal on the smooth flagstones before the hearth, and he and Laure spent an hour that afternoon playing the game that needed no language, while Magda fluttered around them and drove Laure to distraction by wondering audibly what the count would say when he found Laure had taken his carved pieces without permission. "Playing on the floor, too, like a baby!" she scolded.

When Stephen did come in, midway in the afternoon, Magda gave a screech that drove all thoughts of her next move out of Laure's head. He stood over the improvised chessboard and the players without speaking. Marton jumped up and stood at attention. Laure remained kneeling on her cushion, looking up at Stephen's impassive face with some apprehension. She felt so insignificant, kneeling at his feet like that. But she would not jump up and stand before him like a naughty child waiting to be scolded.

When Stephen finally spoke, it was in an unexpectedly mild voice. "There should be a chessboard somewhere around," he said. "Black and white marble—my father brought it from Buda. It is not quite in the same style as those carved chessman of old Tomas's, but you might find it more comfortable than crouching on the floor." He paused and stood looking over Laure's head, stroking his golden beard and apparently lost in thought. The muscles of her legs cramped in rebellion against her stiff posture, but she would not move for him. "You've altered that dress," he said at last. "It becomes you better than it did my mother—she had not the coloring for it. She was as dark as you are fair. My father used to tease her and call her his little Gypsy." He stared at Laure a moment longer, then turned on his heel and strode away.

Jansci had followed Stephen like a shadow. He waited now until the count was out of earshot, looking down at Laure with a malicious grin that was like a parody of Stephen's smile. "The Andrassy men have always favored Gypsies," he said in an undertone. "Ask Magda about His Excellency's tastes—since you seem to have lost the knack of pleasing him! Or ask him yourself—if you see him. Ask him when Zazuela will be back."

Then he, too, was away into the recesses of the castle, after his master.

Laure frowned over the memory of those words. Jansci had dropped a number of stinging hints about Stephen's past. Not that it mattered to her what his tastes were! But the repeated hints about Gypsies teased her curiosity. That was all it was, just idle curiosity. She didn't care if he slept with every dirty, greasy Gypsy girl in Hungary! But in the back of her mind, she was aware that Geza had gone on from cursing his horse to mention of a Gypsy encampment in the woods between here and the village. That was one of the words she had learned well, thanks to Jansci—*cigany,* "Gypsy." She concentrated now, trying to hear what Geza was saying about these Gypsies. But as always when she made a conscious effort to understand the conversation, meaning slipped away from her and she could not even pick out the few words she knew well. She sighed in frustration.

"Come now! You have made some foolish moves, but it's not such a difficult problem as that."

Laure concealed her start of surprise as Stephen moved from the vantage point behind her chair from which he had been surveying the chess game. Damn the man! He could move as silently as a cat when he wanted to.

He looked like a great cat of the forest today, dressed head to toe in clinging black, with the inevitable dagger gleaming at his waist like a claw. His tawny gold hair shone like a ray of light against the somber background of the gray stone walls and the soft black suit.

He jerked his head and Marton immediately vacated his seat. "Stephen will give you a better game than I could, Miss Laure," he said, holding the chair for his master. Stephen laughed under his breath and Laure looked up sharply, but there was no sign of a double meaning in Marton's face.

"No, stay, Marton," she said. "I have no fancy for the count's—style of game." She spoke in German, and was rewarded by seeing a flicker of expression on Marton's face before a well-schooled blankness descended over it.

"Marton does not speak German," Stephen said. He glanced down at the black and white squares of the board and moved a knight forward to a position where it threatened Laure's queen.

"What a pity," Laure said. "A knowledge of languages does so much to enhance one's enjoyment of travel, don't you think?" In his concentration on attack, Stephen had overlooked a vulnerable point. She moved a carved peasant girl onto the knight's square and took both pieces. "It is never wise to underestimate the pawns. Once in your territory, they can be dangerous. When will you let me return to Vienna?"

"You have grown careless, playing with Marton," Stephen reproved her mildly. "I have never had any trouble dealing with the pawns. Ultimately, they help me to capture the queen." As he spoke, he moved his one remaining bishop down the path left open by her pawn, until it directly menaced Laure's queen.

She bit her lip and studied the board carefully. "As you see," Stephen instructed her, "your queen cannot move without laying herself open to attack by my rook. Yet, if she does not move, she is at the mercy of my bishop. You are surrounded, my dear, and there is no way out."

Laure's knight took the threatening bishop. "The queen may have defenders you don't think of."

Stephen captured the exposed knight. "Perhaps. And how many pieces will you sacrifice for the freedom of your queen? Make no mistake—you will ultimately lose. Isn't it better to concede now?"

"I prefer to play the game out," Laure said. "Perhaps you had better tell me how many pieces one should sacrifice for freedom—the freedom of your country, for example?"

"All that one has." Stephen's fist closed about the piece in his hand.

"You have my answer." Laure rose and faced him across the chessboard. "Stephen, you cannot win my love by keeping me prisoner. Let me go! This game is unworthy of you."

Stephen released the pawn in his hand and set it down on the board quite gently. It was a peasant boy in wide, fringed linen trousers and shirt, his head shaded by a big hat. "On the contrary," he countered, "it is the game of kings. And, with luck, I shall bring even my pawns safely out—to say nothing of my queen." He made a mocking bow to her over the board.

A commotion at the door claimed his attention before Laure could reply. Three peasants, holding their wide-brimmed hats before them, were arguing with Geza. Laure could catch only a few words of their broad speech.

"My roof-thatch—."

"Aunt Csolni's white cockerel—."

"Those damned Gypsies—."

"We want to see His Excellency!"

Chapter Nine

WITH AN ABRUPT MOVEMENT, STEPHEN WHEELED AND strode down to the far end of the hall. His embroidered cloak, swinging out behind him as he turned, knocked several pieces off the board and destroyed any semblance of a game. Laure caught the carved chessmen in her skirt and sat looking after Stephen, a slight frown between her brows.

He dealt with the peasants and his own men as if they were a pack of overexcited hounds. A sharp word here, a frown there—and the complainants resolved into two groups: the men who had been set to guard the door, and the original deputation of peasants. Silence fell on them as if by magic.

"That's better. One at a time now—what is the complaint?"

The two younger peasants nodded and backed away, leaving the old man in the center of the group for their spokesman. He gripped his hat by the brim and addressed Stephen, while staring fixedly at a point over his right shoulder.

"With respect, we've come to ask His Excellency the count to carry out his obligations to the village. Hasn't the village served His Excellency the count faithfully these many years, doing all that was required of us?"

"And it's little enough His Excellency the count ever required!" interpolated Magda in a low murmur. The noise at the door had drawn her from her everlasting sewing in the upstairs chamber, to stand by Laure's side and listen to the disputation. Laure was glad of her presence now, as she translated Stephen's words in the same murmur.

"His Excellency is asking what ancient rights he has overlooked. Don't they gather dead wood, and as much live wood as they need, to repair their roofs and make their tools? Has anyone stopped them from grazing their beasts on the common land or feeding their pigs in the forest? Doesn't he pay the fair market price fixed by the county court for their grain and produce?"

The old peasant shuffled and agreed that all these things were true, but as His Excellency was hardly ever in residence, there were other matters that went overlooked. Wasn't it the bounden duty of His Excellency the count to see that the forests were kept clear of dangerous wild game? And didn't he owe compensation to the village for any damage caused by wild animals that he had failed to kill or drive away?

Stephen laughed. "In the Bakony! What ferocious wild animals have you found, my friend? Nothing more dangerous than a few rabbits, I'll be bound. Unless you count my men here—and I'll go bound they've done no damage in your village."

Geza turned bright red and shuffled at this last speech. "My lord, the girl was willing!" he protested. "And I'd have done right by her, but she wouldn't have me. Said I was a worthless *betyar* who didn't know how to work the fields, and she'd have no husband who was off carousing with the count's wild crew half the year—."

Magda giggled as she translated Geza's embarrassed protestations. Stephen's narrowed glance at his man needed no translation.

"Is that the trouble?" he asked of the peasants. "Shall I give this fellow a piece of land and a plow, and set him up with—I suppose it is Juli?"

"Anna, my lord," Geza mumbled.

"Mari," one of the younger peasants corrected.

Stephen threw up his hands. "What do you want? He can't marry all three of them!"

"No need," said the old man, once more taking command of the conversation. "What do we care what the young folk are up to at harvest time? Juli's married now, that Anna is a flighty piece as'll come to no good, and the young master made a good present for Mari's baby as is all right and proper; and a fine, healthy lad he'll be as will serve His Excellency well. No, that's not the trouble."

But having unburdened himself of this long speech, he seemed struck dumb again. A lengthy silence ensued, during which the peasants shuffled their feet uneasily and the old man coughed and spat into his hat several times.

"Well?" Stephen asked, tapping one booted foot on the flagstones. "I assume you had some reason for coming to see me today. Now, what's all this nonsense about wild beasts in the woods? I've told you before that I'll not be responsible for the rats eating your corn. If you don't have sense enough to mend your houses and stop the ratholes, that's your problem, not mine."

One of the younger men stepped forward. "Beggin' His Excellency's pardon," he mumbled, "but it's them Gypsies that come back and camped in the woods. Worse than wild beasts, they are, way they come down on a village."

"That's right!" his mate seconded him. "Taking the straw out of my thatch to start their fires—."

"Three of my best laying chickens—."

"Can't feed my pigs in the forest while they thievin' rascals are there—."

Stephen held up his hand for silence. "Well? And what do you want me to do about it?" he asked, laughing. "Organize a hunt? Shoot them?"

The peasants stared at their boots. Laure was fascinated by the old man's gnarled, knotted hands twisting the black felt brim of his hat.

"His Excellency's grandsire would have done it," he mumbled. "Hunted them down like the wild beasts they are."

"My Excellency's grandsire would also have hanged any peasant with the temerity to make demands in his own castle," Stephen reminded them.

The peasants backed away as one man, stammering and crowding each other in the door.

"Didn't mean impertinence—."

"Beg pardon, Excellency—."

But it was the old man who had the final say, when they were safely outside the great door.

"Aye, but who's to see to our rights now?" he called out in a high, cracked voice.

Geza started forward, his hand upraised.

"Leave them alone, Geza," Stephen commanded.

The peasants' steps retreated down the path, and Stephen came back to the end of the great hall, where Laure sat over the remains of the chess game. He placed one booted foot on the stool he had vacated and stood looking down on her with a quizzical gleam in his eye.

"There was a riding habit of my mother's among those things in the chest," he said. "Has Magda altered it to fit you yet?"

"Why—yes, I suppose she has," Laure stammered, bemused by his sudden interest.

"Good! I thought you might care to ride out with me. I think I had better go down to the village and see to these fellows' complaints. I'll tell Geza to saddle up for us. Be back here in five minutes!" He had turned away and was halfway across the hall before Laure had gathered her skirts to rise.

"And so, having given his orders, His Excellency departs," she muttered, and then laughed at herself. Odiously confident Stephen might be, but for once he was right! She was so tired of sitting in the castle that even the ride down to a muddy village was a treat she would be loath to miss.

It took Magda somewhat more than the stipulated five minutes to lace her into the green riding habit with its complicated, old-fashioned gold clasps down the front, especially as the maid insisted on brushing out Laure's golden hair till it shone to match the gold clasps and on pinching her cheeks to make them red. Finally, Laure had to command her to stop, pointing out that she was not a pig being dressed for market. Since she said this in English, the sarcasm was wasted on Magda; but the biting tone got results.

"I'm sorry I snapped at you, Magda," Laure apologized. The maid beamed under her starched lace bonnet.

"No matter, gracious lady. Of course you're nervous, but don't fret. Just try not to offend His Excellency again, and all will go well."

Laure turned so sharply that the skirts of the riding habit whistled about her feet, and descended the stairs regretting her apology. For just one moment she felt in sympathy with the autocratic structure of this feudal land. Magda would never have dared speak so if she'd been the true lady of this castle!

Halfway to the great hall Laure's sense of humor caught up with her. She was laughing at herself as she came down the last narrow stairs. A stray shaft of light from one of the arrow slits high in the wall caught her there, with her hair floating loose behind her like a nimbus of light. Stephen, standing at the foot of the stairs, caught his breath at the sight. She was so lovely and golden, like the spirit of sunshine breaking into his gloomy hold. And she was laughing. Perhaps she had forgiven him for—for—.

For what? Stephen reminded himself that he was count of these lands, with absolute power of life and death over his subjects—and that this stiff-necked English girl had put him to a deal of trouble, not to mention shaming him in front of his men. No, he had nothing to be forgiven for. All things considered, he had treated her with surprising consideration! His brows snapped together and he greeted her with a frown.

Laure saw the dour expression on Stephen's face. It

effectively stilled her moment of laughter. No doubt he was regretting the momentary weakness that had led him to invite her to ride out with him. Her own lips closed in a firm line, and she descended the last few steps with as stiff a neck and expression as any dowager of the court. To Stephen, it seemed as if the light had gone out.

"I'm glad to see you have overcome your tendency to levity," he greeted her. "For a moment I thought you might actually enjoy riding with me! Are you sure you would not rather sulk by the fire?"

Laure's eyes swept past him to dwell for a moment on the empty fireplace, occupied by nothing warmer than last winter's ashes.

"The fire is no warmer than the rest of your hospitality," she answered. She put one hand lightly on Stephen's wrist and, with the other hand, lifted the trailing skirts of her habit.

Stephen snorted with unwilling laughter. "Now, you are unfair!" he protested. "Haven't I shown the warmest desire to keep you here?"

"Like your other possessions," Laure agreed, "under lock and key!"

Stephen frowned again. *Damn the girl, must she be always quarreling?* "I can't let you go back to Vienna," he said. "Not now. It wouldn't work."

"You think I would betray you," Laure stated flatly. She marched on ahead of him to the courtyard door. "And who knows? Maybe I would. Your treatment of me has given me no very high opinion of your principles. What sort of freedom can you win, when you deny it to all around you—me, your serfs, and—oh!" she gasped, temporarily forgetting what she had meant to say next. "Oh, what a beauty! Do you really mean to let me ride her?"

The chestnut mare stood almost as tall as Stephen's own black horse. Laure ran a hand over her flanks, and admired the perfect lines of breeding as much as the glossy coat that spoke of constant care and grooming. "Arabian?" she hazarded.

"Half," Stephen agreed. "But foaled on a Hungarian mare—yes, one of those scrubby black ponies you saw drawing carts on the roads! I believe that with time, and the importation of the right bloodstock—perhaps from your English horses—we can breed a superior strain of horses here in Hungary. The conditions are right for it—our miles of grassy plain—and every Hungarian is born to the saddle. It is only a matter of improving the strain." He stooped and gave Laure a leg up to the saddle. She crooked her right knee over the upper crutch of the saddle and crossed the reins in her left hand, smiling in pleasure at the mare's instant responsiveness.

"Good," Stephen said. "Geza would have it she was too skittish a mount for a lady, but I told him you were not one to be pleased with an armchair ride."

Laure felt a flush rise to her cheeks at this unsuspected praise.

The path down from the castle to the village was not so bad as the stony route by which they had ascended on that first night, but it was steep enough to demand Laure's full attention to her mare. The horses picked their way in single file down the narrow path, Stephen's in the lead. Laure was glad not to have to keep up a conversation; it was enough to manage a new and spirited mount in this difficult terrain.

At the foot of the hill, where the beech woods began, the path broadened enough to let two horses walk abreast. Stephen reined in and waited for Laure to come up beside him.

"I am afraid this path through the woods is too tricky for us to let the horses go," he apologized. "After I have seen to things at the village, we shall ride down to the fields; and then you shall try your mare's paces."

"Thank you," Laure said. "She's a darling—I shall look forward to that. If you can really breed such horses here in Hungary, Stephen, wouldn't that be a better career than fighting with the emperor?"

Stephen laughed. "So! I thought I had embarrassed you with my talk of bloodstock and breeding. I had forgotten that one does not speak of such things to a young lady—it is so easy to talk to you. But when you were silent so long, I thought I must have offended."

"No," Laure confessed, "only the path was a bit tricky, and I had to concentrate on my riding. What about it, Stephen? Why don't you import more horses and start a farm here?"

Stephen clenched one fist about the reins. The black horse stirred under him and tossed up its head, sensing the rider's mood. "Because the emperor does not approve of his noblemen engaging in trade," he answered at last. "Three times he has refused my application for the necessary permits." He smiled down at her. "Remember I told you, the first day, that my parents would rather I became a brigand than find honest work? I am afraid it is true—not only the emperor, but most of my nobly blind, honorably stupid countrymen have the same sentiments!"

Responding to the suppressed excitement in his voice, Stephen's horse broke into a brisk trot. Laure's mare followed suit, and in a few moments the village was in sight.

Here the path widened again and became a broad street, almost a square, shaded on either side by enormous trees. On either side of this central street there was a line of mud-walled, reed-thatched cottages, their dull brown and tan colors obscured by the riot of flowers that grew around each doorstep and in some cases almost covered the cottage walls. Between these carefully tended gardens and the flat street was an ambiguous area of mud puddles and randomly placed steppingstones, where puppies, geese and half-naked children played indiscriminately. The first deep breath that Laure took confirmed her suspicion that the fenced yards behind the cottages housed the pigs that were the peasants' yearly meat supply.

At the end of the short street was a larger building, of two stories, with a stone terrace shaded by vines and with real glass in several of the windows. A line of old men sat on a split-log bench, just under the shade of the vines. As Stephen and Laure appeared, with one gesture they set their half-filled glasses down on their knees and turned to stare at the new sight.

"The inn," Stephen said, jerking his head toward this building. "Will you wait for me there, or come with me?"

Laure looked at the impassive faces of the old men and decided to follow Stephen rather than be subjected to their passive inquisition.

They left their horses in the care of a grubby, barefoot boy of nine or ten, who had appeared, as if by magic, from around the corner of the inn as soon as they stopped. The other children, except for the babies who played in the mud puddles, had all vanished. As they walked back down the dusty street, Laure sensed their presence in a smothered giggle behind her, eyes peeping from behind a red embroidered curtain, a wisp of rag disappearing around the corner of the cottage just ahead. But none were brave enough to come out and look at the count and the foreign woman face to face.

The first cottage they visited was set in a veritable sea of mud, marked by a line of faltering stepping-stones not much higher than the surrounding puddles. Laure picked up the skirts of her riding habit and resolved to concentrate only on the more attractive elements of the scene—the bright flowers and the even brighter embroidered curtains.

A wrinkled old woman greeted them at the door with a creaking attempt at a curtsy.

"No, don't ruin your knees for me, granny," Stephen said slipping his hand under her elbow to help her up.

The old woman invited them in, in a dialect so thick that Laure could scarcely follow one word in ten, and Stephen answered her using the same local accent instead of the pure Hungarian Laure had been starting to understand at the castle. Unable to follow the conversation, she amused herself with looking around the room and cataloging its contents while Stephen listened to the old woman's complaints. It was not as rich a house as the inn where they had stopped on their journey, but to Laure's mind its cosy simplicity was even more attractive. The walls were white-washed and painted with a border, about seven feet from the ground, of twining flowers and vines.

There was the obligatory bedstead in one corner, piled high with straw ticks, feather mattresses and embroidered coverlets in which the linen could scarcely be seen for the profusion of red wood stitchery; and a spinning wheel sat in the corner nearest the door. Beyond these things, there were no furnishings or decorations. But what need of them, when every article was so exquisitely ornamented in itself?

Finally the long, almost incomprehensible conversation between Stephen and the old woman seemed to have come to an end. After her monologue of screeching complaints they were both laughing, and Laure saw Stephen press some gold coins into her hand as he took his leave.

"That was Granny Csolni," he told her. "She says the Gypsies have stolen three of her chickens, and it's all my fault for not keeping a farm attached to the castle so that the Gypsies can steal from the estate like everybody else."

"So you paid her for the chickens!" Laure couldn't keep from laughing.

Stephen looked down at her with one fair eyebrow lifted in a question. "Well—it's better than keeping chickens myself! Besides," he added, more seriously, "she is right. It is my responsibility to protect my people and see that no one steals from them. I have been away so much that the Gypsies think they can do as they please."

That point was repeated at the next house to which they went, where a crippled ex-soldier had lowered his dignity to mind three tumbling children, while their mother, his daughter, went out to her man in the fields. Old Peter threw back his shoulders with the military precision learned on the drill field, and spoke clearly enough that Laure could follow most of what he had to say. He didn't mention the right of tenants to take what they wanted from the count's estate, but he did emphasize that it was His Excellency's duty to protect the village. If he'd been an able-bodied man himself, he would have organized guards to watch the village while the Gypsies passed through; but what could you do with these thickheaded peasants! They should do their twenty-five years in the army, as he'd done—then they'd learn what it was to stand up to an enemy, to keep your watch and guard your picket lines! But since it was too late to educate the shiftless so-and-sos, let His Excellency send down two or three of those wild boys he had playing at brigands, and he'd soon see to it the Gypsies knew where they belonged!

Laure had to suppress a laugh at Peter's speech, but she was impressed by the way he spoke to Stephen— neither cringing nor insolent, but as a man who knew his rights and expected the count to know his. Stephen heard him out courteously, thanked him for his suggestions and asked if he or his family had suffered any direct losses from the Gypsies.

Old Peter snorted. "Not likely! I can keep my girl's house safe enough. And don't you listen to those other whining no-goods, Excellency. Give them a chance, they'll blame the Gypsies for everything from the child's whooping cough to the harvest of '09 that failed—and expect you to pay up!"

Stephen laughed. "Very likely."

And it seemed to Laure, as she listened to the stream of complaints that poured over their heads in the next hour, that old Peter had been exactly right. This man's pig was thin because it had been poisoned; that woman blamed the failure of her garden on the Gypsy's evil eye, and the cottage at the end of the lane was losing its roof not because the owner hadn't rethatched it in fifteen years, but because the Gypsies were sneaking down to the village at night to pull out the rotten reeds for their fires.

"Very likely!" Laure burst out, after Stephen had promised the owner that the estate carpenter from the manor house would visit the village and assist with the rebuilding of the tumbledown cottage.

"Oh, he'll come," Stephen assured her. "Before the next cold weather, too—I hadn't realized there was so much work to be done here." He looked down one of the winding alleys that led off the main street, and pointed out missing bricks, collapsing fences and half a dozen more houses that lacked great patches of their reed thatches.

"I meant," Laure amplified, "he has a nerve claiming the Gypsies destroyed his house, when anyone can see he hasn't worked on it for years. Why should you take the responsibility?"

Stephen sighed. "Why indeed? But my ancestors made serfs out of his ancestors, and told them where to go and what to do until they'd lost the habit of thinking for themselves. So I can hardly complain, now, if I have to think for them. Only I wish . . ." His voice trailed off and for a moment he looked tired and defeated. Laure felt a confusing urge to put her arms around him and comfort him.

"Wish?" she prompted softly after a few moments.

Stephen's head came up, and he forced a smile. "Nothing. . . . You play chess with Marton. Would you give me a game some time? There's nobody here to play chess with. . . ."

It seemed to be a non sequitur. But as Stephen waded into the next disputed claim, Laure wondered just what he had meant by it. Did he sometimes wish for someone to share his life and concerns on a level that the peasants, or even the men at the castle, could not understand? He must be lonely at times.

Then she watched him laughing and tickling a

pretty peasant girl under the chin. The girl beamed up at him, warming herself in his radiant smile. Laure could remember herself melting in the same way. Lonely! She laughed at herself. The man had his own ways of getting company. What was she worrying about? He could take care of himself.

Chapter Ten

Around midday the complainants who had gathered round Stephen in the main street began to melt away. Some time earlier Laure had retreated to the shaded terrace before the inn, where she sat sipping a glass of sweet white wine and watching the little dramas that were played out before her. She noticed that most of the people talking to Stephen were old folks like Granny Csolni, or young women with babies hanging at their skirts. The men must have been out working in the fields.

The young women slipped away first, leaving Stephen to crack jokes with the old grandmothers who were still screeching complaints into his ears, while the line of old men sat watching on their split log outside the inn. There were usually two or three poeple talking at once, all in the thick peasant dialect, and Laure could not catch more than a word or two of what was said. The general drift was that they blamed Stephen for the Gypsies' passing through and felt he had encouraged them in some way; but it wasn't clear how. Once she heard a familiar name.

"It's that Zazuela put 'em up to stealing from us," grumbled an ancient crone who might have been Granny Csolni's great-grandmother, so dry and withered did she appear. Of all the peasants, she had shown the least shyness in assaulting Stephen's ears with shrill demands for restitution of her property. "Thinks she can get away with anything now, because Your Excellency's favor—."

"Silence!"

Stephen's voice, no longer friendly, cut through the old woman's querulous complaints like a whiplash. Startled, Laure looked at him and thought she saw a sheepish look in his eyes. Then he turned away from her direct, questioning gaze and went on, "You have a lot to say about other people's business, grandmother. Has your house no men to feed, that you have leisure to stand out in the public streets looking for men to trouble?"

The old men on the log burst into laughter. One of them raised his glass in mocking salute to Stephen and called out something unintelligible, but presumably encouraging.

Stephen's abrupt change of mood seemed to signal the end of the impromptu meeting. The peasants drifted away to their cottages, taking care not to look directly at Stephen or Laure as they went. Nevertheless, Laure felt sure that every detail of her dress and hair would be discussed in each cottage over the noonday meal.

Noon! A tantalizing aroma swirled down the street, borne from the cooking ovens of each of the little flower-covered cottages. Laure sniffed the air appreciatively and recognized the paprika-rich smell of *gulyas,* the national dish of stewed meat and sweet red peppers, which she had eaten three times a week up at the castle. But, somehow, it never smelled so good there as it did here in the open air.

Stephen dropped into the rickety wooden chair beside Laure's and sprawled his long legs out with a sigh. "Enough! Thank God, they would rather eat than complain—and so would I," he finished with a smile. He clapped his hands, and a short man with a grease-spotted apron tied about his middle hurried out to bow before the count. "Do you mind if we eat here?" Stephen asked. "It is peasant food, but good of its sort. And it seems I cannot return to the castle just yet." Without waiting for Laure's reply, he turned back to the innkeeper. "Two bowls of that *paprikas gulyas,* Pal. Some fresh bread, sausages, and—a bottle of that Tokay you have concealed in your cellars? Bring it out now, and perhaps I don't have you hanged for serving this inferior stuff to my lady here." With a disdainful gesture he emptied the dregs from Laure's wineglass over the terrace steps. Pal nodded, smiled, rubbed his hands together, bowed several times and backed up the terrace into the dark interior of the inn.

"It's not inferior," Laure said, "I liked the wine very much. Who do you think you are?"

Stephen favored her with a lazy smile that made her heart turn over even while she was trying to stay angry with him. "I know who I am," he replied, "and so should you, by this time. 'His Excellency the count!' "

He nodded approval of the new bottle that Pal had brought out for his inspection, poured a few golden drops into his glass and raised it to his lips. "Better," he nodded. "That stuff you were drinking is local. My land is good for corn and pigs, but not for grapes. You see, I know where I belong. Just as Pal knows his place, and Magda hers. Perhaps that is the trouble with you English." He reached across the table and took Laure's hand in a strong, compelling grasp. "Stay here with me, Laurica. This land is good for you. Can't you feel it? This is your proper place—by my side."

Laure felt her resistance weakening at his touch and the intense blue gaze of his eyes. She lacked even the strength to withdraw her hand. That one contact between them—his work-roughened fingers against her palm—was the only stable point in a dizzying universe. She felt her whole body softening and relaxing. He had not spoken to her, looked at her, touched her like this since that disastrous morning two weeks ago. She had forgotten the power and intensity of his passion.

The table was between them. That seemed wrong. There should be nothing keeping them apart—there could be nothing, not when his eyes compelled her so. She swayed toward him, and felt the edge of the table cutting into her side.

The momentary pain brought a momentary awareness. What had she been thinking of? Would he make love to her here, in the very street? Laure pulled her hand back and picked up her own wineglass. As soon as the contact was broken, she felt like herself again— as long as she didn't look at him, that was.

"A sense of identity," she repeated. "Is that what you have that makes you dress up and pretend to be a

149

highwayman? Forgive me if I don't quite understand. We British have such a naive idea of our places. We think that if a man is a nobleman and a great landowner, his place is taking care of his land and people, not galloping about the countryside with a mask on, scaring people and kidnapping them."

Stephen's frown was safer for her than his smile. All the same, she felt unaccountably cold and comfortless at his bleak expression.

"I think you cannot now accuse me that I do not take care for my people," he said, biting off each separate word as though it were a bullet. "And for the rest—you do not understand my reasons."

"How could I," Laure snapped back. "Your Excellency never lowers yourself to explain anything! All you do is stamp through my life every few weeks, treating me like your personal property and throwing a tantrum if I don't seem to care for the idea. I don't think you have any high and lofty motives. You're just used to acting as if you owned the whole world!"

Still furious, and clinging to that fury as her only safeguard against deeper and more dangerous feelings, she tossed back the wine in her glass at a gulp.

Stephen's angry look dissipated and he laughed at the surprise on her face. "I deserved that," he admitted, startling Laure into choking on the last of her wine. "And you, sweeting—you deserved this wine, the best in Pal's cellars. Now do you see why I would not settle for the thin local stuff?"

Laure nodded.

"Tokay," Stephen said. He raised her glass to sparkle in the sun as he poured in a thin stream of the wine, then handed it back to her with a courtly flourish. "The wine of gods and poets—sweeter than honey, distilled sunshine. The wine of Hungary!" He raised his glass to her in a salute and together they sipped the golden wine. The sun dancing through the green leaves overhead struck sparks of fire from Stephen's hair and beard and from the joined wine-glasses.

"It is a good pressing," Stephen went on in a more prosaic vein. "It should be—I've good reason to think this lot came from the last Tokay I had sent to the estate. Pal was probably afraid to serve me my own wine!"

He laughed, and after a moment Laure joined him. The wine was singing in her veins now, warming her like the bottled sunshine that Stephen called it. Perhaps she had been trying too hard to understand the rules of this strange land. Stephen behaved, sometimes, like an absolute autocrat. But then, he seemed to take it for granted that the people on his estate would steal from him; and he paid for what the Gypsies had taken, as if that, too, were his responsibility. They were afraid of him, always addressed him by the most formal of titles, and yet did not hesitate to crowd around him demanding their ancient rights.

"Yes," Stephen said softly. Laure realized that she had been speaking aloud. "Yes, you are beginning to understand. I told you once, did I not, that I belong to them as much as they to me? Now you begin to see."

Pal brought out two shallow bowls of *gulyas* and a loaf of dark bread on a wooden platter.

"Eat," Stephen commanded her, hacking off a piece of the bread with his long knife. "The wine will go to your head, otherwise, and I want to talk to you."

Obediently, Laure spooned up tender chunks of meat flavored with red paprika, while Stephen leaned back in his chair and talked at the vines overhead. The stew was hot and spicy. She broke off chunks of grainy dark bread from the slice Stephen had handed her, and cooled her mouth with more of the sweet Tokay. There were birds cooing in the rafters overhead, and the filtered light on the terrace was cool and green and rippled with little splashes of sun coming through the leaves. And Stephen, for once, quiet and almost meditative. He sought to make her understand the bitter fight he had been waging, and she tried, not always successfully, to keep her mind on his words and not on his sensual lips or his strong, brown fingers. She could remember with surprising vividness the feel of those long hands moving over her body. His momentary handclasp had brought back all those feelings. But he was talking seriously now. She ought to listen.

"You English have had your Parliament—oh, for hundreds of years! So have we in Hungary. We are not a subject nation, you know, but an equal crown with Austria. Joined under the emperor, whom we Hungarians love and revere as the head of our nation." Stephen broke off for a moment and gave her a wicked, sidewise glance. "As emperor, that is. As a man, I have sometimes found him stubborn to the point of foolishness. Your English king also is a fool," he said, unconscious of offense, "but in England that does not matter, for you have very wisely stripped your king of the power to do much either of good or harm. It is your Parliament that does all. We are not so wise here in Hungary; but we, too, have had our Parliament, called the Diet, and it is through those meetings of the landowners and nobles that we can find a better government for this realm—if one is to be found. But do you know how long it is since our Diet was convened? Twenty years! The emperor is supposed to convoke a diet every three years. But because we offended him in 1802 by daring to ask to use our own language, to export our own products—and had the ill grace to renew these demands in 1805—he has simply refused to convene another diet. I was a child in my father's house when the last diet met, in 1805. Franz—pardon me, the emperor—closed it after ten days, because he could see that our nobles were not going to bow the head to him. Since then, Napoleon has rolled over the world and been defeated, the colonies of South America have risen one by one to declare their independence, even the Greeks have shaken off Turkey's yoke. In the world we have gone from candles to gaslight, from oxcarts to steamships. Only my country remains backward, ignorant, in chains. A rich farmland for Austria to administer. The peasants are ignorant and the nobles waste their lives in Vienna.

"I don't try to change the world overnight. But it is time, and past time, for us to take one little step toward that freedom which the rest of the world is discovering. Let us have our Diet convened again—and let our laws be made and discussed in Magyar, the language of the nation, and not in Latin. How would you like it, if you were tried in court, and told you could plead your cause only in ancient Greek?"

Stephen's languid pose had ended by now. Fired by his own eloquence, he faced Laure across the table, his eyes flashing with an enthusiasm that demanded her response. He pushed the crockery out of the way and took both her hands in his. "Do you see now?" he demanded. "Do you see what this land could be—what I could make it? You talk about freedom, Laure. You in England have been given freedom as your birthright. Here we must fight for it daily. Sometimes you don't like the way we fight, but can you find it in your heart to understand why we must fight? Do you see?"

His hands closed about hers with bone-crushing force. Laure felt herself swept away by the intensity of his passion. "You love Hungary," she whispered, knowing how inadequate the words were.

Stephen beamed. "Yes! And I love you, Laure. And I will win you both!"

He pulled her to her feet. "Come, now. I must ride to talk to these foolish Gypsies, and tell them not to annoy my people. You will like the ride through the woods. Then we will go home, and we will finish our game."

"The chess game? You spilled the pieces."

Stephen drew her close to him for an intoxicating moment. "All our games, Laurica. It is time for an end to playing games."

Those words recurred to her with compelling force as their horses picked their way through the thin belt of beech woods beyond the village. They were very close to the cultivated land here. Sometimes, through a thinning in the trees, Laure could glimpse the broad fertile acres of the TransDanubian Plain, stretching out for countless miles below the hills of the Bakony.

"Let's stop for a moment," Stephen said unexpectedly, at the height of a hill overlooking the plain. They left their horses tethered to trees in the wood, and Stephen assisted Laure over the volcanic boulders that sprouted from the land at the very edge of the hill. From here they could overlook miles of the plain. Laure gazed at it with new eyes, perceiving its beauty for the first time.

When Stephen had forced her and himself through that land at breakneck speed, seeking the sanctuary of his castle, it had seemed a harsh, unforgiving land to her, an extension of her prison. Now, with eyes sharpened by Stephen's love of his homeland, she saw not a vast featureless plain, but a gently rolling, fertile land green with the young growing crops. A subtle dip almost hidden between two hills marked the course of a river; a cluster of darker green branches signaled the treetops rising out of a valley where a manor house lay; a clump of brown, squat shapes on the horizon signified a village like the one they had just come from.

She looked at Stephen, wanting to share her moment of insight, but he was gazing out over the vista with rapt eyes and lips slightly parted. "Yes," he said without taking his eyes off the plain, "it is beautiful." His arm rose and fell in a vast sweeping arc that took in two-thirds of the view to the horizon. "My lands," he said. "Some day soon I will take you to my manor house—oh, no, this crumbling castle is not my only home!" He laughed at her look of surprise. "Did you think this 'estate' the peasants talk of is nothing but a pile of rocks and stabling for a few horses? No, my wealth is in those broad acres; and the Andrassy family home is nestled among them, in a valley beside a swift-flowing river, shaded by many trees. It is not perhaps a palace like those of the Prince Metternich or the Count Zichy in Vienna, but I hope to show you that even in Hungary we do not live altogether like barbarians. There is a library there with four hundred books in French, and my mother caused a spinet to be imported from Paris. For you I will buy English books and English music, and we will plant roses in the garden; and you shall ride every day on the horses I will breed, the fastest horses in Hungary."

Laure was dizzied by the eager, passionate sweep of

his words. So this was what he had been dreaming of while they fought and quarreled their way across Hungary, while he left her locked in his castle to wonder what was to become of her! Why could he not have spoken sooner?

Stephen's hands were on her shoulders now; his burning blue eyes caught and held hers so that she could not look away. She felt like a leaf in the wind, helpless before his passionate intensity.

"Laure," he said. Her name on his lips was like a spell that she could not escape. "Laurica. *Életem, szivem.* My life, my heart, Laure! With you by my side, how can I fail to persuade the emperor? With you to share my life here, how can I fail in anything?"

His hands burned through the thin fabric of her habit. But he did not draw her to him. His eyes stayed on her, with a question in them.

Laure understood. This time he would not force her. He was asking her to come to him, to make a commitment to equal his. To give herself to him, not as a possession, but as a free and equal companion.

"Oh, Stephen, Stephen!" she murmured. Her own hands went up and around his neck. She clutched him as though he could save her from drowning in the sea of passion that rose up and engulfed her. His strong, hard body against hers was the only reality. The sea was lifting her and carrying her away now. She surrendered to it, could hear the surf beating in her ears. That tide of desire, stronger than anything she had ever known, drowned out self and reality, drowned out even the love words Stephen murmured in his own tongue as he carried her back into the shelter of the woods.

His cloak was their blanket, spread over a couch of leaves. The dried beech leaves rustled as they fell together onto the improvised bed, and the fresh ones were crushed under them to fill the air with a pungent green scent. Stephen's hands ranged over her body now, unloosing laces and clasps, ripping the fabric away when his impatience overcame him. Laure helped him with fingers suddenly grown blind and clumsy. Nothing mattered now except that their bodies should be free and together as they had always been meant to be.

A fresh little breeze swept through the wood, cooling her nakedness. She pulled Stephen down on top of her and felt complete at last, his long hands moving over her body, his thighs with their sprinkling of golden hair pressing between hers. He entered her almost roughly, with no preliminary caresses, knowing that this time she was as ready for him as he was for her.

Laure gasped with pleasure as Stephen filled her with his passion. Her breasts were crushed under him and her skin was scratched by the dry leaves. None of that mattered. She wrapped her arms and legs around him and held him closer to her, driven by the same primeval instinct that sent him plunging deeper and deeper into the secret recesses of her body. The tide of desire that had carried her off was a stormtide now, tossing them both on waves of passion that rose and rose without ever cresting. She pushed against him almost fiercely, as though she could hold all of his love and intensity in her body. His hands tightened about her shoulders and his lips sought hers in a long kiss as their bodies strained together. The warmth in Laure was a fire now that consumed her. She raked at his shoulders with her nails. His mouth stopped the air; she couldn't breathe. She didn't need air. She needed something, she didn't know what. She struggled under him, thrusting upward, until suddenly the waves of passion crested and left her gasping on the beach, washed by retreating ripples that made her whole body quiver.

Stephen kissed her from her mouth down the line of her throat, between her breasts, down to her toes and back up again in quick, sucking, demanding kisses that drew out her whole soul with them.

"Laure, *szivem*," he murmured.

Laure stretched out one lazy arm and drew him back down to lie beside her. Her passion sated now, she desired nothing more than to lie beside him, sunning herself in his warmth like a cat in a sunny window. She curled into the curve of his body and made little inarticulate sounds of pleasure and contentment. Stephen arched his arm protectively over her, and they lay together in the warm nest of his body and his wool cloak over the beech leaves, while the sun sank in the sky.

Stephen was the first to return to himself. He leaned over Laure, still half-dreaming, and wakened her with little, nibbling, teasing kisses. She floated up through a lazy sea of contentment to open her eyes on his face bending over her, protective, loving and somehow apologetic.

"If you apologize," she murmured, "I will be angry."

Stephen smiled. "How do you know what I am thinking? Why do I bother to talk to you, if you are a witch who can read my mind? I don't want you to think I take you casually, like a peasant girl."

"Mmm." Laure stretched. "Just stay out of the woods with your peasant girls!" There was a chill in the air now, as the sun sank lower in the sky. She reached out and fumbled in the leaves for her discarded clothes.

"Let me." Stephen had already slipped into his black trousers and clinging black shirt.

"Men's clothes are so simple," Laure complained. The many pieces of her riding habit, from the breeches underneath to the flowing skirt, with its inset to cover her right knee when she sat with it raised on the sidesaddle, were impossible to manage without Magda's help. And Stephen was a very inept lady's maid, and easily distracted!

"I think you don't want me to get this fastened," she teased him, when his fingers slipped once again from the gold clasps of the bodice to caress her breasts under the lace-covered chemise.

"Mmm, could be right." But eventually they had the many layers of flowing garments arranged to Stephen's satisfaction, if not Laure's. Two of the gold clasps had been ripped from the fabric, so that the bodice gaped open halfway down the front, and there was another gap in the seam of her skirt where Stephen had torn it off with fingers too impatient to fumble with the lacings.

"Oh, Magda will fix all that," Stephen assured her blithely.

"Then she'll know—she'll guess—." Laure stumbled over her words and blushed.

"She would have assumed, anyway," Stephen told her. "Don't you know half the castle has been asking if I'd lost my manhood, to let such a beauty as you sleep alone? It hasn't been easy, Laure."

Laure gave him a wicked, three-cornered smile. "So that's why you inveigled me into the woods—so you would not have to break your vow?"

Stephen looked blank.

"You promised that you would not enter my room again without invitation," she reminded him.

"So I did." Stephen pulled at his beard and looked uncommonly sheepish. "Well, then——."

Laure leaned closer to him. "Dear my lord," she whispered, "will it please you tonight to enter any room in your castle?"

Stephen laughed and swung her up over his head in both hands before settling her lightly on her horse. "That it will!"

Before mounting his own horse, he looked over the damage to her garments more closely, shrugged, and tossed her his cloak.

"Better wrap this around yourself," he advised. "You are still better covered than many a Gypsy wench, but you might not wish to ride through their camp in such a condition. *I* don't wish it. They steal enough without giving their men open invitation to covet such a prize as you."

Chapter Eleven

A CIRCUITOUS, NARROW PATH WINDING AROUND THE base of the hill brought them to the Gypsy encampment in about half an hour's ride. At first sight, the camp presented a rather cheerful appearance, with brightly painted wagons drawn up in a semicircle around the clearing, naked children playing in the dust at the horses' feet, and the blue smoke of the cooking fires spiraling upward to meet the shadows of the forest overhead. As they drew closer, Laure saw that the paint on the wagons concealed their ramshackle condition and that the finery of the girls consisted for the most part of rags brightened by a few cheap, bright scarves and a profusion of glass bangles. One listless girl of about thirteen languidly bumped a

tambourine with her elbow, a black-garbed crone
stirred the cooking pots, and two or three men slept in
the shade of the wagons. The children seemed too
tired to run and shout like the village brats, and
several had great running sores on their arms and
legs.

The old woman roused herself at Stephen's approach.

"Hola, count! Come to tax your subjects?" She
followed her jest with a raucous burst of laughter that
echoed in the forest behind them, increasing the air of
brooding stillness that lay about the place.

Stephen bowed as though he were addressing royal-
ty in the Viennese court.

"I come to pay my respects, grandmother." From a
pocket in his trousers he extracted a packet wrapped
in yellow paper and handed it over to the old woman.

She unwrapped it with greedy, trembling fingers
and exclaimed over the contents. "Good Latakia
snuff! His Excellency is generous." She popped a wad
of the dark snuff into her cheek and settled down
happily over the cooking pots.

The word *generous* seemed to have aroused the
children. Two naked little boys advanced with palms
held out in the traditional begging gesture, while the
girl swirled her skirts to expose a length of skinny,
flea-bitten leg and bumped the tambourine with a
little more energy. Laughing, Stephen reached into
his pocket and scattered a handful of copper coins
among the children.

"You spoil the brats," mumbled the old woman.

"They can do with it," Stephen retorted. "Why not
settle down on my land, grandmother? I will give your
people enough land to farm to feed them all, and the
children can go to the manor school."

The crone lifted a rag of black veiling before her face while she spat into the dust away from the cooking pot. "I think your *serfs* might not agree, Excellency. Besides, we are the free people. We don't live on Count's land and raise corn for Count!" She cackled again.

"The people don't like your being here now," Stephen said. "There's talk in the village. What will you do if they come to burn you out tonight?"

One of the men who had been apparently asleep under the wagons opened one eye, grinned and produced a wicked curved knife from nowhere. He balanced the blade point-first on his palm, then let it fly in a deadly circle across the clearing to land, still quivering, in a tree beside the cooking fire.

"No fighting on my land," Stephen said. "That applies to you as well as the villagers. Don't steal any more from the village. It irritates them."

The old woman opened her hands, palm upward. "A little flour—a morsel of oil," she whined. "We need so very, very little to live, Excellency!"

"Two pigs, three cockerels and a load of kindling wood," Stephen added.

"The pig was dead, Excellency. Villagers too proud to eat dead meat—we did but take it away to save them the trouble."

Stephen leaned over the cooking pot, took the wooden spoon from the old woman's hand and fished out an unmistakable portion of backbone with the boiled pork still clinging to it in shreds. "Dead now, anyway," he allowed. "But that's enough—you hear? Come up to the castle tonight and dance for me. Perhaps we can find 'a little flour, a morsel of oil'— and whatever else it takes to keep you good-for-nothings out of the village. And, dammit, gather your own firewood! The forest is full of dead trees—there's no need to steal from the villagers!"

"Ah, didn't I say as Excellency wouldn't forget us?" the old crone praised him. "Will Zazuela come up before his Excellency now? She is sleeping, but she'd like fine to ride his Excellency's great powerful . . . horse."

"Zazuela may come up with the rest of you, and not before," Stephen snapped. "I've a fancy to entertain my lady here with a night of your music and dancing. Otherwise, I've no use for the lazy lot of you."

He turned back to Laure and slapped her horse on the flank. "Come! I want to get back to the castle before it's dark." He wheeled his horse and trotted off on a narrow path through the trees. Laure followed at a more sedate pace, puzzling over the implications of the little scene she had just witnessed.

I should like to see this Zazuela, she thought.

It was a wish she was to have granted more thoroughly than she had desired.

By night, with the leaping flames of a bonfire illuminating the castle courtyard, the Gypsies looked much more as Laure had imagined them. The girls' bright cotton skirts and cheap scarves shone like real satin; their glass bangles could have been jewels as bright as any she had seen in the Austrian court. They said that you could support an army in the field through one campaigning season with the diamond necklace and armlets that had been stolen from the Princess Bagration and were worn everywhere. But could Katharina Bagration buy any jewels as bright, as flashing, as darkly mysterious as Zazuela's eyes?

Zazuela had been easy enough to pick out; she was the center of the dance, the loveliest of the four or five young girls who twirled and stamped their feet to the sweet, sobbing music of the Gypsy violins. Her dark hair hung below her waist and the ends were weighted down with tiny bells. Anklets of the same silver bells decorated her shapely legs, bare beneath a skirt that fluttered out almost to her waist with the sharp turns of the dance. Her hands and feet were long and slender and delicately arched, and the palms and soles were emphasized by designs drawn on them in some dark red dye. More bells hung from her ears, tangling themselves in the long dark hair. Her face was a perfect oval of dark gold. Her eyes were enormous, and further emphasized by lines of dark paint and by a glass jewel that dangled from a ribbon round her head, hanging right in the center of her forehead, between the lovely arched brows.

The Gypsies had made a carefully staged entrance long after dark, leaping into the courtyard with shouts and skirls of joy that would have brought gunfire down on them if they had been an attacking force. Without a pause for breath they streamed into the courtyard, the men already playing their fiddles or clapping in rhythm, the girls dancing on delicate, little bare feet that could have graced a king's palace. They wove an enchanted pattern around the fire, leaping with joyous abandon, throwing their arms and tossing their long hair from side to side in time with the wild call of the music. At once Zazuela dominated the group. She prowled between the lines of girls like a hunting cat, keeping a slow sensual rhythm in counterpoint to their quick flashing steps.

"Jaj Zazuela!" Geza called. She pulled a flower from her bodice and threw it at him, laughing, but by some miscalculation the blossom soared over his head and fell before Stephen. Erect, frowning in the firelight, he made no move to pick it up, and his hand clasped Laure's convulsively. Geza and another of the young men dived for the flower simultaneously, and in their laughing struggle the fragile petals disintegrated, leaving Geza the victor with nothing but a thorny stem for trophy. The awkward moment passed in laughter at his empty victory.

When the girls were breathing deeply, their slender sides quivering with the effort of the fast-paced dance, the violins slowed to a more sensual rhythm. Zazuela danced up to first one man, then another, beckoning, flirting, inviting with a flash of her white teeth. But whoever moved to take up her invitation found himself abruptly spurned, as she whirled away to try her wiles on the next victim.

She had gone halfway around the courtyard before Laure worked out the pattern, and saw that her next target would be Stephen.

"Don't worry," murmured a voice in her ear.

Surprised, she looked around and saw Marton, standing at attention like the old soldier he was.

"We'll soon sort that hussy." He raised his voice. "Hola! Gypsies! Enough of that foreign slop; now give us some music a man can dance to—a good *csardas,* or a *karikazo!*"

The leader of the Gypsy men glanced at Stephen, saw his brisk nod, then resettled the violin under his chin and began a new, fresh melody that was like a cool wind blowing away the oversweet scents and humors of the Eastern music. The snapping rhythm appealed to Laure, and she found herself moving up and down on her heels in time to the quick, crisp notes.

Stephen's men moved into the courtyard now,

forming a circle about the fire, arms on one another's shoulders. They were singing.

"Elvesztettem a zsebreválo késem . . ."

"Walking in the fields," Stephen translated in her ear, "I lost my pocketknife, and after that I lost my handkerchief. 'Azt sajnálom, nem a régi szeretömet.' That's all I am weeping for, not for my lost sweetheart." He grinned at her, looking young and excited in the flickering golden light. "We Hungarians are very proud you see—and very passionate. But it's a dance for couples. Will you join me? It's simple—you have the rhythm already." He showed her the basic *csardas* step—to the side and back, heels clicking, knees bent—and swept her into his arms and into the circle of firelight. The circle of singing men opened to let them through and became a line between them and the fire, singing, swaying back and forth in time to the strongly marked melody.

"Aszt sajnálom, nem a régi szeretömet . . ." The rhythm was intoxicating. As he saw that Laure had caught on to the steps, the violinist speeded up the music. First one man, then another dropped out of the line, but Stephen and Laure danced on. In his arms she felt light as a feather, able to go on forever. The red boots that were part of her peasant costume clicked and stamped as lightly as the little kid slippers she had worn to balls in Vienna. The billowing petticoats and skirts no longer seemed clumsy; when Stephen lifted her hand to spin her out and away from him, they gave her balance for the concluding steps of the dance. She spun back into his arms, he met her with a long kiss and the violinist, recognizing a natural climax, signaled the end of the music with a long, drawn-out sobbing chord that might have been the

Hungarian youth of the song, wandering out in the fields to weep for his lost sweetheart.

When Stephen released Laure, the music changed to a more martial tone. Now the men came back into the courtyard, but as individual dancers, not part of a line. Geza danced forward before the others with quick, short steps. Faster than Laure could follow the movements, he was down on his knees, then up again, then squatting and kicking out like a Cossack. The eight bars of the melody gave place to the simple rhythm of the chorus, and he jumped up and resumed the short, regular steps with which he had begun.

When the melody began again, another man jumped out and took Geza's place. He imitated the last kicking step and introduced a variation of his own, spinning on fingertips and toes like a human top.

After that, the competition was so fierce that Laure could hardly keep track of the different steps. Each man had his own athletic feat to contribute, always in perfect time to the demanding music, always rejoining the standing group without seeming the least bit tired or out of breath.

A muffled sound beside her drew Laure's attention from the wonders of the dance. It was old Marton. He had not joined the competing men.

"The *Verbunk*," he whispered, "the recruiting dance. See, the emperor would send his soldiers through the villages to dance, and any village lad who was foolish enough to join them, he had joined the army and found himself marching away the next day. Ah, we are a foolish race! Who else would be mad enough to leave home, parents, sweetheart, crops in the fields, for a mad dance by firelight and the chance of being shot in an Austrian emperor's service? But it was a fine life—a fine life, for all that. I served twenty years, and then, because I caught a bullet through the kneecap and could no longer march, they sent me back to my village. What was for me there? My sweetheart was a grandmother, and I was fit for nothing but to sit on a log with the old men and tell stories. But young Stephen remembered me—old Marton, who used to be young Marton, and who put him up on his first horse when he was not breeched yet." Marton blew his nose on a sleeve that was already in some need of washing. "He's a good man, your Stephen. But—I cannot dance with them anymore."

Laure put her hand on his arm, somewhat timidly. She was shaken by this outburst of confidence from the reserved Marton.

"Ah, don't worry about an old man," growled Marton, shaking himself free rather roughly. "Look at your man, there. I warrant he'll put the rest o' them to shame!"

Stephen had taken up the challenge of the dance now. Laughing, he faced the line of men, taking the quick staccato steps of the basic dance back and forth while he got into the rhythm. Then, springing forward in the firelight, he copied and topped Geza's original Cossack dance, balancing himself backward and forward on fingertips and toes, bending his body like an arch of fine steel, and then, as rapidly, upright again to beat out a rapid tattoo with his boots. His supple, black-garbed figure was as lithe as any acrobat's. Laure caught her breath in admiration as he followed one seemingly impossible feat with another. His endurance seemed inexhaustible.

"And he was wounded two weeks ago!" she murmured, half-inaudibly; but Marton caught the words.

"Aye," he said, "that is why he must show them

what he can do now. That was the way of the *betyárok* in the old days. A man who was not fit to lead in every way could not long be a mountain chief. Oh, he'd still be count"—the dismissing tone in his voice showed how little Marton valued the title—"but would these lads follow him anywhere, as they'll do now? Ah-ah, the young fool!" he broke off.

Stephen had backed off to the very edge of the courtyard. The Gypsies parted to give him a clear running space.

"What's he going to do?" Laure tugged at Marton's sleeve.

"Leap over the bonfire. Ah, but he'll never make it! Not enough space for a clear run." Marton waited in uneasy silence, chewing the ends of his grizzled mustache, and Laure gripped his arm and held her breath. The music was rising to a crescendo. Four—five—six running steps, and Stephen's legs gathered under him for the effort. He launched his body into the air without a pause. His boots brushed the top layers of the fire, and scattered embers in the courtyard; but he was down, safely down on the far side, grinning and panting with the last effort. He waved at Laure and called something unintelligible to her, the words lost in the roar of the crowd.

Marton seized Laure's arm above the elbow and yanked her back unceremoniously to the shelter of the castle wall. "Young fools—fools, all of them!" he shouted in her ear. "Now we're in for it."

Stephen's men had chosen to accept his last feat as a challenge to be taken up. Five of them in unison backed up, not half as far as he'd gone, and launched themselves, running, at the fire. The Gypsy girls screamed and dived out of the way, throwing their arms around the necks of any men who happened to be standing nearby. Two of the boys made it almost through; one landed on the fringes and jumped up, howling, with his hand clapped to the seat of his pants. Geza and Jansci, who had aimed for the very center of the fire, crashed down in the midst of the flaming sticks and scattered them about the courtyard.

"Are they alive? Oh, are they all right?" Laure pushed herself up on Marton's shoulders and tried to see into the crowd.

The dispersal of the bonfire had left the space dark, erratically lit by flickering flames. But she heard more good-humored laughter than screams of pain. The one lad who'd had the seat of his pants put on fire was drowning his pain with a skin of wine, while Geza and Jansci seemed to be getting enough petting from the Gypsy girls to make up for any singed mustaches and burnt boots. And Stephen—where was he? She'd lost sight of him in the confusion.

Two booted figures kicked the scattered remains of the bonfire back into the center of the court. "Play, damn you, Gypsies!" shouted Geza's voice.

A slow, sobbing tune began, the sort of thing the Gypsies played for themselves around their campfires at night. The quietly sensual music calmed the crowd. Most of the men and girls had paired off by now and were melting away into the shadows of the courtyard.

"Come on within, my lady," Marton urged. "This is no place for you now." Muffled laughter and the gurgle of wineskins had replaced the earlier hilarity.

"I'll wait for Stephen," Laure insisted.

A tattered, scorched figure reeled out of the darkness and paused before her. It was Jansci, his fine white trousers scorched to rags and his long hair frizzled by fire. Smudges of soot blackened his face and hands. But he was in good enough shape to have commandeered one of the few good bottles of wine to be found, and one of the prettiest of the Gypsy girls.

"Wait for count," he hiccupped, "have a long wait, lady! Didn' I tell you t'ask'im about Za—Zha—Gypsy whore?" With a loud, drunken laugh, Jansci stumbled off to find a quiet corner, pulling the girl after him.

The reconstituted bonfire gave one last dying blaze. In the spike of light Laure could make out Stephen's tall, black-clad figure. He seemed to be looking away from her, at something moving in the shadows by the gate. Before she could call to him, the moving shadows came out into the light. Glint of firelight on green satin skirts and silver bells, sparkle of a jewel in the forehead, shadowed eyes enlarged by kohl.

It was Zazuela.

She prowled up and down before Stephen with slow, almost hesitating steps, light-footed and graceful as a cat. With a pang Laure saw the match of that lithe-limbed grace she had so often admired in Stephen's movements, and remembered his comment on his mother: "She was dark. . . . My father always called her his 'little Gypsy.'" Did Stephen find something in these dark people of the forest that she could never offer him?

The music subtly shifted, rippling like a forest stream or like a bird in courting time. Zazuela's steps quickened to the new beat. Here was no overt seduction, no flashing of skirts and deliberately gaping bodices such as the other Gypsy girls engaged in. Her proud bearing proclaimed that she, Zazuela, had no need of such cheap tricks. Was she not the daughter of the forest and the queen of her people? She offered Stephen all the dark mystery of her world, and when he came to her, it would be the mating of equals. All that was implicit in her cat-footed, barefoot steps and in the proud curve of her neck.

Like a man in a trance, Stephen reached forward to take her hands. But the music grew louder and mocking, and Zazuela whirled away from him in the quick, evasive steps of the ancient dance. No, it was not to be so easy! This was a dance of courtship and conquest. Let him follow her, let him desire; and then—only then—he might conquer.

And follow her he did. With deliberate steps that matched hers, pacing around her with his arms held high as if to catch and cage his wild bird, Stephen was drawn into the wild, singing magic of Zazuela's dance.

Laure caught her breath on something like a sob. The wild beauty of the dance had enraptured her for a moment. The hypnotic effect of the violins, the clouds of aromatic smoke rising from the bonfire where Zazuela had dropped a handful of herbs, the darkness and mystery of the night all clouded her brain. It seemed as though nothing existed but the perfect pair dancing there in the middle of the silent courtyard.

What place did she have in this world?

As if in answer, a cold breeze from the mountains swept the smoky air from her face, and left her with a moment of aching clarity. She had no place here. That was the answer. She was a stupid English girl who was out of her place by a thousand miles. Someone Stephen had toyed with in Vienna, and whom he found amusing to bring here, treating her with the autocracy he showed to the peasants on his estate. But not someone who really belonged.

A thousand years of heredity and tradition bound Stephen to this land and these people. A deeper magic than any she understood drew him to the Gypsy girl, who could beguile him without a word spoken.

And she, because in a few weeks she had begun to understand some words of the language, because Stephen looked at her with those burning blue eyes that promised everything and gave nothing—she dared to think she had some place in his heart and his life?

Laure gave a dry laugh. If anything had been needed to show her how little she belonged here, Zazuela's demonstration had provided it. That Stephen could forget her very existence so completely, only hours after she had given herself to him without reservation! She laughed again, turned to go inside, and painfully dragged herself up the stairs to her room.

Chapter Twelve

"No, Magda. *No!*"

Laure put aside the flowing silk *robe de chambre* that Magda had laid out for her. A delicate confection of peach-colored silk trimmed with scallops of blond, it was a nightdress for a princess—or a countess.

"It is not suitable for a prisoner." Laure spoke the thought harshly, aloud, not caring whether Magda understood or not. Wearily, she raised her arms so that Magda could unlace the embroidered bodice of the peasant dress, which Stephen had suggested she wear for the night's festivities. The red boots in which she had danced so happily lay empty and discarded in a corner, their tops of soft leather falling over as if they, too, were tired to death of this masquerade.

"I don't know what I am, who I am, do you see?"

Laure rambled on as she sponged her arms and shoulders down with cold water. The chilly water and the coarse towel raised goosebumps on her skin. A small penance for the dreams she'd allowed herself to indulge in. The weightier penance would mark her heart forever. She had allowed herself to love a man who used her as his plaything. Who had carried her off from Vienna in a moment of passion, wrecking her life for a whim. "And I love him!" Laure scrubbed herself with the coarse towel as if, by rubbing her skin raw, she could erase the memory of those moments in the woods when she had given herself to him so completely.

"Maybe he was right. He knows where he belongs and who he is. This is his place. And I—I'm lost. Wandering in a dark wood where the road is obscured." Wasn't there an Italian poem that started out something like that? Suited her mood. Laure could feel herself tipping over into extravagant self-pity. "I'm not the first girl who's been made a fool of by a man, and I won't be the last."

No. Such astringent common sense didn't suit her mood tonight. Besides, the trappings were hardly ordinary. A seduction carried out in the Black Castle in the heart of the Bakony demanded a touch of high drama. "I love him!" Laure declared. "No, I don't, I hate and despise him!" She threw the coarse towel on the floor and burst into tears.

A hesitant touch on her shoulder roused her. Magda's round face, topped with the coronet of fat blond braids, hovered over her. *"Wein?"*

Magda had been unable to understand Laure's disjointed ramblings in English. But it was clear enough that the foreign mistress was unhappy, and clear enough why—His Excellency still down there in

176

the courtyard, drinking and amusing himself with that
Gypsy slut, and the poor lady waiting! Magda lacked
the vocabulary to tell Laure not to take on so, that this
was the common lot of the nobility. The lords always
amused themselves with willing girls, and the ladies
were supposed to wait and embroider and pretend
they noticed nothing. This foreign miss was silly to
make such a fuss, when the Gypsies would be gone
tomorrow. But foreigners were all mad, or so they
said.

Still, Magda had a real affection for the blond girl
who talked so much and used so many funny words.
After all, it was serving Laure that had got her this
soft life in the castle, instead of working in the fields
like the rest of her father's fourteen children. So she
would offer what comfort she could—the flask of red
wine that Stephen had sent up to the bedroom against
his coming that night.

Laure sat up, dried her face with the back of her
hand and accepted the wine with a sniffle of thanks.
There were no glasses; Stephen's forethought had not
extended so far, and neither Magda nor the cook was
accustomed to serving gentlefolk who would need
such refinements. Laure took a healthy gulp out of the
flask. The wine was warm and smooth, not sweet like
the Tokay they had drunk that afternoon, but fiery
like the sun on the plains and the sweet red paprika
that flavored everything. She took another long drink
and discovered that she felt much better.

"*Gut.* No, I mean *jó.*" She giggled, pleased with
herself for remembering the Hungarian word; and
Magda smiled. "Here, try some." She passed the flask
back to Magda.

What? Drink after the noble lady? Magda was
scandalized. But—foreigners were all mad. She com-

promised by pouring a thin stream of wine from the flask into her open mouth. Then, for good measure, she wiped the neck of the flask with her apron before handing it back to Laure with a curtsy. *Jaj Isten*, but that was good wine! She'd never drunk any but the thin local vintage before. This stuff could make you feel like singing and dancing on the rooftops. The next time Laure handed her the bottle, she forgot to pour the wine without letting her lips touch it.

The flask was three parts empty, and Magda and Laure were sitting on the carved chest with their arms round each others' necks, when a pounding on the oaken door announced that Stephen had remembered his lady.

"Go away," Laure shouted. "I hate you." She could no longer remember exactly what Stephen had done, but she assured Magda that it was something entirely despicable.

"Have to let 's Excellency in," slurred Magda. Her devotion to Laure was not enough to override twenty years of training in absolute obedience. She stumbled to the door and fumbled with the heavy iron bar that Laure had slotted across it earlier that evening.

Muffled thumps and curses from the other side of the door stirred Laure to tardy action.

"Magda, no!" She steered an uncertain course across the wavering oak floor of the room, caught Magda's frilly sleeve and pulled her back. There was a ripping sound as the worn fabric came loose in her hands. Magda staggered backward, a surprised look on her silly face, and sat down heavily on the floor with her legs sticking straight out in front of her.

"Obey—s' Excellenc'—," she slurred. She slumped against the door and began snoring heavily.

Laure reeled backward with the torn sleeve in her hands, steadied herself against the wall and stared at the door. It seemed to be swaying back and forth, but then so did the rest of the room. The iron bar still held.

"I hate you," she called again. "Go away!"

Without waiting to hear Stephen's reply, she steered an erratic course across the room and fell face down across the bed, still clad in her chemise and petticoat.

Laure awoke to a pounding headache and the stertorous sound of Magda's snores. But neither of these matters seemed worthy of attention. She groaned, fumbled for the water ewer and realized it was all the way across the room. Too much trouble.

All the candles but one had guttered out in their untrimmed wicks, and the last flame was hardly more than a sliver of light. But it hurt her eyes. She threw one arm over her face and tried to go back to sleep. Why didn't Magda snuff the candle? Oh, that's right. Magda was drunk. Stupid woman. And there were rats rustling in the walls; Laure could hear them clearly now, the subtle scratch-scratch-scratching all along the wall behind the great tapestry. She could have cried for the pity of it all.

The tapestry billowed out from the wall. Laure squeaked in alarm and sat up. No rat could have done that! Nightmare visions of ancient monsters tormented her. And her head ached abominably.

"Go 'way, monsters," she murmured. "Not fair —assault a dying woman."

The tapestry gave a muffled curse and a thump on the wall. The hairs on the back of Laure's neck prickled. She was coldly sober, all at once, and very much afraid. That had not been a rat, or a drunken dream.

She was feeling around the bed for something to throw when Stephen ripped the tapestry from its hooks and stepped forward over the dusty folds. Behind him, the stone wall was solid as ever.

Laure rubbed her eyes, as if that would drive away this sudden apparition. When she opened them, he had vanished. A dream? But from the far side of the room she heard the murmur of voices. The door squeaked open and then was shut again. When she looked, Magda had disappeared, and Stephen was dropping the iron bar into place again. He came toward her silently, a half-smile of anticipation on his lips.

"You're no ghost," Laure said.

Stephen bowed without speaking.

"Get out," she added, but without much hope that he would obey.

He advanced on the bed, one hand outstretched. Laure's nerve broke at the last second. She scuttled back to the farthest corner of the bed, clutching a feather comforter around her.

"What are you doing here?" she demanded in a voice shrill with tension. "I told you to go away! I don't want to see you any more!"

If only he would speak! That silent, catlike, menacing stride; the one candle flickering as though there were a draught from nowhere blowing through the room; the solid stone wall behind him! Laure risked one glance over her shoulder. The iron bar was still in place over the door, and Magda lay slumped against it, snoring.

"How did you get in?"

Stephen's hand reached across the bed to caress her bare shoulder. Laure flinched violently away from the touch, pressing herself against the wall. But it was a real hand, warm and slightly rough with calluses—not cold and clammy from the nether regions. The bed creaked as he settled his weight on the edge. And he smelled most vilely of stale wine.

The certainty that it was a man and not a ghost she had to deal with renewed her courage.

"How did you get in?" she asked again.

Stephen smiled. "This is my castle." He lifted the long plaits of golden hair that lay across her shoulders. "Do you know, Laure, you are beautiful tonight, huddled under the comforter like a scared little child, all big eyes and bare shoulders and long golden braids. Did I frighten you?"

"You surprised me," Laure said. It was hard to achieve an air of chilly dignity when she was hunched up under the blanket like a child afraid of the bogeyman. It was even harder when Stephen kept caressing her in that blatantly intimate way that made the pulse beat so hard in her throat. "Don't you believe in keeping your promises?"

Stephen looked blank. "What promises? I promised to come to you tonight. And so I have."

"You said," Laure reminded him, "that you would not come again to this room without my invitation." Her throat had gone suddenly dry. It was the way he kept running his fingertips along the top of the comforter, dipping down every now and then to explore the warm swelling of flesh under her chemise. What did invitations mean to a man like this? Every line of his body proclaimed his intention. He meant to take her tonight, like a peasant, like a serf, with or without her permission. He knew his skilled hands and lips, the pressure of his body, would wring that permission from her body even though her heart remained unwilling.

Laure licked suddenly dry lips. She could envision all too clearly the way in which he meant to assert his rights over her. And she would be helpless—not because of his superior strength, but because of the treachery of her own body. Even now she was aching for his caresses. If he didn't stop that teasing pressure of his fingertips, she would throw off the coverlets and beg him to ravish her whole body with that tantalizing skill she could not resist.

"You did invite me," Stephen said. His voice was so soft she could barely hear the words. "In the forest, under the beech leaves—remember? Have you forgotten so soon? Shall I refresh your memory?" His hands slipped farther down under the coverlet, playing with the laces of her chemise. The traitorous cloth parted for him and her breasts rose out of their imprisonment, full and ripe and ready for the touch of his hands. He pushed the coverlet down about her waist and gazed with satisfaction on the white curves thus exposed. Laure could feel her nipples stiffening and contracting as he watched. His face was indistinct in the light of the one candle; all she could see was the blue glitter of his eyes and the hint of a smile.

"I think you do remember."

Before she could guess his intention, his head dropped and he gently flicked his tongue across first one, then the other nipple. Returning for a longer caress, his lips encircled the tip of each breast in turn, pulling and teasing until her nipples hardened into throbbing peaks of desire. All unwilling, Laure moaned with the sweat pleasure of it.

Stephen raised his head and gave a soft triumphant

laugh. The break gave Laure strength to push him away for a moment. She snatched at the coverlet and tried to hide her arousal under it.

"*No*, Stephen!"

She put up her hands to hold him away from her. He caught her wrists in an unbreakable grip and forced her arms down on the pillow above her head.

"Why?" The single word was more menacing than any threats.

"You can't force me!" she cried out, in defiance of the odds. Who was to stop him?

"I thought," Stephen said, "I did not need to." He freed her hands and turned half-away from her, sitting on the edge of the bed. "What happened, Laure? Don't you care for me at all?" He sounded genuinely bewildered.

"Care? As much as you for me!" Laure said between her teeth. She sat up in the bed and made her points to his unresponsive back. "You ask for too much! You kidnap me, you rape me, and then you ask me to enjoy it! You ask me to trust you and believe in you, and then you come to me straight from your Gypsy slut's bed! Care for you? How does a prisoner care for his jailer? Do you love the emperor? You—."

She stopped at the realization that Stephen's shoulders were shaking with poorly suppressed laughter. Words were no longer enough. She flung out her hands in exasperation.

"That last charge, at least, I can refute!" Still laughing, Stephen caught her hands with a quick turn of his body. This time he showed no mercy, but held her wrists pinioned together above her head while, with his free hand, he unbuckled his heavy belt with the dagger in it and unfastened the tight, black knitted trousers. Laure squeezed her eyes tightly shut and turned her face into the pillow to escape the indignity that was about to be forced upon her.

"Look, you little fool!" Stephen's voice was rough with passion. "Does a man come from his mistress in such a state? *Jaj Istenem,* you must think me more stallion than man, if you think I could satisfy a grasping slut like Zazuela and still be ready to play the man to you! All right—if you won't look, then feel!"

He forced one of her hands down the length of his body, along the rough black shirt, then the smoothness of his bared hip, to the nest of coarse curling hair from which his passion sprung, erect and hard. Laure trembled at the feel of the sensitive, quivering rod beneath her fingers, the instrument that had caused her such joy and such anguish.

"Well? Do you really think I've been pleasuring Zazuela this night? Scant hours since we were together in the woods, too!" Stephen's laugh sent vibrations down into his belly. "I should be flattered."

Laure cautiously opened her hand and stroked the erect rod with the tips of her fingers. Stephen caught his breath, and she had the satisfaction of knowing him caught in the toils of that same passion with which he had sought to entrap her.

"Ah, *Isten!*" he groaned as her fingers fluttered up and down. "Laurica, do you know what you are doing to me?"

He released his hold on her wrist long enough to tear off his shirt and to throw back the coverlet. Laure opened her eyes to see the evidence of desire written on his face. He looked serious, intent, almost sad as he bent over her again. The golden hairs on his chest and thighs sparkled in the candlelight like a sprinkling of gold dust over his intensely masculine body, and the long lines of muscles in thighs and flat stomach were exaggerated by the shadows. She caught her breath, overwhelmed by the sheer beauty of his male body.

With trembling, almost reverent fingers he laid back the lace ruffles of her chemise. She raised her hips slightly to help him slip off the linen petticoat with its seven embroidered flounces. When she was quite naked and exposed to his gaze, she lay trembling with the passion she herself had aroused, waiting for him to throw himself upon her.

Instead, he turned away for a moment. She almost cried with disappointment. But then he was back, carrying the one candle that remained alight, fitting it into a carved holder in one of the posts of the bed.

"You are so beautiful," he whispered. "Laure, Laurica *engem,* my Laure, you are mine now. I will not hurry this moment. I will remember it forever. I will love you forever. I will love you forever—tonight. Tonight will last a thousand years. Empires will grow great and crumble, the forest will grow over the castle and cover it, and I will still be loving you."

With each word he caressed her from head to toes with delicate kisses.

He raised himself on one arm and gazed down at her with a look in which intense tenderness was blended with rough, almost frightening desire. She could feel the heat of his passion through his fingertips as he lightly caressed her smooth, satiny skin. He took his time gently tracing every sweet curve, every muscle in her body with his free hand. He no longer spoke but concentrated fully on enhancing her sensations, until she felt like crying out with her impatience and her desire to have him once again.

She was drowning in a sea of erotic sensations as his fingers traced lightly over her white stomach and dipped down to tease the golden curls below. She gasped and reached blindly for his manhood. "Oh, Stephen, please . . . ," she whispered as her body arched toward him, taut with the unreleased desires he had aroused in her.

"Please . . . what, *szivem engem?*" His voice was low and throaty with repressed passion, but he smiled with pleasure at the obvious aching desire he had aroused in her.

"Are you inviting me in?" he inquired in a soft voice that promised the delights to come. As he spoke, he delicately caressed the insides of her parted thighs, coming ever closer but never quite touching the burning center of her desire.

"Yes, oh, yes, Stephen! I want . . ." Her voice trailed off, and a shudder of desire racked her body as his caresses suddenly became very intimate.

"Tell me what you want, my beautiful Laure," he insisted, his voice filled with passion and desire. Without waiting for a reply, he leaned down and kissed the throbbing bud that his fingers had aroused into passion, tongue flickering lightly over her exposed center.

She writhed in ecstasy under his touch. Her mounting desire only spurred him on as he caressed her with lips and tongue and fingers until she thought she could stand it no longer. She cried out as wave upon wave of passion surged through her, each one starting before the previous one had subsided. And still he continued until she felt completely limp and drained of energy. Dimly, through the haze of exhaustion, she felt one last deeply probing kiss before he released his hold on her.

She opened her eyes to the sight of Stephen's golden body leaning over her.

"Oh, *kedves Laurica,* dearest Laure, my sweet, you are so beautiful," he rasped as he gazed tenderly down at her. Suddenly his mood changed, and a wicked amusement lit his eyes as he said, "Now I have found at least one way to please you. How many more ways are there? Will you tell me, or must I make an experiment?"

He ducked his head suddenly, and she gasped as his teeth nipped the tip of her exposed and sensitive breast. The nipple hardened under his touch, sending piercing waves of sweetness in circles spiraling out from her breast. He buried his face in her white softness and she felt something hard and warm brush the inner surfaces of her parted thighs.

"Please invite me in, Laure," he groaned. "I want you so!"

"Oh, Stephen. . . ." A new wave of desire swept over her as he moved against her. "I want you too."

In an instant he plunged deep inside her moist and ready cleft, filling her with his passion, taking her aggressively with long deep strokes that raised her already heightened desire to an almost unbearable peak of tension. He buried his face in the curve between her neck and shoulder and wrapped his strong arms tightly against her as he possessed her totally and completely.

His breathing became shallow and uneven and his thrusts more rapid as he neared the peak of his desire. Laure clung to him as if her life depended on it, as his passion gave way in a series of violent tremors that coursed the length of his manhood and vibrated within her.

Stephen held Laure's body firmly against his as he rolled over on his side to rest, but his spent shaft still buried deep inside her. His breathing slowed to normal, but his blue eyes still radiated a strong desire for her. She lay quietly, speechless after the intensity of their lovemaking, helpless in his embrace.

"Tired, *galambom*, my dove?" teased Stephen. "I thought you Englishwomen could ride for hours!"

Laure caught her breath and her eyes grew wide with astonishment as she felt him stiffening inside her once again. He chuckled low in his throat. "Yes, *kedves* Laurica, tonight will indeed last forever as I promised you." And he began to love her again with slow, controlled movements that filled her with an indescribable pleasure. His hands roamed gently over her slender body, pausing to cup the soft breasts that spilled out with such surprising abundance, trailing down across her flat stomach, reaching around to caress the sensitive place at the base of her spine and tighten over her hips. He clutched her to him with a moment of uncontrolled passion, then recovered himself and continued the slow, gentle stroking that was awakening her senses to new heights of pleasure. His hands traveled up her back with smooth, fluid strokes until he reached her neck, trailed across the fine line of her throat and cheekbones until he was holding her face gently between his hands. He kissed her tenderly, deeply, his tongue searching the depths of her sweet warm mouth. And all the time he was still loving her with maddeningly slow, deliberate movements.

Laure was caught up in the mood he created; she felt entranced, as though she were floating on a billowing cloud of pleasure. She wanted nothing more than for the patient, tender arousal to go on forever. But her treacherous body had a will of its own. She felt her own hips moving to meet his rhythm. As Stephen felt her passion rise he responded in kind, fanning the flames of their mutual desire to the point of no return. Laure cried out as the first explosion ripped through her body, followed closely by another, then another, till she forgot who or where she was. As if from far away, she heard Stephen calling her name as he joined her in her ecstasy, and then she knew no more.

His hand tenderly stroking the damp hair away from her brow roused her from immeasurable depths. As if slowly floating up through deep waters, she returned to consciousness like a swimmer breaking through into the surface of a sunlit pool. "Not quite forever," he murmured with a tender laugh of apology, and then, "Laure, we have to talk. Zazuela—."

Laure stopped his mouth with a kiss. Whatever he wanted to tell her about Zazuela, she did not want to hear it now. The last flickering candle had finally sputtered to death in its own wick, and all she desired was to snuggle into his arms like a contented kitten.

But that last, sighed word stayed with her in the darkness long after Stephen had succumbed to sleep.

Chapter Thirteen

STEPHEN FELL ASLEEP ALMOST IMMEDIATELY. FOR LAURE sleep was long in coming. She lay awake, Stephen's arm across her breasts, staring at the darkness above her head and listening to his uneven breathing.

Once again she had given in to Stephen's seductive techniques. And she would do so again and again, as long as she remained within his power.

This time she had not even the excuse of believing that he loved her. Their coupling on the mountain had been swift and sure and perfect, two lovers coming together—or so she had believed at the time. There was something beautiful in that.

There was nothing beautiful, nothing to take pride in, in what had taken place that night. Stephen had simply demonstrated his power to have her in his arms and in his bed, willing or unwilling, at any time or any place he desired. No locked door, no bitter words could keep him away. He could even come to her smelling of wine and the caresses of his Gypsy woman; it made no difference. Within minutes she had been naked in his arms, begging to be taken—just as he had predicted. And she knew she would surrender to him in that same way again, whenever he wished it.

What could explain her total helplessness in his arms? Laure had danced and flirted with young men, in London and in Austria. There had been waltzes and galops and lancers, soft words on terraces and conservatories, even an arm about her waist here or a stolen kiss on her cheek there. It had all been a delightful game—nothing more. But Stephen had only to lay his hand on her arm or lift her into her saddle to set her whole body trembling in anticipation of his caresses.

Staring dry-eyed into the darkness of the canopied bed, Laure faced the bitterest knowledge of all. She loved this man who had taken her so casually. Loved him helplessly, hopelessly, with a passion that left no room for pride or independence or any of the other things she had once valued. If they had been still in Vienna, she would have been looking for him at every ball, finding parties flat that he did not attend, going with him out onto the balcony without thinking of the shocked whispers and amused stares of the people who saw them go. The Viennese would have said that she was lost to propriety, that she was Stephen Andrassy's latest flirt, and would have wondered with slightly malicious amusement what the little *Engländerin* would say when she found she was but one in a long string of women.

And now—now, imprisoned in his castle, hearing his voice every day, touched by him whenever and in whatever manner he chose, how much greater was her bondage! In Vienna, separated from him by all the rules of an ancient and formal society, she might eventually have found the courage to break her bonds by fleeing back to England. There, she supposed, in a few years of a life devoted to good works and the happiness of others, she might eventually have forgotten the handsome young Hungarian nobel who wore two faces and who stirred her blood and troubled her sleep.

Now such a flight was forever impossible. She had sensed her fate coming on her when he abducted her from the Metternichs' ball. In the little roadside inn where they stopped to treat his wound, she had known her fate and had made one blind attempt to escape it—that doomed and desperate flight into the heart of the Danubian plain.

Ever since he came after her that day on the black horse, ever since she had accepted his rescue and had ridden before him back to the inn, she had been his. Heart and soul, body and mind. He had set his seal on her, and there was no place she could flee to where she would be free of him. His making love to her had not been the final bondage. She had belonged to him since that day at the inn.

Ever since then she had been fighting against a fate that was already sealed. Pretending that she could resist his lovemaking when he approached her. Pretending that she could make him so angry that he would not approach her again. Pretending that she did not quiver at the very sound of his voice across the hall, that she was indifferent to his presence. Pretending that she suffered his approaches only because she was his prisoner, that all she really wanted was the freedom to go back to Vienna.

And—the last and bitterest pretense of all—pretending that he loved her as she did him, that his glowing words to her that afternoon had been the sign of an equal commitment on his part, that they were equals and lovers rather than master and slave.

The taste of old wine was sour in Laure's mouth, and Stephen's arm crushed her breast. She longed to be free as she had been, riding in the Vienna woods, galloping in the cool morning, tasting the pure intoxication of speed and freedom. Those had been her last moments of pure freedom, the last moments of her girlhood, before she met the man who called himself Csikos. Everything since then had been part of a web that radiated inward, leading her inexorably to the center of this stone castle in the heart of the Bakony, to this bed where she lay with a man to whom love made her a slave.

And he—he did not love her. That illusion had not lasted long! Oh, he wanted her. That was true enough. Before and after his Gypsy girl, as hors d'oeuvres and dessert. And he was His Excellency the count, unaccustomed to giving up anything he wanted. So he would come to her at night, when he was not otherwise occupied, he would take her in the forest when he had leisure during the day, and he would keep her here to serve his pleasure—as long as he wanted her.

How long did she have? A few more weeks? The whole summer? A year or more? Surely not more than a year. She remembered the gossip in Vienna. Stephen Andrassy never stayed faithful to the same flirtation for two seasons. Before the new green leaves came out in the beech woods, then, she would be replaced. She must be prepared for that.

She supposed, dully, that he would send her back to Vienna then, when he no longer desired her. He would find it embarrassing to keep his castoff mistresses around the castle. But then, this castle was not his regular abode. There was the manor house that she had never seen. Perhaps he would go back there and permit her to stay in the castle. He might even ride up from the plains from time to time and visit her for a night. The Gypsy Zazuela had been his love last year—so much was plain from Jansci's hints and sneers—and he still wanted her enough to spend an evening with her and grant some favors to her band.

The thought of dragging out a dreary existence in the castle, as Stephen's pensioner, was bitterly sad to her. Tears filled her eyes and ran down her cheeks. She dared not lift a hand to wipe them away for fear of waking Stephen. Could she bear to stay on those terms, when at last he tired of her? Yes—better than exile. If he sent her back to Vienna, she could no longer stay with Josef and Juli. There would be too much scandal about her. She would have to go back to England, where she would never, never see him again.

But all this was still in the future. For now, Stephen still desired her, and she could be with him every day and take what mixture of pleasure and pain she might from his presence. This one summer—if they could only have this one summer! If they could ride out under the new green leaves of the beech trees, hear the birds singing and pluck the wild roses in the hedges. Just for this summer, let him not tire of her; and she—she would pretend that he loved her, and she would be happy and would not think of the cold winds of autumn. She would no longer importune him to send her back to Vienna, no longer pretend that a freedom without him in it could be anything but husks and ashes. Let them have only this one summer together, before he tired of her, and she would make it do for all the happiness she would ever know.

Stephen stirred, mumbled something in his sleep, and rolled away from her.

Laure realized that she could dimly see the outlines of objects in the room, and that the window slit glowed with a dim blue light. It must be near dawn.

A bird fluttered along the wall, found precarious foothold somewhere among the crumbling stones and let out a tentative trill of song.

No use, now, to lie abed and court sleep. Soon the castle would be stirring. Laure slipped from the bed without awakening Stephen, put on her chemise and petticoat, and dashed cold water from the ewer over her face and shoulders. A glance at the door showed that Magda was no longer there. She must have awakened during the night and let herself out, to find a pallet somewhere else in the castle. The iron bar hung loose from its hinge beside the door.

The sight of the heavy bar reminded Laure of the puzzle of last night. She frowned, trying to remember. Yes, Magda had definitely still been asleep against the door, and the iron bar had been in place, when Stephen appeared at her bedside. He had not come from that side of the room, either, but from the far side, where an ancient tapestry of hunting scenes covered the wall.

Yes—the rotting tapestry had been ripped from its hooks and now lay in dusty folds on the floor. That had not been a dream, then. But the wall behind it was solid, with no door or hallway, not even a niche where he could have been standing concealed.

Could there be a secret passage of some sort? The puzzle intrigued Laure. Her natural resilience was returning with the morning light. Better to try to solve this puzzle than to sit limply like a sack of flour, weeping over her lost innocence. She loved Stephen; he didn't love her. Someday he would tire of her. That was a continual pain deep in her heart. But even when one was in pain, the minutiae of daily life had to go on. She had to wash and dress and eat breakfast as if this were a normal day. She had to go on and be as happy as she could be for this one summer, or however long she had. And one way to do that was to keep busy. . . .

Laure pushed and pulled at the rough projections of the stone wall with more determination than science. Nothing gave to her touch. If there was a passageway, wouldn't the wall be hollow somewhere? Perhaps she could find out by knocking—no, that would wake Stephen. Look for a pattern, then. A place where the stones were set evenly, in a rectangle like a door, instead of haphazardly piled one on top of the other like a child's crazy puzzle.

As the light in the room grew stronger and clearer, it was easier to discern the way in which the stones were fitted together. But she could see no pattern. Only when she felt all along the wall did she find the straight line of a join, cunningly concealed by a series of rocks that had been split down the middle and set back together as neatly as any stonemason could have done it. Her fingertips traced the line up one wall, nearly five feet, then across and down again. Yes, that must be the door. But, push and pull as she might, she could not find the key to open it. Perhaps it could not be opened at all from this side. Perhaps she had dreamed that apparition last night, and Stephen had really only come in through the door. But the memory was so vivid!

A secret door that Stephen could open, and that she had no power over! It was uncomfortably reminiscent of the problem that had set her to prowling around the room in the first place. Laure knelt on the floor beside the wall and rested her hands in her lap. She had never felt so utterly helpless.

"I won't think about it anymore," she promised herself. "I'll just take each day as it comes, and—and be happy!" And the tears flowed unchecked down her cheeks, splashed on her bare neck and bosom and trickled down between her breasts in a salty rivulet. She was sitting four feet from the only man she had ever loved, and she was utterly alone.

Quiet though Laure had been, her movements along the stone wall and the little sounds she made while pushing and pulling at the stones had awakened Stephen some moments earlier. He did not move, but watched her attempts at opening the passageway through slitted eyes. He suppressed an involuntary frown when the movements of her fingertips showed that she had found the minuscule cracks around the door, but smiled as she failed to discover the secret of opening it. But his momentary pleasure was short-lived as he reflected on what this search must mean.

So she was so determined to escape him that she could not even wait till he was out of the room before searching for the secret passage! The thought hurt Stephen like a knife in his heart.

Up to then he had largely discounted Laure's demands for freedom, relying on the passionate bond he sensed between them to bring her to her senses.

When she was so sweet and yielding in his arms, how could she truly want to leave him! She had even helped him escape from Vienna. She must have known then what her actions implied.

Stephen had succeeded to the lands and title of Andrassy *puszta* when he was a boy of twenty-three in the emperor's guard, following the tragic death of both his parents in the epidemic that had swept the Hungarian countryside in that year. For ten years he had lived a double life—an absolute autocrat on his Hungarian estates, the spoiled pet of the nobility in the Viennese court. His involvement with the Hungarian independence movement, real though it was now, had originally grown out of nothing more than his frustration at being refused a permit to import and export horses because the emperor thought it an unsuitable activity for a nobleman. It had been the first time in his life that anything he truly desired had been denied him, and he had reacted with the anger of a spoiled child coupled with the stubbornness of a Hungarian aristocrat. Only as he began organizing gestures of resistance had he begun to realize how thoroughly his homeland was under the thumb of an Austrian ruler, and to see that there were wider issues at stake than the momentary frustration of one spoiled and wealthy man. Now he was devoted, heart and soul, to the cause of freedom, even if the cost were the forfeiture of his estates and his own freedom. But it was humbling to reflect that this, the one great cause of his life, had begun in nothing other than his own selfishness.

And Laure? She had been the second person ever to oppose him. When he first encountered her in the Vienna woods, she had enchanted him immediately— so gay, so brave and proud, neither bending her head to him in submission nor shrieking and fainting like the ladies of the court. Riding like an Amazon, too, on that great horse! A smile curved Stephen's lips as he remembered that first encounter. Like all Hungarians, he valued personal courage and good horsemanship above all else. How could he fail to love Laure?

But love to him meant only desire, quickly aroused and as quickly satisfied. He had seen with satisfaction his effect on her in the guise of "Csikos." It had seemed an amusing game to complete the flirtation and conquest under his own name of Stephen Andrassy. The ever-present risk that she might recognize and betray him had added that necessary spice of danger without which no *affaire de coeur* was complete.

He had been surprised when Laure remained obstinately remote from him. His efforts at flirtation progressed just so far and no farther. He could sense that she was deeply attracted to him, yet there was a will of steel in her that he could not break. She held herself always just that little bit in reserve, and so kept him fascinated for far longer than he was used to dance attendance on any woman.

Then there had come the shattering night when both his worlds seemed to crumble about him. Wounded in that scuffle with the emperor's guards, he had arrived late at the Metternichs' ball only to be greeted by Josef's smiling announcement that he and Laure were affianced. To lose Laure, his lovely Laure, so proud and free, to that—that uniformed popinjay, that bourgeois policeman in soldier's dress, that petty clerk with his pretensions to nobility! Stephen ground his teeth at the memory. It was not to be borne. And yet there was his duty to the cause. He must recapture the lost dispatches, and he dared not return to Vienna to be subjected to police search and questioning—

perhaps to be questioned by Josef himself, who had ill concealed his suspicions. What could he do?

The chance meeting with Laure in the study had resolved all that, or so it seemed at the time. He had used her as cover to escape Metternich's trap, had seized those few moments in the moonlight to plead with her not to accept Josef's offer until he could return to Vienna and court her properly.

But even then she had refused to yield to him. Damn these English and their cold pragmatic blood! No woman of his country, no real woman with blood in her veins instead of milk would have been able to resist such a situation—the wounded lover pleading in the moonlight for one last favor, the danger, the imminent parting. A real woman would have given herself to him there in the gardens and would have promised her eternal fidelity. To be sure—a cynical smile curved Stephen's lips—she would probably have married Josef while he was hiding in the country. But you could not expect fidelity of a woman—and he would have had the satisfaction of knowing he had her first surrender.

But not his damned, stiff-necked, entirely lovable little *Engländerin!* No, she had to rail at him for the double game he had played with her—as if there was ever truth between lovers! How naive could she be?

It had been a mad impulse, to sweep her off with him on his escape. A mad, unreasoning impulse. But he could not remain in Vienna, and the thought of leaving her to that Josef—intolerable! Besides, she would never have been really happy with that stuffed figurehead. She needed to lie in a real man's arms, to learn what loving was really about.

Her passionate response, that first night in the castle, had seemed to justify his actions. Couldn't he make her happy as a woman deserved to be? What more did she ask? But the very next morning she'd been railing at him again, complaining about having been kept prisoner against her will, demanding to be set free. What nonsense! How could it be against her will? Hadn't she wanted it as much as he? It would serve her right to be left alone for a while. She'd be glad enough of his company when he favored her again.

It hadn't worked out quite that way, though. Laure had made herself quite at home in the castle, sewing and gossiping with Magda, playing chess with old Marton, picking up enough words of Hungarian to ingratiate herself with the men. It was he who'd been uncomfortable. A sorry two weeks he'd had of it, inventing errands away from the castle to be out of range of her scornful eyes, sleeping on straw in the great hall while his men laughed at him behind his back. And lonely—he hadn't known how much her company meant to him until he willfully deprived himself of it. All in all, it had been a relief when she'd accepted his proffered olive branch yesterday.

Stephen rolled over, flung one arm across his face and groaned. Was it the Tokay he'd imbibed so freely over their meal, or the relief he felt at being no longer in her bad books, or—or something else, some feeling deeper than he'd known before? He couldn't tell. But something had intoxicated him into speaking to her as he should not have done. Mixing his declaration of love with a vision of their life together as it might have been.

He had no right to speak to her that way! He knew how paper-thin was the disguise of "Csikos." At this very minute, in Vienna, his enemies might have put together the evidence to unmask him. Already they were working to discredit him—this tale of "Csikos" becoming a common robber and jewel thief. That had been a clever move. Who would believe him if he confessed to the political robberies but not to the rest? At this very minute his estates, his very life might be forfeit to the emperor. He had no right to talk of marriage and sharing his life with a woman, when that life might be cut short at the end of a rope the next time he showed his face in Vienna.

For the first time Stephen began to see the wrong he had done Laure, and to wonder how he might make amends. He had carried off the girl, ruined her reputation. He could not marry her—he could marry no one while he was in danger of being attainted for treason. What was to become of her? He had delayed sending her back to Vienna because he could not imagine life without her, and because he was afraid she would marry Josef. But Josef would never have her now—and if he did, he would make her life a perpetual penance. What had he done?

All the same, she must go back. Vienna, England— it hardly mattered. If the gossip Zazuela had carried to him were true, it was not safe for her to stay here. A troop of Austrian soldiers searching for the castle, bribing the peasants for information! He had faith in the castle's ability to withstand any seige that could be mounted against it, but he dared not subject Laure to the horrors of a private war. If the worst should happen, and the castle fell, her fate would be unthinkable. And in his heart Stephen knew, whatever the strength of his castle and the loyalty of his people, there could be only one end to an open rebellion against the Austrian forces. The nation was not ready yet to rise with him, to throw off the shackles of the usurper. It would be a generation yet before that could happen. No, the emperor's forces would crush him like a nut between two stones. And Laure—gentle, proud, courageous, loving Laure—she must not be connected with him in any way. She would have to leave at once, today, and well escorted, even if he stripped the castle's defenses to do it.

He had come last night to tell her of his decision, after hours of drinking with the Gypsies and coaxing information out of them. But she had angered him by barring the door against him like that—and by the time he groped his way up the secret passage and forced himself into the room, his thoughts had taken quite another turn.

And now—now they had lost a night in which she could have been riding to safety. And for all she'd yielded herself to his lovemaking last night, here she was now, bruising her hands against the stone wall like a bird in a cage that batters its wings against the bars, and weeping quietly into her lap. So much for his vaunted skill at lovemaking! What use was it to bring a girl warm and willing into your arms, if she woke to these quiet, hopeless tears? Stephen cursed himself. He knew now that he wanted more from Laure than the momentary satisfaction of his desires. He wanted to share his life with hers, to protect her from the blows of fate and keep her happy forever. Instead, he had made her miserable. What a fine lover! The least he could do, having come to this moment of despairing honesty, was to let her have the freedom she craved. And to try, if he could, to arrange it so that he did not drag her own life down amid the ruins of his.

He swung his legs over the side of the bed and stood up unsteadily. Laure stopped her weeping on a sharp, indrawn breath. The quick turn of her head as she looked up at him, the instant blankness of her expression reinforced his feeling that she felt only fear of him. What a fine muddle he had made of things! Anger at himself made his face harsh and his voice expressionless as he spoke to her.

"It's time for you to go back to Vienna."

Well, at least she had stopped that continuous, silent weeping. But why did she stare up at him without moving, as if she feared some further blow?

"So? It's what you wanted, isn't it?" Disappointment made his voice harsh. He realized that subconsciously he had been hoping she would change her mind, want to stay with him. Not that he could allow her to do so—but it would be something, to know that she had come to care for him.

"For the last three weeks, all I hear is 'Let me go! Take me back! I want to go home! You can't keep me prisoner!'" Viciously he imitated a woman's high-pitched tones, whining the words out. Unfair. Laure had never whined. Well, it was bad enough to lose her. He didn't have to be fair too. "All right—so I am giving you what you wanted. Don't you have anything to say to that?" He stared down at the still figure crouched on the floor.

Laure looked down at her clasped hands. So soon! Even the summer she'd prayed for, then, was not to be.

"Laure, Laurica." Stephen knelt on the floor beside her and took her hands. *Isten!* They were as cold as ice. How long had the girl been out of bed?

"Listen, Laure. Do not be afraid. It is not a trick. You have been begging me for your freedom—very well, I give it you. Oh, I'm not going to simply turn you out." Could that have been bothering her, the prospect of being left to make her own way, alone and friendless, back across the border? *"Jaj Istenem!* What kind of a bastard do you think I am? No, don't answer that; just listen to me." He could just imagine what Laure's sharp tongue could do with a question like that. In his imagination he could already hear her, pointing out with caustic words that a man who would abduct and rape a young woman might be supposed to have few scruples about his later treatment of her. He didn't need to hear that. He would never be able to convince her that his original selfish impulse had turned into real love, the kind that shows itself by caring more about the beloved than about oneself. All he could do was act on his feelings, protect her by sending her away and hope that one day she would come to understand.

"You will travel in my coach, with an escort of my best men—Marton, and Geza, and six men picked by them. You will travel as the honored guest of the Count Stephen Andrassy, and no man will lay a finger on you. When you get back to Vienna, you can put it about that you have been ill—exhaustion from the season—and I offered you the use of one of my smaller estates to recuperate and enjoy the country air. I, of course, was not there." It was a thin enough story, but the best he could concoct on the spur of the moment. When he was unmasked as "Csikos" and it was known that he had been hiding at the Black Castle all this time, Laure's insistence that she had been at the manor house might save her reputation. And if, by some miracle, he escaped from this coil— well, then he might return to Vienna bearing his own name and title; and if Laure had not married the stodgy cousin by then, perhaps he might have another chance. But he had no right to speak of that now. You could not ask a girl to wait for someone who might be dead within the month—particularly, he thought, with a mental laugh at the ironies of fate, if you had already made the girl hate and fear you! No, let her find a respectable life with the cousin, if she could. If she could not, she might consent to take him to patch up her reputation; and perhaps, in a few years, she might learn not to hate him.

But it was very unlikely that he would get the chance to make amends. The presence of Austrian soldiers in the Bakony could mean only one thing—that the fatal connection between Andrassy and Csikos had been made. No, the best that he could do for Laure now was to send her away, out of danger, and hope that some day she might forgive him. At least she had brightened up now that he had promised her a proper escort back to Vienna.

For one wild, despairing moment Laure thought of begging Stephen not to send her away. But what was the use? He had taken her for his pleasure, on a whim of an instant, and tired of her almost as quickly. No doubt her distaste at sharing his favors with the Gypsy had speeded the inevitable end. What would be her life if he did allow her to stay with him? To drift round the castle, waiting for the rare moment when his glance fell on her, and be laughed at by such as Jansci and Zazuela?

Generations of inherited pride came to her aid. She might have loved unwisely, but she deserved better than this. Far, far better to return to England and wither into spinsterhood than to stay here and be despised, and inevitably cast off anyway in a few years.

She squared her shoulders and looked at Stephen with almost dry eyes. This might be her last chance to memorize his countenance, the piercing blue eyes, the leonine mane of tawny hair and beard, the sensual lips.

"Thank you," she said. "I'm glad you have finally come to your senses. As you say, you could hardly keep me a prisoner here forever."

She rose to her feet and turned away from him to hide the sudden trembling in her lips. "Will you find Magda and send her to me? I will want her help to pack for me."

Chapter Fourteen

MAGDA WAS MERCIFULLY SILENT WHEN SHE TIPTOED IN, a few minutes after Stephen's departure. Like Laure, she assumed that this abrupt decision meant that His Excellency had tired of her. Jansci must have been right after all; the Gypsy's hold on His Excellency was too strong to be broken by a milk-faced *Engländerin*. But what a pity, what a pity! Miss Laure was a true lady, not like that dirty Zazuela, who would make eyes at any of the men when His Excellency wasn't looking, and threw things and screamed in tantrums when she thought she wasn't being served with the proper degree of respect. That one was all right for a hot-blooded young man to amuse himself with; but Miss Laure might have been lady of the castle, and Magda as her maid might have shared in the soft life.

A thousand pities she'd angered the count by screaming at him and turning him away last night!

When it came to the point, Laure realized that she had very little packing to do. She would have liked, in fact, to have made the grand gesture of refusing to take from the castle anything that was Stephen's. But she could not do that. She had literally not a stitch of clothing that was her own. She compromised by telling Magda to pack two of the simplest muslin dresses in a basket, with the ivory-backed hairbrush and comb. For the journey she would wear the green cloth riding habit; it might make her feel better to ride partway, rather than being cooped up in a stuffy coach all the way.

Magda frowned and clicked her tongue several times at these orders. "It's not right, my lady," she complained. "His Excellency would never send a lady away without making her a present. Very generous, the count is. Are you sure he didn't mean you to take some of the jewels?"

The jewel box had been at the bottom of the chest, with the hand-carved chessmen. It contained a barbaric display of gold and silver chains set with heavy gems, far too massive and ornate for modern taste. To Stephen they were trinkets not worth considering, jewels his mother had not cared for enough to bring to the manor house. To Magda—and to Laure—they represented a small fortune, but one that Laure would not touch. She had refused to take more than the bare minimum necessary for her daily needs while she was here, and she would leave with no more than that.

"Seems a pity," Magda sighed, holding up a gold collar set with dull blue, round-cut sapphires. She ran the heavy links through her fingers with longing. Never could a poor peasant girl wear such a thing, but it would give her almost as much satisfaction to see it around Laure's neck. "Besides," she added on a more practical note, "you'll be needing something for your dowry, after . . ." She paused.

Laure gave a hard, dry laugh. "It doesn't matter, Magda. Put it away! I'll take nothing from Stephen. All I want is to forget this experience as quickly as possible."

Magda nodded. "Yes . . . but a good dowry will help the others forget." She took the simple, practical view of her village. Laure was not worth as much in the marriage market, because she had been with the count; therefore it was the count's duty to make up the difference to her prospective husband. The old count, Stephen's father, had been a great one for the village girls after his wife died—almost as bad as that Geza! But never a girl had gone back to her village without a purse of silver heavy enough to find her a good husband. This count didn't take the village girls, but that wasn't to say he didn't know the rules. Considering that Laure was a lady, she should have been given whatever it would take to buy a husband in her world. Magda thought the gold-and-sapphire collar would do nicely, and when Laure was not looking, she stuffed it in between the folds of a muslin dress in the basket. Miss Laure would be glad enough of it later, when she'd got over the count and was looking about her for a husband.

"There now," Magda said, offering awkward comfort. "Don't you be grieving over him, Miss Laure. You'll be home soon enough."

"Home. Yes. . . ." Better not to think of what lay ahead of her in Vienna, or of what she was leaving behind here. Better not to think at all, except of such trivialities as which dresses to pack. Thankfully Laure seized on a distraction.

"Magda, the count came here last night."

Magda gave a reminiscent giggle. A mistake it had been, but she would always treasure the memory of Miss Laure shouting through the barred door that Stephen should go away. Never seen anyone stand up to him like that, she hadn't!

"Yes, and us sent 'un away with a flea in his ear, didn't us?"

"Not then." Laure dismissed the memory with a wave of her hand. "Later. . . . You were asleep against the door; he couldn't have got in that way. Magda, he seemed to come right through the wall!"

Magda's eyes were wide, and she nodded solemnly. "They do say as the old count's mother was a real Gypsy witch," she whispered, "and she knowed spells to fly through the air."

"Rubbish. There must be a passage somewhere. Do you know anything about it?"

Under pressure, Magda searched her memory and recalled stories from her mother's day, of how the old count, when he was a boy, would appear at village dances and commandeer the prettiest girls, when all at the castle believed him safe in his bed. "Only fourteen," her mother had said with a fond smile, "but a lord already, and a lord with the girls! I was eighteen and fancied myself quite grown up, but your father— he was walking out with me then—threatened to beat me soundly if I let the young master dance with me again! He used to come slipping through the woods— the young master, not your father—with mud and slime on his boots, as if he'd been crawling through the cells."

"Cells?" Laure queried Magda at this point.

"You know—where they used to lock up the prisoners. Down under the castle." Magda was impatient at being interrupted. She had just remembered something else.

"Used to say he got out by the moonbeam. Well, they do say as his mother was a witch."

By the moonbeam . . . crawling through the cells. . . . Laure couldn't make anything of the story. The first part sounded as though there really was a secret passage through the four-foot-thick stone walls of the castle, one that led down into the underground cells and then, perhaps, out by a tunnel. But that bit about moonbeams—what could it mean? Well, no matter! Why should she puzzle over it? She would hardly be here long enough to make use of any knowledge she could glean from Magda's confused stories. It had only been something to occupy her mind while she packed.

And now? Stephen had disappeared without a word as to when she should be ready for the carriage. Her basket was packed. Perhaps he meant to send her away with no more farewell than this. She should go down to the hall, act as if she were delighted to be set free at last.

No. Her spirit winced at the idea of facing the whispers and giggles of such as Jansci. And—if she were to see Stephen again, let it not be in such a public place! Perhaps, if she waited, he would at least come up himself to tell her when the carriage was ready. Laure settled herself in a hard wooden chair beside the ruins of the tapestry, crossed her wrists in her lap, and waited. There was, after all, nothing else to do.

All through the long hours of the day she waited

there, unmoving, reliving the few sweet moments of the past weeks. There had been that day at the inn when she had to change the dressing on his shoulder, when she had first known the force of her feelings for him and had run away from that knowledge. There had been the first night after they arrived at the castle, the ride through the woods together and last night— the night he promised would last forever. Laure gave a wry smile. It seemed that the memory, at least, would last her forever.

At intervals during the day she was plagued by Magda's urging her to take a glass of wine, to eat some cold chicken and bread, to answer her, to walk around. Laure nodded and answered whatever was polite and sent the girl away again, sipped the wine and played with the plate of food, and lapsed into her waking dream again as soon as she was left alone. Strange, how her memories seemed more real than this barren room with its stone walls and its incongruous trappings of luxury. It would be pleasant if she could stay within this dream forever, if she could not be quite conscious of the parting when the coach moved off with her and left Stephen behind.

He came at sunset.

The long chamber had been in shadow for some hours; the narrow window slit caught only the morning sun. Magda would have lit candles, but Laure had stopped her with a wave of her hand. Better to sit in the dark, better not to be seen too clearly.

Stephen's booted feet rang on the stairs and on the stones of the narrow hall with an odd sense of urgency. He thrust the heavy door open without knocking and strode into the room to stand over Laure like the messenger in a play.

"The coach cannot be ready until morning," he

said. "Some trouble with the harness. You will have to stay here another night. Be ready to set out at first light."

He sounded furious. Laure's own temper rose up at his angry tone. "I'm terribly sorry for the inconvenience!" she snapped. "Why are you so discommoded, Your Excellency? Had you promised this room to your new mistress for tonight? Shall I ask Magda to find me a pallet in some corner, so that I shall not be in your way?"

To her horror, she felt tears prickling behind her eyes at the end of this speech, and her voice had a slight but definite quiver. Thank God it was dark! Perhaps she would be able to carry out her pretense of indifference until he left her alone again.

"You must leave as soon as possible," Stephen said.

"Yes." This time Laure had schooled her voice to a fine indifference. "I had gathered you were eager to be rid of me. But spare me your temper, Count Andrassy! It's hardly my fault if your servants can't keep the harness in repair."

Stephen seized both her wrists and drew her up to face him. "Eager—to—be rid of you?" he rasped, shaking her on each word. "You little fool! Eager to save your life, is what I am! Do you understand nothing? Last night Zazuela—."

Laure freed one hand with an effort and brought it up against his cheek with a resounding slap. "Spare me the stories about your Gypsy whore!" she shouted. "You tired of me soon enough; I'm going—what more do you want? My blessing on your next mistress?"

Stephen caught her hand and forced it back down behind her back, pulling her close to him. "It's too much," he said between gritted teeth. "I had not

meant to tell you—but a man can only bear so much!"
His arm pressed Laure's hand into the small of her
back with agonizing force, and held her so close to
him that she could feel the rise and fall of his chest
under the linen shirt and black vest. The silver
buttons on his vest pressed into her skin and cut her.

"I love you, Laure. Do you understand? I know it's
no excuse for the way I've treated you. God forgive
me, I've been a selfish fool. I thought you might come
to love me in time—might forgive me. But there's no
more time. The Austrians are looking for this castle.
My men can hold it, but I'll not have you here during
a seige—and maybe worse. Don't you see? They
know who "Csikos" is. They mean to hang me. And
you must be far away from here. I've done you
enough damage already; but only to your reputation,
my darling dove, not to your life. And that may be
rescued—if your cousins believed the letter I sent,
they will not have gossipped about your absence, and
you may go back to Vienna without a scandal. But
God knows what the secret police would do with you
if you were caught with the notorious rebel. I won't
risk you rotting your life away in one of the emperor's
prisons. You must go—and some day, try to forgive
me."

Laure's heart ached for the passion and the love
behind the anguished words that Stephen dragged
out, one by one, as if he were tearing out the roots of
his heart. "Stephen—oh, Stephen!" she whispered,
and put her face up for his kiss. He crushed her to
him, his kisses fierce and passionate. Laure's heart
pounded as suddenly; he caught her shoulders and
held her at arm's length. His eyes blazed with passion
and devoured every inch of her trembling body.

"Oh, Laure *szivem*, to think that I might never

again . . ." The words caught in his throat. He shook his head impatiently. Words were not enough. With fingers that shook with desire he undid her bodice, pushing the soft fabric off her shoulders to expose the white, soft curves beneath. He buried his face in her swelling breasts. Her hands caressed the back of his head and held him to her as, with an urgency that could not be denied, he freed her from her remaining garments. Laure clung to him and they kissed fervently as he ripped off his own clothes. And then the only things between them were the sprinkling of crisp golden curls that covered his chest and thighs, and the hard evidence of his desire rising from his golden nest.

Laure's own desire mounted swiftly as she returned his prolonged, probing kisses, each one a promise of the joys to come. He gently lifted her eager body in his arms and carried her across the room to the fur rug beside the bed. The soft fur caressed her naked skin as his kisses burned a trail of passion down her body.

She cried out in ecstasy as he came to her, probing her body now as he had taken her mouth before, stirring her desire till it reached the boiling point. Their bodies strained together, heedless of time or space, blindly seeking the satisfaction that comes only from being one with the other. And together, they found their release, in a shattering explosion that tore through their bodies with the force of a lightning bolt.

Laure clung to Stephen as reality returned in the aftermath of their sudden explosion of passion. His rock-hard body and the firm clasp of his arms steadied her as their passions abated. Slowly, sated for the moment, they drew apart and Laure's head fell back onto the soft furs beneath them. Shaken and exhausted though she was, she felt a deep contentment such as she had never known before.

"*Kedves* Laurica."

Had she been asleep? Stephen was rousing her with sleepy, teasing kisses. Laure rolled over and gently returned them. He sighed and drifted back into his dream, a happy smile on his sleeping face.

It occurred to her that in the violent passion that had consumed them both, she had still not told him that she loved him. Well, time enough for explanations later. Time for everything, now. Now that she knew Stephen loved her and was not sending her away because he had tired of her, she had no intention of going anywhere.

But it was getting cold. She groped for a rug to pull over her, but Stephen's weight firmly pinned down the pile of furs. She slipped away from him and fumbled in the shadows for her dress. It was awkward dressing without Magda's help and without any idea where her petticoat and chemise were, but eventually she managed to get the skirt fastened and the bodice covering her shoulders. The ornate gold clasps of the bodice, as usual, defeated her.

"After his blood horses," Laure muttered to herself, wrestling with the stubborn clasps, "the next thing I want Stephen to start importing is buttons. Maybe before the horses. Maybe I'll become a button smuggler." She gave up the effort to manage the refractory clasps. What if her bodice did gape open? It kept her warm, and Stephen, when he woke, would probably say he liked her better this way.

A mischievous smile touched Laure's lips. Perhaps she had better find a scarf to disguise the gaping front of the bodice, if she didn't want Stephen's awakening to lead directly into another passionate interlude. Not that that was such a bad idea—but after her long day of waiting and being unable to eat, she was feeling almost as interested in a steaming bowl of *paprikas gulyas* as in Stephen's embraces.

Their lovemaking and the brief sleep afterward had bridged the gap between afternoon and night. The moon was up now, and a bright silver shaft of light pierced the room, falling on the stone wall that had once been hidden behind the tapestry.

"The moonbeam. . . ." Laure recalled Magda's fanciful story of how Stephen's father used to escape the castle as a boy. In the narrow beam of silvery light the stone wall looked quite different. Minor irregularities were exaggerated into a landscape of mountains and valleys, and a smooth patch of stone that she had not even noticed before seemed as round and artificial as if it had been carved by a stonemason.

Laure moved into the moonlight to see the wall more clearly, and as she did, the stones opened before her onto a dank space full of darkness and ill-defined movement.

A shadow sprung out of the space and caught her round the waist, covering her mouth with a filthy hand that smelled of onions. Even as she was pushed back into the corner, other shapes followed the first, revealed in the moonlight as armed men. Laure watched over her captor's hand, helpless with horror, as two of them knelt over Stephen's sleeping body. A hand rose and fell twice, sharply. That gleam—was it a knife? She struggled violently against the encircling arms. The man holding her chuckled and ran his hand over her bared breasts. Nausea swam up and threatened to overpower Laure. Stephen was lying so very still. . . .

The last figure to come out of the passage was that of a tall, well-built man growing slightly paunchy with middle age. He swung the door shut behind him and the wall was solid again. In the moonlight, Laure could not even see the hairline cracks that betrayed the presence of a door.

This last man's stiff, formal bearing and the short, iron gray hair worn *en brosse* proclaimed the professional military man. His back was toward Laure as he bent over Stephen's still figure.

"So. He will give no more trouble—for a time." He spoke in German. There was something vaguely familiar about those clipped accents. He straightened and turned toward Laure, and her eyes widened as she recognized Baron von Staunitz.

"So! Miss Standish." The baron clicked his heels together and favored Laure with a stiff bow of military precision, as though they were meeting at a ball in the Rennweg instead of the room where he had just captured her and her lover. "I am desolated that we were not in time to rescue you from"—his eyes just flickered over her disordered dress with a greedy look—"an unpleasant experience."

The man holding her hand slightly relaxed his grip when the baron greeted her with such courtesy. As soon as the hand fell away from her mouth, Laure took her cue.

"Unpleasant, baron, but over now—thanks to you and your gallant men." Was she laying it on too thick? "But—your man—is this really necessary?"

Upon a sharp word from the baron, Laure was released altogether. She bent her knees in a token curtsy, pretending to ignore the way the baron's eyes fastened on the soft curves revealed under her open bodice.

"My apologies, Miss Standish. My men could not know, you see, who you were—or how you might

219

react. An outcry at the wrong moment, however well-intentioned, might have fatally damaged our surprise."

Laure inclined her head regally. "I understand perfectly, baron. Permit me to congratulate you on a successful conclusion to your endeavors." Mad, quite mad, to stand here talking as if in a drawing room! But von Staunitz returned her compliment with another bow. He was pleased; dared she risk asking for further concessions?

Rapid footsteps outside in the hall, a hammering on the door. Laure's heart leaped up in hope. Jansci, Geza, Marton?

An unfamiliar voice called out, the words somewhat muffled by the thick oaken planks of the door. "Baron—beg to report—all under control."

The Baron gave a death's-head grin in the moonlight. "Excellent!" He turned to Laure and offered her his arm. "May I escort you to pleasanter surroundings, my dear young lady? I am sure this room must have many unhappy memories for you? Below, we shall see if we cannot add a touch of Austrian civilization to this Hungarian barbarism."

Laure drew back involuntarily at his touch. The baron frowned and she seized upon the first excuse she could think of. "Baron, I should be delighted to join you in your victory celebrations, but as you can see, the state of my dress is not adequate to do you honor. Might I beg you to send my maid to me here? I shall attend you presently." If only Magda was still alive!

The baron gave a curt nod. "Very well." Laure held her breath, rejoicing at the success of her stratagem. A soldier opened the great oak door and the men who had filled the room filed out.

Stephen stirred and groaned, and Laure felt renewed hope. If only she could be left alone with him here! She raised her voice to cover the sounds of his movement.

"I beg of you, baron, do not forget my maid. And have her bring hot water and candles. You would hardly expect me to dress for your victory feast in cold and darkness!" She made herself sound pettish, as though the only thing on her mind was the difficulty of arranging her hair and doing up her gown.

A louder groan from Stephen frustrated her efforts. The baron smiled and beckoned two of his men back into the room. "Our prisoner wakes. Take him below, will you? See that he is clothed. The lady has been offended enough by the sight of his filthy body. Then—bring him to me, in the hall." He smiled at Laure. "I think I can promise you some rare entertainment tonight."

The two men heaved Stephen roughly to his feet, an arm dangling over each of them. His head still hung limp, but as he passed Laure his eyes opened and he gave her one intense glance. She started forward involuntarily, longing to reassure him.

"Take a last good look at your lover, Miss Standish," the baron told her. "I fear he may be sadly changed by the next time you see him."

Only one possible answer to that. Laure lifted her hand and slapped the helpless man across the face, so hard that his head rocked back. "No lover of mine, baron." She wiped the back of her hand on her skirt as if to cleanse herself of his touch. "Nor do I desire to see him again. If you have any pity for the sufferings I have undergone, pray keep him from my sight."

"Oh, I think he may yet afford us some amusement," the baron promised. He motioned the remaining soldiers out of the room, save for one whom he told to remain on guard duty. "For your protection," he assured Laure.

She forced herself to smile and curtsy, as though he were doing her an honor. No chance of being alone with Magda, then. But—she could not escape now, anyway. Not until she learned where those two soldiers, now shuffling across the floor with Stephen suspended between them, were taking him.

His questioning glance hung between them as the soldiers dragged his limp body out of the room and down the hall.

Chapter Fifteen

SHORTLY AFTER THE DISAPPEARANCE OF THE BARON'S men, the door was thrown open and Magda almost fell into the room, staggering slightly from the force of the push she had received. Her face was flushed and the neat coronet of braids had come undone, but she retained enough spirit to slap the grinning soldier who started forward to catch her in his arms.

"*Esel!* Ass!" She cursed him. "Make yourself useful, fellow, and help to carry in the hot water for my lady. Then take yourself off."

"Magda! You're not hurt?" Laure took her maid's hand and drew her over to the far side of the room to wait while two more soldiers staggered in with buckets of steaming water.

Magda tucked the ends of her braids back into place and smoothed her apron. "Nothing to signify. They're swine, but not drunk yet. And the Gypsy is keeping them busy."

"The gypsy—Zazuela?"

Magda nodded vigorously and dislodged one of her braids again. "How do you think they took the castle so quiet and easy? That slut opened the main gates for them when all downstairs were drunk. Boasting of it, she is now, and sitting on the baron's knee while he goes through the best of the wine the old count laid down. I tell you, my lady, your message came none too soon. I was glad to be out of that hell downstairs."

"They came through here too," Laure told her. "There is a secret passage. . . . I suppose Zazuela told them of that also." The Gypsy must have spent her share of nights in this room. Better not to think of that now. She must find out, while the soldiers were busy bringing in the hot water, what else was going on downstairs. "Did you see Stephen?"

Magda nodded soberly. "They dragged him down to the old cells, I heard one say."

The old cells. A faint hope began to tug at Laure's mind. But first she must find out more. "The men?"

Magda looked down and twisted her hands in her apron. "There was fighting. . . . I didn't see all. It was quick. They were mostly unarmed, you see, and drunk."

Even the baron, surely, would not kill unarmed men. They must be prisoners with Stephen. "Geza?" Impossible to imagine that quicksilver spirit submitting to be taken prisoner.

"Dead. I saw him fall at the door to the great hall. He had only his knife, and they spitted him like a turkey."

The picture was unbearably vivid. "Jansci?"

Magda shook her head, and Laure turned away to hide her tears. She'd never liked Jansci—but so young! Did none of Stephen's men survive?

"Marton is alive," Magda volunteered. "I know, 'cause they were talking about putting his feet to the fire to find out where the count's gold was. Then—I'm sorry, miss, but you'd best know what they devils plan. When they saw His Excellency was still alive, the baron said he'd make better sport than an old soldier, and you'd enjoy watching."

Watching. The baron's mocking words came back to her. "He should provide us some rare entertainment." Dear God, they meant to torture Stephen, and make her watch! The gold must be merely an excuse; there would be no saving him. Laure's hard-won control broke at last. The muscles of her stomach and throat revolted, and her head spun with a whirling black dizziness. She fell to her knees on the floor and retched agonizingly, her empty stomach trying to turn itself inside out. Her forehead rested on the rough stone wall. The stones were cold and hard, they scratched her face and hands. Someone was bending over her, trying to raise her shoulders. She resisted feebly. All she wanted was to lie here in total collapse.

Dimly, through the roaring of her ears, she could hear Magda shouting at the soldiers on the other side of the room. "Now see what you've done, frightening my poor lady almost to her deathbed, you clumsy oafs! Go on, get out of here, let me clean her up. Did you think the baron meant such as you to watch her in her bath? Shoo!"

The door thudded shut behind them and Magda quickly slotted the iron bar into place. Then she was back beside Laure, wiping her face with a cool cloth.

"Now, my lady. At least we've a little time to think what to do next." She cast a distracted eye at the window slit. "I could never make it through there, but you're slim enough. Do you think—."

Laure shook her head. Even if she could have squeezed through the impossibly narrow slit, it was a drop of twenty or thirty feet to the ground—and then she'd only be in the castle courtyard, where the baron must surely have stationed some of his men. Besides —leave Stephen, and Madga?

"It's what His Excellency would have wished," Magda insisted. "As for me, don't worry yourself. I can flatter and amuse the swine till they're drunk, and then slip away quietly. They'll not trouble themselves about a village girl." But her pale face and tightly compressed lips belied the calm of her words.

"There might be a better way." Quickly Laure explained her deductions about the secret passage. It must lead down to the cells below the castle. If Stephen and Marton were held there, could she possibly slip down that way and free them?

"You say you looked for the way once and could not find it?" Clearly, Magda thought this a slender hope. But then, Magda had not seen the tide of armed men pouring in through the wall.

"That was before the moon came up. Remember what you said—about getting out by the moonbeam? I think the first moonlight shows where to push. There's a round space, almost carved smooth—one would never notice it in daylight."

"Or by a candle." The moon had risen too high by now to shine in at the window slit, and their only light came from the branch of candles standing on the dressing table. Magda raised the candles above her head to flicker on the wall. "You can't remember exactly where it was?"

Laure felt and thumped along the wall over her head. "It may take time."

Laure's poundings on the wall were echoed by fists on the oaken door.

"And time's just what we don't have," Magda finished. "Quick—into the bath!" She pulled Laure's bodice and skirt off while shouting, "Would you disturb my lady in her bath? She'll be down when she's fitly attired for your master!"

"Advise her not to prank too long before the mirror," a gruff voice returned. "He's nasty when crossed." But the footsteps receded down the hall, and both Laure and Magda exhaled long sighs of relief.

"I'll have to go down," Laure said. "Even if we find the door now, they'd be looking for us too soon." She splashed water from the tub over her face and shoulders while Magda combed out and braided her long hair. "The rose satin, do you think?"

"It's not a good color for you," Magda protested.

Laure managed a watery chuckle. "All the better. I want to seem to be doing him honor, not to set my cap for him." She adjusted the folds of lace about her shoulders with trembling fingers while Magda fastened the back of the dress. "Do I look properly happy to have been rescued?" She pinched her cheeks to bring color back into them. "Very well—open the door. I'll wait for a proper escort. You bar the door after me, and wait till I come back. If I plead exhaustion, he may let me come back soon enough; and then we'll have the rest of the night to work out the entrance to the passage."

"And if there are guards below?"

Laure shrugged. "All the more reason to go down now. I'll see what I can find out about the disposition of his men."

"And if—His Exccellency—." Magda could not go on.

"They'll not kill him," Laure said, with more assurance than she felt. "The baron wants to bring him back to Vienna as a sort of trophy."

That view of the matter was one that had not actually occurred to Baron von Staunitz until Laure suggested it to him, over their midnight feast of half-burnt roast meat and excellent wine.

"To Vienna—eh?" The baron sucked at the end of a rib bone and tossed it down on the floor behind him. "Quite medieval, this place," he commented, as if in extenuation of his bad manners. "One quite expects to see rushes on the floors and a minstrel playing in the gallery. I expect you'll be glad to make it back to civilization—eh?" His free arm encircled Laure's waist and pulled her closer to him.

Laure managed a revoltingly girlish giggle and snuggled up to the baron. "If you knew how I have dreamed of this moment!" she confided. "Vienna— the Prater—the Rennweg—balls, *redoutes*—it sounds like a dream after a nightmare!" As she spoke, the fine buildings and parks of Vienna seemed to rise up before her, looking mightily like the walls of a prison. "Only one thing lacks to make my happiness complete. I vowed to myself, when that monster first"— she looked down and raised a hand to cover her face—"when he abused me so vilely, I promised myself that one day I should see him dragged in chains through the streets of Vienna. As I am sure he deserves, for his monstrous crimes."

The baron gave a hearty chuckle and wiped his greasy fingers on Laure's skirt. His hand lingered over the curve of her thigh with an unmistakable pressure. "Chains in the street, eh? How—medieval. I fear the barbarous spirit of this place has begun to affect you, Miss Standish. And to think I feared you might have fallen in love with your captor!" He spoke lightly, but his small bright eyes searched her face.

"Indeed, baron," Laure answered with as much calm as she could muster, "I fear I have grown barbaric indeed—in my desire for revenge." She clasped her hands together in her lap and faced him with hard, bright eyes that showed no hint of mercy or weakness. "My dearest wish is to see him degraded in the place where he first fooled me into trusting him."

The baron's rumbling laugh started from his toes and swelled into a convulsion of amusement that shook his entire body. "Why wait so long, my pretty English miss? I promised you some entertainment tonight, I believe." He clapped his hands, and two men who had been lounging on a bench at the far end pushed themselves somewhat unsteadily to their feet and went out.

"It amuses me," the baron said, still watching Laure's face carefully, "to see a nice English girl express such savage wishes. Your sufferings must have been incredible." The arm about her waist stole upward until one hand was caressing her breast. "You must tell me all about your dreadful experiences . . . later."

The difference in his manner since she had seen him

in Vienna made his meaning obvious. As Miss Standish, a respectable English girl under the chaperonage of her cousins, he had treated her with at least surface courtesy. As the defiled victim of a Hungarian bandit, he assumed she ought to be happy to share his bed. Laure remembered Geza's retort, when Stephen chided him for spending nights out of the castle with a village girl who'd already had two children by different fathers: "What's one more slice off a cut cake?" Her stomach twisted and threatened to rebel again. She reached for the rough wooden cup before her and recklessly poured a measure of wine down her throat.

"That's my girl!" The baron released his hold on her breast to give Laure an approving slap on the back that knocked her sideways. She bent over the table, exaggerating her coughing and sputtering at the wine that had gone down the wrong way, and managed to inch herself a little further away from the baron.

"Drink up, forget y'r troubles, let's all be happy." The baron filled her cup again and pressed it into her hand. "Like t'see a pretty girl enjoying herself."

His speech was growing slurred and his head wobbled from side to side as he spoke. Laure began to hope that he would drink himself into a stupor, forgetting his plans for her and Stephen. She glanced around the hall for some distraction to keep him occupied through a few more bottles of wine.

There were fewer than ten men in the hall, and of those, four were already passed out on the floor, snoring with their heads in pools of their own vomit. Three more were clustered on a bench, arms about each others' shoulders, singing a drinking song with a fine individualistic disregard for words and notes. And the remaining two were trying to tease the sullen

Zazuela into lifting her skirts in another flashing Gypsy dance. Her pouting face and the dark looks she directed at Laure showed how much she resented the English girl's getting the baron's attention away from her. If only she knew how gladly Laure would trade with her! And that gave Laure the germ of an idea.

"Look, baron." She tugged at his sleeve and pointed at Zazuela. "The Gypsy is dancing." It was an optimistic way to describe the lazy shuffle and occasional swish of her skirts with which she was indulging the soldiers. "Have her entertain us?"

"Ah, to hell with the lazy slut!" The baron's words were clearly audible across the room. Laure could see Zazuela's back stiffen and the proud black eyes flash. "She's served her turn, getting us into the castle. I've no more use for her. Why fondle a dirty Gypsy when I can have a clean pretty girl like you? Let the men amuse themselves with her."

The words were all the encouragement the two soldiers needed. With a whoop of delight, one of them caught Zazuela's skirts and yanked her backward into his lap, while the other fondled her breasts. Laure held her breath, expecting to see the flash of a knife from the Gypsy girl's sleeve, but to her surprise the girl only laughed and called for wine. Perhaps all she had wanted was attention, after all.

But her ploy had not worked to distract the baron. His groping hand reached for her again, and Laure, not daring to struggle, was pulled across his lap and subjected to a long, greasy kiss. The stench of sour wine and garlic threatened to overpower her. She closed her eyes and held her breath and waited passively for the baron to tire of mauling her.

A shout from the door caught his attention. He

dropped Laure unceremoniously, and she had to catch at the table leg to keep from falling off the narrow bench as he stood. She blessed the interruption and then shut her eyes again as she recognized what it was.

Stephen stood in the door, between the two soldiers who had left a few minutes ago. He was dressed in a torn pair of wide fringed linen trousers, with his feet and chest bare. There was a terrible red swelling on one side of his forehead, with matted blood sticking his hair together, and there were new thin red lines across his bared chest that Laure did not understand at first. His hands had been brought before him and tied together with a length of rope.

"So! His Excellency the count!" The baron laughed and jerked Laure to her feet by one arm. "Look, my dear. How do you like your fine lover now?"

Laure did not dare to look directly at him, but she could feel his eyes searching her face. There was only one way to lull his suspicions of her.

"He looks better than when I last saw him," she answered, "but he'll look better still swinging from the end of a rope!" And she put one arm around the baron's neck and pressed her lips to his in a lingering kiss that left her feeling sick and faint with revulsion. The baron put his arm around her and ground her body against his, squeezing her buttocks till she thought she must cry out with the pain.

"So our little English miss has some fire in her after all!" He gave an approving grunt when at last he released her.

Laure gave him a languishing glance. "For you, my liberator—all my heart!" She slipped from the baron's hold and stepped forward to examine Stephen. She halted a bare pace from him. He had seemed half-dead, but at her approach he raised his head to stare at her with a burning blue glance that spoke of hatred replacing love. Laure fought down the impulse to cry and cast herself upon his shoulder. Instead she stared intently at his face and body, cataloging details while she rehearsed in her head what she wanted to say to him.

His chest and shoulders gleamed with beads of sweat, though it was a cold night. The scar of his bullet wound stood out unnaturally white, and there were white and red swellings of flesh around his wrists where the rope bit too deep. If he didn't get free of those bonds within the night he would be permanently crippled, whatever happened after.

Laure took a deep breath, raised her hand and slapped him viciously across the face. "Hol van a titkos tur!" she shouted into his face, while he still rocked backward from the force of her blow.

He replied with a few muttered Hungarian words, hanging his head now as if afraid to look her in the eye.

"Es hol a foghaz!" It was only pidgin Hungarian, but his first response showed that he had taken her meaning well enough.

Stephen raised his head and spat in her direction with his next answer. His eyes were glittering with some strongly suppressed emotion.

At once the guards jerked him back by the shoulders, so that he fell backward onto the stone floor. While he tried to get up, hampered by his bound hands, one of them lashed at him with a whip of thin wires. Laure understood the thin red lines that covered his body now. She backed away, afraid to face the baron for fear the disgust she felt would show on her face.

"Not a pretty sight." The baron evidently took her disgust for granted, and misunderstood its reason.

Laure forced a laugh. "Better so, than lording it over this castle!"

There was a flurry of skirts from the corner where the two men had dragged Zazuela down. Laure glanced over and saw the Gypsy girl extricating herself from their grip. One of the men was already snoring, his breeches half-unbuttoned, and the other was too muzzy to do more than wave a feebly protesting hand as Zazuela freed herself. She came running across the stone floor, the glass bangles in her hair flashing and floating behind her, and gave Stephen a kick in the ribs while he was still on his knees. "There's for you, you bastard Excellency!" she declared in a shrill voice. She dropped to her knees beside him and thrust him viciously back down onto the stone. Her long hair floated over the two of them, and Laure could see nothing but that sparkling, glittering mass of black hair interwoven with bells and glass beads. But when Zazuela stood, Stephen was still breathing. He even managed to close one swollen eye in an audacious attempt at a wink.

Zazuela turned from him as the soldiers dragged him out, and enveloped Laure in a tempestuous hug. "I used to hate you," she declared, "but now I love you like a sister, because we hate the same man!" But her eyes went over Laure's shoulder to the laughing baron as she spoke. Laure felt a tiny packet being pressed into her hand.

"A pinch of this in his wine," Zazuela whispered.

"'Twill put him to sleep like those swine in the corner. I wish I had what my grandmother used to poison the pig!" She looked at the baron again. "Promised to make a lady of me, and throws me to his men. You've got the better man, foreign girl. See if you can save him for us?" She laughed and released Laure, but her quick movements and the fluttering of her draperies screened them both for long enough for Laure to hide the packet in her sleeve.

Laure turned back to the baron and made her curtsy. "Thank you for the entertainment, sir! Now, if it pleases you, I am sore fatigued from the excitement of the day." She pressed one hand to her head with a look of pain that did not have to be faked. Her forehead was throbbing abominably, as if in sympathy with the blow Stephen had received. "Might I beg your permission to retire to my chamber?"

The baron laughed. He was always laughing, and for so little cause! "Your chamber? I beg pardon, Miss Standish. As the conqueror of the castle, I naturally take the master's room. Any less would not be due to my dignity. You are, of course, free to rest elsewhere." His glance surveyed the great hall, filthy with vomit and scraps of food, and with soldiers sleeping in the corners. "If you find a place where you think you would be—comfortable. Or you may, if you desire, share my room."

His room! That would ruin everything. But she couldn't—.

Yes, she could. Laure looked down and made herself stroke his arm, as if unbearably excited by the prospect. "Please, baron—spare my blushes!" she whispered. "Of course I owe everything to you." She looked up at his face and made her eyes wide. "Shall—we—retire, then?"

A salacious grin overspread the baron's face. "We shall indeed." He hooked his arm firmly about her waist and half-dragged, half-carried her up the narrow flight of stairs leading from the great hall.

Chapter Sixteen

MAGDA HAD TRIMMED THE WICKS OF THE CANDLES around the walls of the room and lit them anew. The bed was straightened and the basket Laure had packed so many hours ago was out of sight. So was Magda. Laure glanced around the room and suppressed a start of surprise when she saw that the tapestry Stephen had pulled down and the two fur rugs were piled together in a far corner of the room, half-hidden behind the carved chest. The height of the pile was greater than could be accounted for by her memory of the rugs and tapestry, and it seemed to Laure that it moved slightly in the candlelight. Hastily she averted her eyes, hoping that Baron von Staunitz would not notice the direction of her gaze.

The baron was far beyond noticing subtle hints like that. The jovial mood in which he had celebrated the easy conquest of the castle was only accentuated by the delights of humiliating Count Andrassy and taking his woman to bed. "And such a pretty little piece, too!" He drew Laure to him and caressed her limbs with the insolent familiarity of a nobleman honoring a barmaid with his attentions. "All white and gold, ivory and g-gold!" He hiccupped over the words. "Lift y'r skirts, m'dear. I've a fancy t'see whether y'r white and gold all the way up—you take my meaning?" He laughed uproariously at his own jest and belched up a quantity of sour, wine-tainted breath. Laure turned her momentary recoil into a movement of acquiescence, walking over to the carved chest and raising one foot to take off her stocking. Perhaps if she could draw out the show, the baron would fall asleep before he tired of watching her and making her obey. But even with her back turned, her flesh crawled at the thought of his greedy little eyes enjoying the sight of her body.

"Gold, spun gold!" Von Staunitz had lurched off the bed and followed her over to the chest. His fingers fumbled with the tight coronet of braids Magda had created, and yanked out the hairpins. Laure suppressed a wince of pain at his rough treatment and turned to smile at him over her shoulder.

"Let me do it, sir. Great soldiers like you cannot be expected to act the lady's maid!"

"True enough." The baron belched again and sat down heavily on the chest. He overbalanced and leaned his weight on the pile of furs to steady himself. "Where's that stupid maid of yours?"

Laure cursed her careless words. And to have led him to that corner of the room! She dropped her skirts and walked casually back toward the bed, hands busy with her braids as she spoke.

"Who knows? Doubtless the slut has found some of your soldiers to amuse her by now."

"I'd like to know where," the baron mumbled. "All I've got is those drunken fools in the hall, and the two guarding His Excellency the bandit. Those sots below are too drunk to do a woman any good, and I'll flay the skin from the guards if they neglect their prisoner."

Only eleven men! Laure filed the information away and shrugged, as if the whole discussion was a matter of indifference to her. "So? Who troubles about what the servants get up to? I vow, baron"—a touch of petulance would not come amiss— "if you go on so, I'll begin to think you like my fat maid better than myself!" The last pins were out of her hair now. She shook her head until the golden mass flew about her face and shoulders, and gave the baron a coquettish smile. "There, do you like me better this way?"

The baron grinned and reached forward. "Better and better. Come here! As long as y'r under my protection, you'll wear y'r hair loose like that." And, as Laure made no move to come to him: "What, did you think I'd want you only for the night—a little beauty like you! Spoiled goods you may be, my dear, but well worth taking back with me. Best prize in this stinking castle—unless your bandit count tells me where his gold's hid. *Donnerwetter!*" He swore as a new thought struck him. "F'rgot t'ask him. What d'you say? Shall we have him up again now? Jurgen, the fellow with the whip—he's got a rare way with a hot poker. We could make y'r count dance a pretty tune before he gives over his fortune."

Laure shrugged and turned away, pretending indifference. She fiddled with the bed hangings and began to pick an embroidered tulip out of the curtain with her fingernails. "I think y'are mistaken about the gold, baron. This is a poor castle. If Andrassy has wealth, it's in his land and people—not in gold and jewels. Why, he never so much as gave *me* anything but castoffs to wear!" She infused a note of indignation into her voice, and jerked at the curtain so viciously that the tulip and a long trailing embroidered stem came loose in her hands. "As for jewels—you saw the Gypsy whore, his other mistress. Would such as that be content with glass bangles if there was wealth to be had out of him? I tell you, he's one of the starving nobles, the 'sandal nobility' they call them here. Why else would he take to the road?"

The baron leaned forward and propped his greasy chin on his fist, as if pondering the force of her argument. Laure fancied she could hear a sigh of relief from the pile of furs.

"You make a fine case, my dear. Perhaps too fine. Could it be you don't want to see your fine lover tortured? I should think the game would amuse you, even if there's not gold at the end."

Laure forced a laugh. Coming from a throat constricted by fear, it sounded appropriately harsh. "I was but warning you, baron. Don't you think the fellow fooled me finely? From the way he peacocked it in Vienna, I thought there'd be fine pickings on his estates. Instead, here I am kept prisoner in this moldering castle, no society but a handful of flea-bitten serfs, no music, no dancing—and no jewels."

"Ah, so that was the way of it." The baron gave a thoughtful nod. "I wondered how he'd seduced you into this mad flight. Some girls might have been stirred by the romance of a—robber count."

Laure laughed again. "Not I! If I'd known he financed his tomfoolery on the high road, I'd never have listened to his sweet promises. You'll deal with me more generously, baron, I trust."

"Aye—but have you thought he might be fooling you still? All these Hungarian nobles have generations of family wealth. I've heard it said there's enough bullion on the gold clasps of their cloaks to finance an army."

"May be," Laure countered swiftly, "and in Vienna, they say the Princess Bagration's diamonds could keep that army in the field through a six-month campaign. But I've had neither diamonds in Vienna, nor gold here." She yawned. "And I've not had much from you either, baron, except this vastly boring discussion. First my slut of a maid, now Andrassy's mythical fortune." She pouted. "I thought it was me you came to rescue." Anything to distract him from his plans to torture Stephen.

The baron lunged to his feet and put an arm about her waist, pawing with his other hand at the lace that covered her bodice. "Shall I show you how much I want you, pretty thing?"

Laure slapped his hand away and retreated. The baron's eyes bulged out at this affront to his pride and he raised his two hands, squeezing convulsively as though he meant to put them around her neck.

"Not so fast, baron!" Laure made a production of arranging her flounces. "I thought you were a gentleman of parts who knew how to treat a lady, not like these barbarians. Come now!" She bent toward him with a coaxing gesture, incidentally giving him a good view of the delights inadequately concealed behind a fall of lace and a low-cut bodice. "Let us drink a glass of wine together, and do show me that you have not forgotten how to court a lady. I promise"—she bent even farther forward on the pretext of stroking his hand—"you will not find me ungrateful." Her coquettish smile promised all manner of lubricious delights.

The baron clicked his heels and bowed. He lost his balance and staggered forward, one hand outstretched. Laure neatly sidestepped and let him crash into the wall. His head hit the stones at the bottom of the wall with a satisfying thud.

Laure stared down at the prostrate figure. He seemed to be lying quite still. But she could not be entirely sure that he had knocked himself out. He had already demonstrated impressive powers of recuperation.

Just to be on the safe side, she knelt beside him. "Oh, dear, oh dear," she quavered, her hands fluttering over his prostrate body. He did seem to be thoroughly unconscious. "Baron von Staunitz! Are you all right? Oh dear, what am I to do now?" She covered her face with both hands and burst into noisy sobs, peeping through her fingers to see if the baron moved or changed color.

After a few seconds she put one hand on his shoulder and rolled him over onto his back. His face was purplish red, and he gave a strangled snort when she moved him; he then began snoring.

A hand brushed her shoulder. Laure gasped and felt the blood draining from her face.

"A pity he did not break his neck," Magda said. She was a little rumpled from her long spell of hiding under the furs, but otherwise quite cheerful. "We had best make sure." She casually swung back the heavy candlestick she had brought with her and struck the unconscious man on the forehead. The force of the blow rolled his body halfway over again and a strange clattering sound came from beneath him.

Laure stood with the back of her hand against her mouth. Later she would find bruises where she had bitten her hand to keep from crying out. "Magda, you've killed him!" she whispered in horror.

"I'm afraid not." Magda looked down at the helpless figure with a shade of regret. At least, Laure thought, she was not entirely devoid of human feelings. "A pity I don't have a knife. We should make sure of the swine while we have the chance." She knelt and began going through his clothes with experienced hands. "Take that scarf," she ordered over her shoulder. "Tie his hands and feet. And gag him. It'll buy us the night before they think to give chase."

Fighting down her sense of horror and repulsion, Laure followed Magda's orders, using the baron's own silk scarf and some linen strips ripped from the bed hangings. Before she had finished, Magda was through with her search. "Here," she announced, handing Laure a purse of gold coins and a silk packet wrapped around something hard and heavy. "We'll need money, and there's no reason to leave the other with him."

Laure took the silk packet by one corner. The wrapping unraveled and a glittering chain of precious stones fell to the floor.

"Diamonds!" Magda scooped up the treasure and weighed it in both hands. "No doubt he was meaning to put these round your neck. We'll just call it payment in advance."

Laure laughed unsteadily, and was shocked to discover how near to hysteria she had come. It was hard to stop. She felt as though she could go on laughing and laughing forever. "I don't think so,

Magda. Those are too good for—what did he call me? 'Spoiled goods.'" She reached out and stretched the necklace between her two hands. The double chain of diamonds hung free, with heavier diamond pendants swinging from every fourth link. "The Bagration diamonds. They were stolen a month ago, when the Princess's coach was stopped outside the city. They said—." Her breath died away as she realized the meaning of the story. "They said that Csikos had taken them." She stared down at the bound man at her feet with undisguised loathing. "Stephen swore he never stole jewels. He thought it was a plot to discredit his political actions." With trembling fingers she rewrapped the diamond necklace in its silken covering and handed the package back to Magda. "Here. Can you put this back where you found it? So that he'll never know we had it?"

"Trust me." Magda knelt and restored the packet to its place in a cunningly sewn inner pocket. "But— why leave it?" Every fiber of her being revolted against leaving treasure with an enemy.

"I can't explain. But it might be more use to us there." Laure took a candle from the wall and turned away from the baron's snoring body. "The first stone on the right, he said. . . ." Murmuring to herself, she reached high on the right side of the wall and felt with her fingers along the rough surface. Yes, there it was, the smooth circle she'd marked when the moon shone on it! She pushed once and the door glided smoothly open. A draft of cold, dank air came out of the passageway and almost extinguished her candle.

Magda was staring. "How did you go right to it?"

"Stephen told me," Laure explained. "When they —oh, I forgot you weren't there. They dragged him into the hall when I was down there. I pretended to be insulting him in Hungarian. Nobody understood. So I asked him how the passage worked, and where he was being kept."

Magda laughed soundlessly, clutching the fat over her ribs with shaking hands. "And you a foreigner! Almost smart enough to be a Hungarian." It was her highest praise.

Laure paused at the entrance to the passageway and looked back. "I don't understand, though. The baron passed out before I even had a chance to give him Zazuela's herbs." She shook the little packet out of her sleeve and showed it to Magda. "She was angry with Stephen for not loving her anymore; but the baron meant to pass her around among his men for amusement, and that made her angrier. She slipped Stephen her knife and gave me these herbs. But I never had a chance to use them."

Magda crossed herself. "Just as well. Who knows what sort of magic they are! . . . Besides, we can use them on Stephen's guards." She picked up the bottle of wine that had been sent up for the baron and sprinkled the herbs into it. "As for the baron, when I was downstairs they were calling for water to mix with their wine—our good Hungarian wine is too strong for them! So old Georgi in the kitchens, he brought out a cask of *Egri víz*. Half of that in a bottle of wine would put out stronger heads than the baron's."

Egri víz—water of Eger. It was a joking name for the clear distilled spirit made in eastern Hungary. Laure had sipped some once, when Jansci handed it to her as a joke. Smooth going down, the single sip had exploded into fire in her stomach. But the baron and his men would have been already too drunk to notice that the clear fluid being poured into their cups was far from innocent water. She could almost find it in her heart to feel sorry for them.

"Hurry." Magda handed Laure the wine bottle and herself snatched the basket out from under the pile of furs. Then, on an afterthought, she reversed the burdens. "No, I'd best offer them the wine. They'll know something's up if they see a lady like you down there."

The basket seemed heavier than Laure remembered. She almost dropped it in surprise. "Don't drop it!" Magda spoke sharply, then remembered herself and sketched a curtsy. "My lady. Can you manage the candle, too? Best if I go ahead; then you hold the candle and light us both down."

The single candle cast a wavering circle of pale light over steep, narrow steps that wound down into darkness. Magda moved ahead of Laure with quick, sure-footed steps. Her shadow loomed like a grotesque figure over the circle of candlelight until it was swallowed up in the darkness below them. Every once in a while Laure glanced back over her shoulder; there, too, the darkness reigned absolute. Her last act had been to close the door behind them. It might well have been a mistake—the last mistake she would ever make. They had no idea how to open the door from this side. If the passage were blocked below for some reason, they might have condemned themselves to a living death within the thick stone walls of the castle.

Laure told herself not to entertain such fears. The baron had led five of his men up this very passage not six hours earlier. How could it have been blocked up since then?

But the dankness of the air and the slippery mold on the steps and walls made the passage seem more like a tomb than a way in and out of the castle. Only the torn spiders' webs on the rough ceiling bore mute witness that men had recently passed that way.

"Uhg!" Magda, rounding a corner, walked into a web near the wall that had been left undisturbed by some chance. She flailed about with her arms, trying to scrape the clinging cobwebs off her face. Laure hurried to help her. On the narrow, turning stair Laure's foot slipped on a patch of mold and she pitched forward. She fell with shattering force on her left arm and her face. There was a stinging, burning sensation in her hand and the world seemed to have gone dark.

"Miss Laure." It was Magda helping her up. "You're not hurt?"

Laure managed a shaky breath. "Nothing broken. But—I can't see."

"Well, of course not. You dropped the candle!"

Laure laughed under her breath. Once again it was difficult to stop. She concentrated on the pain of the scrape along her arm, on the different pain in her hand. "I must have put it out with my hand."

"But you didn't drop the basket." Magda was patting her all over, exploring for breaks and sprains. "Good!" Her voice held a peculiar note of relief. How much difference could a pair of muslin dresses and a dresser set make to their safety? Laure hadn't been thinking when Magda shoved the basket at her, or she would have refused to be encumbered by such a burden.

They groped their way around the circle of the turning stair, and a dull yellowish glow appeared ahead of them in the darkness. "We would have had to put out the candle anyway, in a minute."

After a moment of peering at the glowing light, Laure realized why Magda was whispering. It must be the reflection of a lantern in the cells. Of course, that was why they had so many stairs to come down. They were coming out well below the level of the great hall.

A few more steps, and the stairs leveled off into a low, slanting passage broken by short steps at irregular intervals. The two girls tiptoed toward the light. Before they reached the mouth of the passage, Magda put out a hand to stop Laure. "You wait here," she mouthed, the words barely a ruffle of air in the darkness.

Laure waited, pressed against the damp wall of the tunnel, scarcely daring to breathe, while Magda glided like a ghost out and around the bend in the wall. From the soldiers' shouts and the slap of cards that she heard, she guessed that they did not see Magda until she was standing beside them.

"Hola! Come to comfort a lonely soldier? Sit here on my knee, sweetie, and give us a kiss!"

Laure relaxed imperceptibly. The first barrier was passed; they had not guessed that Magda did not come from the stairs that led directly down from the courtyard.

She tried to shut her ears to the smacking sounds and drunken laughter that followed. But that wasn't fair. Magda might need help. She had to listen.

"The baron doesn't forget a pair of brave fellows," Magda was saying. "Didn't he send me down with a bottle of the best wine for you?"

There was more laughter, and a gurgling noise. Then Magda, giggling and protesting. "No, no, *Her-*

ren, you'll be the ruin of a poor girl! . . . All right, just one then. Now drink up, and let's all be merry."

"You drink too, sweetie," proposed one voice.

The other quickly contradicted him. "Hell, no! This's good stuff—out of 's Excellency's private cellars. Don't worry, girlie. Me and my mate can make you happy wi'out the wine."

Magda giggled. "Don't you even want to give the count some—seein' it's out of his private cellars, and all? Where is 'e, anyway? I'd like to see our great former master with the tables turned on him."

"Over there." The lantern light rose, wavered and shone brighter, almost exposing Laure where she huddled against the wall of the tunnel. She slipped back into the darkness as quietly as she could, but her foot dislodged in a stone in passing.

"What's that!" Footsteps. Both men were on their feet now.

"Scared of a rat?" Magda laughed. "An' I thought you were such bold, brave fellows, set to guard this dangerous count."

"Huh! Don't look so dangerous now, not after me an' Jurgen worked him over," boasted one of the voices. "Have a look." The circle of lantern light moved again, as if the lantern were being held high to show Magda a choice sight.

"Don't look too lively, and that's a fact," Magda admitted. "You an' your mate must be tired, after workin' so hard—just two of you to beat up one man, and him tired." Her voice was so flatly innocent that it was hard for them to take offense. "Dry work, too. Have some more of this good wine the baron's sent?"

"Don't mind if I do."

"Hey—share th'bottle!" There was the sound of a scuffle, and then the noise of breaking glass.

"Clumsy!"

"*Esel!*"

A single cracking sound, like a fist on someone's jaw. Then footsteps, slower than before, shuffling away from the tunnel.

"That's taken care o' Jurgen—greedy bastard," the remaining man boasted. "C'm 'ere, girlie. I'll show you a good time—soon as—as—." His voice trailed off into incoherent mumblings, and silence reigned in the tunnel.

Laure waited and counted her breaths. Fifty, a hundred, and she would look out.

Long before she reached that number, the circle of lantern light brightened again, and Magda appeared as a silhouette in the tunnel mouth.

"Works fast!" she said. "I hoped that Zazuela never takes a grudge against me. That Jurgen, he's alive. But the other one hogged most of the bottle, and I doubt he'll wake again this side of the devil's dinner table. Good riddance." Her tone dismissed him.

"And Stephen?"

Magda raised the lantern. Laure saw Stephen's half-naked figure behind an iron-barred door, horribly stretched out on a pile of straw. His wrists were tied to hooks on opposite sides of the narrow cell, and the stretching had made the whiplashes on his chest open and bleed again. But he was alive, and conscious enough to open one sardonic blue eye at the lantern light.

"Keys—in Jurgen's pocket," he whispered.

Laure was already going through the unconscious

man's pockets. It was the work of a moment to find the ring of heavy iron keys and try them in the cell door. She threw the rusty bars back and knelt by Stephen's side.

"The knife?"

"In my waistband."

Laure felt around the band of his wide linen trousers with trembling fingers, all too conscious of how the slightest motion could put additional strain on the ropes that held his body taut. The minute handle and viciously sharpe blade seemed to leap into her hand. She slashed at the rope nearest her and Stephen sagged down onto the straw with an involuntary moan of relief. Two more cuts, and he was free and chafing his strained wrists.

"Give me that." Magda held out her hand for the knife. "I'll make sure of the bastards."

Stephen shook his head and took the knife from Laure. "I owe them either more or less than a quick death, my dear. And—I'll settle my own debts." He pinched Magda's chin and won a smile from her. "Including, I think, a very great one to you." He turned to Laure. "Can you walk?"

"Can you run?"

Stephen nodded. "All right. But we'll all be crawling first. There's another way from here than through the courtyard, or else my father would never have got out for his midnight excursions. But it'll not have been used for years."

Magda opened her mouth as if to speak, then checked and busied herself with trimming the wick of the lantern.

"God send it's not blocked by an earth fall!" Stephen caressed his beard with one hand. "Perhaps we'd best try to slip out by the courtyard. They might not have set a watch."

"The tunnel will be all right."

Stephen gave Magda a sharp glance and then, as if accepting her authority, bent and picked up the lantern. "Very well. Come with me."

Chapter Seventeen

MARTON WAS IN THE CELL BEYOND STEPHEN'S. HE WAS an even worse case than Stephen, having been brutally beaten by the guards before they shoved him into his cell; but he could walk with the support of Laure's shoulder.

"No matter!" Stephen reassured him. "We'll all be crawling soon, if I remember the tunnel. Lucky if we haven't to dig the earth out with our hands."

Magda opened and closed her mouth again, and subsided into silence at the back of the little procession. She was carrying the lantern now; Laure had enough to do, with the oddly heavy basket of clothes on one arm and Marton on the other.

The entrance to the tunnel was not cleverly concealed like the door upstairs. It was just a narrow crack in the walls of the passageway down which Laure and Magda had come. Laure had been standing in the draft of cold air from the opening even as she waited for Magda to get the soldiers drunk. Two steps farther back, and she would have put her hand on it.

A jutting outcrop of rock half concealed the narrow opening to anyone coming down the passageway from the castle. Stephen raised his candle and illuminated the jagged black opening. A draft immediately blew it out, and Magda squeaked in alarm.

"Good!" He sounded satisfied. "There's air coming through—it can't be completely blocked."

Without pausing, he disappeared into the blackness of the crack in the wall.

For the first few steps, the tunnel was so low that Laure had to stoop to avoid cracking her head on the overhanging rock, and so narrow that Marton could not walk beside her to lean on her shoulder.

"No matter," he assured her with a wheezing attempt at a laugh. "I can lean on the rocks, since they are so kind as to come close on both sides they may as well give me support."

That was the worst moment for Laure. The irregular roof of the tunnel sloped steadily downward until she was indeed crawling on her hands and knees as Stephen had warned. When she put out a hand to either side, she felt earth walls damp with trickling underground springs. Magda, with the lantern, was so far behind that Laure got only flickering rays of light to illuminate the darkness, and the shadows and scattered glances they gave her seemed even worse than total darkness. If Stephen had not been just ahead of her, steadily moving on through the dark, she would have been tempted to refuse to go farther. What if—as he feared—a fall of earth had blocked the tunnel entirely, farther up? Would they be able to crawl backward out of this narrow space, or would they be stuck forever? Were they pressing forward into their own tomb?

Laure felt the weight of earth and stone above her like a crushing physical presence. The darkness added its own weight. The arching overhead walls of the tunnel came together so sharply that her shoulders brushed them. She felt as if all those tons of earth were lying on her back, pressing her into the ground, constricting her chest so that she could not breathe. The darkness was like a foul beast that filled her mouth and nostrils. And still this everlasting, painful scraping forward on hands and kness! She couldn't go on—she would not go on! She would have to scream and batter at the walls with her hands. The walls were closing inward on them—

"Not much farther now." Magda's voice, so calm and matter of fact, gave Laure back a modicum of sanity. "It should open up soon. And at least there've been no more of those nasty spider webs!"

Marton gave a dry chuckle. "Trust a woman! Best hope there's none of them nasty foreign soldiers at t'other end!"

"There won't be," Laure said. "He had only the eleven men. Nine of them are drunk in the hall." Or dead. What had been in Zazuela's packet of herbs? "The other two are behind us." Having to count the men she'd seen steadied her. Her breathing relaxed and she realized that while they'd been talking, the tunnel had been growing imperceptibly wider and higher. And it was true, too, what Magda had said.

However narrow the space was, it was remarkably smooth and clean for a secret tunnel unused for years. There were no spiders spinning their webs in crevices, no falls of earth and stones on the hardpacked earthen floor they'd been crawling over.

Ahead, Stephen gave a sigh of relief, and there were scrambling sounds as he stood up. A moment later, his hand found hers, and he pulled her to her feet. Instinctively Laure put one hand up to protect her head from knocks, but she touched nothing above her.

"It's a natural cave," Stephen explained briefly. "This region is known for them. The tunnel was only a device to connect the castle to a string of underground caves." He bent to help Marton out, and after him, Magda.

"Raise your lantern, Magda, and let's have a look. I've not been down here since I was a boy." There was an odd note, almost of exhilaration, in his voice, and Laure realized with a shock that he was actually enjoying this.

"Adventures indeed," she muttered, as she brushed the dried mud off her sleeves. "Bandits. Secret tunnels. Spiders! Why couldn't I take up with a nice, boring, young Englishman?" But her sotto voce grumblings died away as Magda raised the lantern and revealed the glory of the cavern they were standing in.

On either side vast fluted arches, stained red and yellow by the chemical action of the underground waters, soared upward to meet in the darkness like the vaulted ceiling of a cathedral. Majestic stone figures, worn smooth and carved into grotesque shapes by the centuries of trickling water, loomed in the shadows all about them. Where the walls of the cavern were not colored, they were bright with a myriad of twinkling particles embedded in the soft stone.

Laure gazed, speechless with wonder, as Stephen took the lantern from Magda and raised it higher, turning as if to show off the miracle of nature that surrounded them. The stone outcroppings were thrown into relief as he turned the lantern beam on them, taking on in the brief moment of illumination a fantastic semblance of light—here a dragon and mounted knight, there a praying bishop, there a plain rounded form like a wine cask—.

Laure looked again. That mound of stones in the corner did look most uncannily like a pile of wine casks. They even were colored dark brown, like seasoned wood. And beside them, that formation was as white and fluffy as a stack of sheepskins.

Magda stumbled and fell heavily against Stephen. He put out his hands to save his lacerated back from the rough stone walls, and the lantern crashed to the floor. The candle inside went out and they were left in absolute darkness.

"I am a clumsy fool, Your Excellency," Magda said. "You should beat me."

"I think perhaps I should!" Stephen said. "No wonder you were so sure the tunnel would not be blocked."

"My lord?" Magda's voice was all meek subservience; but Laure knew somehow that she was smiling in the darkness.

"Oh, never mind." Stephen sounded resigned. "Just tell me, someday, how many of my men are in it with the villagers. No wonder this estate never produced enough to pay its own way!" He reached out and took Laure's hand. "Marton, you hold on to Laure," he ordered. "Magda, I think you had best lead the way, since you seem to feel we can do without light."

"A thousand pardons for my clumsy mistake!" Magda did not sound the least bit penitent. "No— bear a little to the right, Your Excellency."

The little procession made a stumbling, shuffling progress forward under Magda's guidance. She did seem to know where she was going; only once did she lead them so near an overhanging ledge of rock that Laure had to put out her hands to protect herself. It was a desperately nerve-racking business to shuffle forward in the dark like this, forced to trust Magda's sense of direction not to lead them down a slope into the river or into a cul-de-sac; but as they went on, Laure felt her confidence growing. She even thought her eyes must be growing accustomed to the dark; Stephen and Magda ahead of her appeared as slightly denser patches of blackness in the surrounding dark, and she began to sense the outlines of rock piles on either side marking the edge of the path.

They rounded a corner and a pinpoint of light expanded before her astonished eyes. One moment it was only a point in the blackness, a few steps later it was a round hole filled with light; and then she was blinking in the gray light of dawn.

A stand of young trees with thick-clustering leaves covered the mouth of the cave. They squeezed between the trees and found themselves standing on a rocky hillside covered with sparse, coarse grass. Above and behind them the rocks became the cliffs on which the Black Castle perched. Before them, the hillside stretched down to a wall of beech trees. A boy was standing just inside the trees, watching two pigs rooting in the mast. When he saw the strangers emerge from an apparently blank cliffside, he gave a whoop of astonishment, turned two rapid somersaults, and took to his heels into the forest, leaving the squealing pigs to fend for themselves.

"Jaj!" Magda sounded annoyed but resigned. "That was young Tomas, Mari's boy. Now the whole village will be in on it."

"I rather thought they were," Stephen remarked. "From the looks of things, there's been enough goods passed through there to feed an army. I think it's time I paid more attention to this most unprofitable of my estates."

Magda looked down at her boots, and Stephen laughed and pinched her chin. "No matter, *kicsi!* I think this may turn to our advantage. Do you know a place where we can lie hidden, while you explain to the villagers that if the baron's men keep the castle, there'll be no more rich pickings for all?"

"I think there'll be no more in any case," Magda said glumly. "Still, they do say the devil you know is better!"

Stephen laughed. "Insolent, too! Tell me, would the villagers really like it if I came back and took up residence here—at least part of the year? I have a suspicion they've been well content to see me spend half the year in Vienna and the other half on my rich *puszta* in the lowlands, leaving them free to take what they want from the estate."

Unexpectedly, Marton put in a word. "Well managed, my lord, this estate could produce enough for all. But if you'll forgive me, when I served in the army they told us to defeat the enemy first, before we quarreled over dividing the spoils. We're free now, but the baron holds the castle. Do you have a plan?"

Stephen took the rebuke without resentment. "Our first plan must be to get shelter, and find out what help we can count on in the village. Magda?"

"There's a cottage in the beech wood where Granny katika used to live," Magda said. "Nobody will go near it. She was a witch, you know."

Stephen nodded, instead of laughing, as Laure had expected. "I remember. She gave me a charm for warts, and cured the blacksmith's girl that had a crippled foot. But I thought she was dead years ago."

"There's dead, and then there's dead," Magda said. "She's been *seen*. But you're gentry. I'll show you where her cottage is." Her tone made it clear that she had no intention of taking shelter there herself.

They followed a narrow, overgrown path through the beech woods, which was scarcely more than a track for animals. Twigs caught at Laure's hair and gown, and her feet slipped from time to time in the damp leaves underneath; but she could still spare a glance at their motley, bedraggled procession. No wonder the pig-boy had run! The cuts on Stephen's chest and shoulders had reopened, covering him with drying trickles of blood, and his fringed peasant trousers were only fit for a pigsty. The side of Marton's face was blue with a massive swelling bruise, and his dark coat had been torn half off his shoulders. All of them were mud stained from the crawl through the tunnel. Only Magda, leading the way with her braids tucked neatly back into place and her full skirts brushing the twigs out of her path, was incongruously tidy. Her plump little legs in their red boots stumped ahead as if she were doing nothing more out of the way then walking down the main street of the village, and she was not even breathing heavily from the brisk uphill pace she set.

Stephen glanced back and surprised the smile on Laure's lips. "Ah, well, you're no picture yourself!" he teased, correctly interpreting her amusement. He looked up and down the pink satin dress, now sadly mud stained and somewhat torn about the neck and shoulders. "Why are you always dressed for a party when we run away?"

"My mistake," Laure replied meekly. "I should have learned by now to wear a suit of armor when I am anywhere in the vicinity of Your Excellency!"

Stephen gave a shout of laughter that was quickly hushed by Madga's placing a warning finger to her lips. She motioned them to stop while she tiptoed ahead, although her progress through the wood, leaves crackling and twigs breaking at her every step, would have given ample advance notice to a waiting army. While they waited for her to return, Laure patted the handle of her straw basket with renewed appreciation. She began to look forward to this deserted cottage, where she could change into clean clothes and maybe even have a wash of water from the well. That would make Stephen eat his words! Silently, she blessed Magda for making her bring along the basket. At that moment, tired, dirty and bedraggled as she was, the pleasures of washing her face and combing her hair outweighed every other desire. If she could once comb the tangles from her hair, she thought, she could face anything they might be called upon to do next—even if they had to flee the length of Hungary on foot.

"It's behind those trees," Magda pointed.

By craning forward, Laure could just catch sight of a tumbledown mud hut with half its thatch of reeds fallen in. In style and construction it was no different from the peasant houses she'd seen in the village; but here, crouched under a towering, bent old tree whose branches leaned protectively over it and cast a dark shadow around it, the simple hut looked indescribably sinister. A broken-down fence of wooden poles enclosed a narrow, shady space before the house, once a garden but now growing only the seedlings of young trees among a fine crop of nettles. The windows of the hut were innocent of glass or any other covering; they were simply dark, empty holes in the mud wall, like two blank eyes.

"I'll—come back." Magda had edged to the rear of the little group. "After I visit the village. I'll—bring food."

"Here, lass," Marton said unexpectedly, "I'll go with you. Perhaps an old soldier can get some spirit into those worthless lumps of peasants."

"Marton, no!" Laure protested. "You must rest first." All the way up the path the old man had been leaning on her, his wheezing breath sounding loud in her ears. He had changed color alarmingly, from flushed to pale and back again, and now the hand he extended in farewell was trembling uncontrollably.

"Let him go," Stephen cut in. He extended his hand to Marton's and clasped it briefly. "God go with you, old friend! Bring us what news you may."

"He's too tired," Laure whispered, as the ill-assorted pair moved away on a path of Magda's choosing. "You shouldn't have let him."

Stephen put his arm round her waist and pulled her close. "Should I make him say in a witch's house? Oh, yes"—he smiled at her look of surprise— "Marton's a traveled man and a soldier, but he grew up in a village like this one. He wasn't trembling from fatigue, Laure. If we'd made him stay here, he would have insisted on sleeping outside under the trees, and would have said it was so he could stand guard." He looked back, frowning, at the half-collapsed hut. "And he might have been more comfortable, at that! No matter; we're better off inside. It's one place the villagers won't come willingly, whatever tale that pig-boy spreads."

"Stephen!" Tardily, Laure understood the drift of his words. "You don't think they'd betray you—your own people?"

Stephen shrugged. "They are used to doing what the man in the castle tells them. Right now, the baron is the man in the castle. We'd have done Marton no favor by keeping him here, Laure. He's better off away from me, if the villagers decide to betray us. I should have sent you with them, in fact. It's not too late—."

"No." Laure held his arm with both hands. "I'll not be sent away from from you."

Stephen gave her a long, level look, as if assessing the extent of her determination, then smiled at last. "And I'm too weak, God forgive me, to make you go. Laure—you are my strength." His lips met hers in a long, desperate kiss, their two bodies straining together. When they drew apart, Laure's knees were shaking, and there were fresh stains on her bodice from Stephen's blood.

He gave her one more gentle kiss and set her away from him. "And that, my dearest, is all the lovemaking your exhausted kidnapper is good for. We'll have to find some other way to while away the time." He stretched both arms over his head and yawned mightily. *"Isten!* I hope there's straw in the hut. I don't know which I want more—sleep or a wash."

The well behind the cottage had a leaking pail attached to the rim—fortunately, by a length of chain rather than rope, which would have long since rotted. The first few buckets Stephen brought up were full of rotten leaves and twigs, but with perseverance he got almost half a bucket full of relatively clear water, with which Laure could sponge off the dried blood from his head and chest. She was relieved to find that the wounds were all superficial and that most had clotted long since, so that no bandages were required.

"Now for this mess," she said with satisfaction, after she had rinsed the mud from her hands and knees, shaking out the tangled mass of her hair. "There should be a comb and brush in here." She opened the basket and shook out a muslin dress that had been rolled around something heavy. "I'm glad, now, Magda made me take—oh!"

A fortune in gold and silver and rough-cut gems rolled out of the muslin folds and blazed up at them from the beech leaves, touched to fire by the rays of the rising sun. Laure picked up one of the gold chains and ran it through her hands. At her feet, the collar of gold and sapphires winked up at her, and a ruby pendant on a chain of silver filigree caught the light like a fresh drop of blood.

"My mother's jewels." Stephen picked up the ruby pendant and swung it back and forth on its chain. "The old-fashioned stuff. It was never brought to the manor. But—you wouldn't wear them when I asked you to?"

"Magda." Laure was recovering from her first shock. "She was alone for a time, while I was down in the hall with—." She didn't want to remember those hours by torchlight in the great hall, fending off the baron's greasy fingers and waiting in agony for some word about Stephen.

Stephen laughed. "So she packed a few trinkets for the journey! A girl of forethought. We may need to distribute a few bribes before this affair is over. The villagers might need some encouragement to fight."

Laure stared at him in shock. "You mean to fight? Now—here?" Her hand swept round the muddy yard and the poor house. Her eyes took in the bruise and the matted blood on Stephen's head, the white lines of fatigue in his face. "I thought we would go to the *puszta*." Surely at Stephen's rich manor in the lowlands they could get all the help they needed. Why would he stay to fight it out here on this barren mountainside, with his men dead and the baron in possession of the castle?

Stephen gave a sober nod of acquiescence. "It may yet come to that. But we don't know, Laure, what the situation is on the *puszta*. These eleven men of the baron's—are they all, or did he leave an army in the lowlands? It doesn't make sense that he should come with so few. And if he has found out my secret, who else knows?" He kissed her again, swiftly. "I may have to become a true *betyár* of the mountains, living in a cave and washing in a stream while I fight to get my inheritance back again."

There was that suppressed note of excitement in his voice. Part of him, Laure recognized, was looking forward to the freedom of just such an existence. To forget the hampering chains of respectability, tradition, the needs of his people, and to enjoy the old savage pleasure of harassing his enemy directly. She opened her mouth to make a sarcastic comment and then closed it again. She should have learned by now that Stephen could never be argued into anything—and that he would not forget his own responsibilities for long. They were both tired. They should rest for the remainder of the day. By the time Magda came back with news and food, Stephen would be ready to take the sensible point of view.

The interior of the hut was empty and, thankfully, clean of spider webs and other forms of insect habitation. The pile of straw at one end was not even unbearably musty. Stephen prodded the straw experimentally for rats and smoothed it into a low mound that they could sleep on. "All the comforts of home." A gigantic yawn smothered the end of the sentence as he stretched out on the low couch of straw.

Laure stripped off her mud-stained dress and lay down beside him in her underclothes, using one of the muslin dresses from the basket to cover herself. Stephen's arm encircled her shoulders and within seconds his deep, regular breathing showed that he was fast asleep. Lucky for him! She herself was far too overset by the events of the night to even think of sleep. But she would have to lie quietly so as not to disturb him. . . .

Baron von Staunitz was chasing her through a meadow honeycombed with treacherous holes. Laure stumbled and dodged this way and that like a cornered hare while he shouted, "What are you crying for? A pocket handkerchief or a knife? You won't find your lost sweetheart here." Behind him, Geza and Jansci, their faces horribly bloodstained, swayed with arms round each others' shoulders and chanted, "Azt sajnálom, nem a régi szeretömet." Laure was watching them, when she slipped into one of the gaping holes in the earth. She slid down, down, endlessly falling, while above her the baron shouted. "All right—I'll bury you with your lover, unless you come out now! Come out! Come out!"

Laure's throat closed around the scream of terror that she wanted to let out. She jerked upright and the comforting, warm straw rustled about her. Slowly, her panicked breathing quieted and she recognized the shadowy outlines of the hut. Beside her, Stephen was still sleeping peacefully.

"Come out! Hsst! Come out!"

That had been part of the dream. No. It was real. Laure peered out of the window and saw Magda standing just beyond the broken fence, calling as loudly as she dared. Quickly Laure scrambled into her dress, dashed water from the bucket over her face and hands, and went out to meet her.

"I've brought food." Magda flipped the napkin from a large wooden bowl and revealed steaming mugs of soup, a flat round loaf of dark bread, and a leather skin half-full of wine. "His Excellency—?"

"Still asleep." Laure picked up the bowl. "Come inside?"

Magda shook her head. "Not me! It's all right for you. You can eat after I've gone—there may be time. Marton is looking for horses. You'll have to be away as soon as it is dark."

Although Laure had been urging the sensible course on Stephen, she felt oddly dashed by Madga's acceptance of it. "The villagers?"

"Worthless. And there's worse." Magda drew nearer and lowered her voice. "You must get His Excellency out of here before he does something foolish. The baron—."

Laure waited for an agonizing moment before Magda decided it was safe to go on.

"He knows now that you've both escaped. He's vowed to recapture you both. He says he may keep you for his mistress yet, if you beg for his mercy. But he'll hang His Excellency from the castle tower. A reward to any peasant who finds you. I don't think any one in the village will claim the reward. They're stupid and afraid to fight against the baron, but they'll not betray His Excellency." But her tone was not as certain as her words. "And—they won't need to, once Stephen hears—."

Again, the agonizing pause. Laure took Magda by the shoulders and dug her fingers into the plump flesh. "Tell me!" she commanded in a voice quite unlike her own.

"Jansci," Magda whispered. "He's not dead."

Laure's fingers relaxed and her hands dropped to her sides in relief at this anticlimax. "But that's good news! Stephen will be happy to hear it!"

"Perhaps not so good. The baron vows he'll kill him—slowly—unless His Excellency gives himself up. He means to start at dawn tomorrow. He said to let it be known that his man is very skilled. Jansci should take at least three days to die, so His Excellency will have plenty of time to think it over."

From the corner of her eye Laure caught a flash of movement in the doorway of the hut. It was Stephen. His tattered trousers were indescribably filthy, the lines of pain and fatigue around his face had deepened and he was leaning against the doorpost for support.

But he had never looked more like His Excellency the count.

"The baron has always thought that all Hungarians are very slowwitted," he said. "I will actually require no time at all. I shall meet him at the castle courtyard at dawn tomorrow."

Chapter Eighteen

THEY ATE OUTSIDE, SITTING ON THE GROUND. MAGDA had brought a thin blanket as well.

Laure could hardly swallow the food that had smelled so enticing when Magda uncovered the bowl. She took a few sips of the soup, crumbled the bread between her fingers and sat staring at the trees that surrounded them. Stephen's hand covered hers in a warm clasp.

"Eat," he commanded. "You have a long way to go." He turned to Magda. "You can get her out of here?"

Magda nodded. "Marton will get horses. He can take her as far as Poszony."

The name of the border town brought their half-formed plans into sharp focus for Laure. She turned to Stephen. "I'm not leaving you."

"You'll do as you are told," he responded, absently, not even looking at her. "Now, eat."

Laure sat down the mug of soup carefully on the ground. It seemed very important not to spill a drop. The crust of bread she balanced on top of the mug. "No."

Stephen's hands were heavy on her shoulders. "*Laurica.* I brought you into this. Don't add to my shame by refusing to let me bring you out again. Do you think it will make me happier, tomorrow, to know that you will be von Staunitz' plaything after—." He stopped and looked away from her for a moment, before beginning again. "I've thrown and lost. Let me know that you are safe. I will not go to the castle until Marton has you well away."

It was an unanswerable argument. Laure nodded, her eyes blinded by tears. When Stephen released her, she sat staring into the forest again, trying not to think of anything at all. This time tomorrow—no, she mustn't think!

The long shadows among the trees seemed to flicker in the fading light. Strange forests always seemed full of life, little unexpected sounds and movements, menacing because they were unknown.

Movement solidified at the edge of the trees. A tall beech with a double trunk shifted and split into two sections. One of them became a dark man in a greasy jerkin and leather breeches.

"Stephen!"

Laure cried out and threw her mug at the unexpected apparition. With the dexterity of a juggler, he caught the mug, holding it well to one side to avoid the splash of soup, bowed, and tossed it into the air again, where it was mysteriously joined by two spinning knives that he caught by their hilts and juggled up in the air again.

"Ex'celens." The juggler brought his trio of toys to rest and bowed, a knife in each hand. The mug had vanished somewhere, but there was a suspicious bulge in his jerkin.

Now the woods were alive with them—lithe, dark men in once-gay rags. And behind them, Marton's gray head lifted in the shadows.

"I went to trade for horses," he addressed Stephen directly. "They had other ideas." A smile split his leathery face. "I think they don't like the baron much."

The juggler spat on the ground and threw one of his knives at a log where it stuck, quivering with the force of the throw. "Told us to move on," he confirmed. "Keeping Zazuela. Didn't pay." He looked up at Stephen. "I'm your man, count, if you want some help."

Now Laure recognized the men she'd seen lounging around the Gypsy camp. Then they'd been torpid with afternoon sun and sleep. Now, moving quietly through the woods, they gathered an almost palpable sense of menace with them in the clearing.

"Count never fussed about a few chickens," chimed in one of the other men.

"Kind of like having this place to camp in. An' he shouldn't have made Zazuela stay. *Rom* girls go where they want. Not property."

They stood round Stephen in a silent ring, a few paces away, appraising him with bold, black eyes. They'd said their piece; now it was for the count to speak.

"The passage will be guarded now," Stephen said slowly.

Laure's heart leaped. He was considering it!

The juggler retrieved his knife and balanced both knives on his palms. "There's ways. He doesn't have so many men. Less now, if I know Zazuela." A flashing grin lit the darkness of his face, but his eyes never left Stephen's. "Course, some ways don't come free. . . ."

"How many men?" Stephen asked.

The juggler gestured to the circle. "If it's worth our while . . . all these. Eight!" He spoke like the leader of a small army.

Stephen ran his fingers through his beard. "Eight. . . . It can be done. Have you thought of the risk if we fail? I don't want men who'll change their minds at the last minute."

The juggler grinned again. "That's why it will cost something, Ex'celens'. Hard for poor men to risk their necks in another's cause."

Stephen nodded. "I can pay—after we take the castle."

The Gypsy shook his head. "Before, Ex'celens'. Baron promised pay after, then turned us out."

"Then, what's my security that you don't take the pay and run away?"

"Like count better. Count always treated us fair. You pay now, promise that after, you let us stay here even after what that slut Zazuela done." The knives spun through the air in bright arcs, the rhythmic flashing of their blades almost hypnotic.

Stephen smiled and caught one of the glittering knives in midspin. "Zazuela's paid her debts. Done!"

But there was still a long session of bargaining to go through. Stephen and the Gypsy leader squatted on their heels in the clearing and passed the leather wineskin back and forth, counting on their fingers and arguing in a mixture of broken Hungarian and Romany. Finally a price was settled, and Stephen called Laure to his side.

"Bring out a gold chain and the sapphire collar," he whispered in German. "Don't let them see the rest."

The moon was high when Stephen and the Gypsies set off, with Marton bringing up the rear. The sapphire collar winked and flashed on the bare chest of the juggler, above his dirty jerkin, and the gold chain was wrapped around the wrist of one of his men. Magda and Laure watched them, out of sight.

"You'd best stay inside." Magda looked at the tumbledown hut, its windows blank in the moonlight, and shivered.

Laure shook her head. "No, I'll wait out here." They could not see or hear what was going on at the castle from this forest glade, but it was better to wait outside than to be shut into that dark little hut, wondering if the next footsteps they heard would belong to Stephen's men or the baron's. Stephen had not been happy at leaving her like this, but Laure had argued down his objections. Marton could not be spared, and as for the Gypsies, she would feel safer with no guard at all. The only alternative, she told him firmly, was to take her with him. And this he absolutely refused to do.

Laure perched on the one remaining rail of the wooden fence and hugged her knees as she stared into the impenetrable gloom of the forest. Somewhere high above them on the hill, Stephen and the Gypsies were staking their lives on a last, desperate chance. The Gypsies were to swing by their camp on the way up to the castle, pick up their fiddles and a few of the girls' bright skirts and blouses. What the baron's men would see would be a party of Gypsy men and girls, playing music and dancing in the moonlight and offering to entertain them in return for wine. Only after the gates were opened and all were inside would the "girls" draw bright knives from their full skirts, and the men toss away their fiddles. While they hunted the soldiers, Stephen and Marton would make their way into the castle to look for the baron himself. Once he was their hostage, the soldiers could be ordered to give in peaceably.

The hastily cobbled-together plan could fail at a dozen points. And even if it succeeded, what would Stephen's position be? If the baron had announced before leaving Vienna that he had discovered the identity of Csikos and meant to hunt him down as a common robber, Stephen might dispose of the baron's men only to face the entire might of Austria against him.

Suddenly Laure realized that she had forgotten to tell Stephen the one thing that might save him. The Bagration diamonds! She jumped to her feet and shook the dozing Magda by the shoulder.

"Can you help me find the Gypsy camp?"

"Ah—wha—why?" stammered Magda.

"I have to join Stephen."

"He told us to wait here."

"And I'm telling you to take me to the Gypsies."

Magda stumbled to her feet, rubbing her eyes. "Now?"

"Of course now!" Laure stamped her foot with vexation. "Would I have waked you in the middle of the night to make plans for a picnic?"

"Could be," Magda mumbled. "No crazier than

asking me to take you to the Gypsies in the middle of the night. And His Excellency won't be pleased. All right, all right—."

She led the way down another of the narrow paths that wound among the roots of the beech trees. "Though I don't know what you'd want with the dirty Gypsies," she complained.

"Clothes," Laure said.

"Clothes?" echoed the grandmother at the Gypsy camp, when Laure had at last succeeded in waking her and explaining her errand. "And the men making off with half my girls' skirts, as it is! What do you want my poor girls to wear tomorrow?"

"They can have this." Laure indicated her simple muslin dress.

"Not much fabric in it," grumbled the old woman. "Pale, too; no color."

"And this." Laure slipped a chain from around her neck and held up the ruby pendant. It glowed like one of the embers in the Gypsies' campfire.

"Ah-h!" Greedily the old woman fondled the jewel. "Skirts you wanted, my lady? Some pretty shawls, and a glass bangle to jingle nicely? Just you wait here, lady. Old Annika will find whatever the ladies require." She scuttled into the nearest wagon and was back shortly, almost invisible under the pile of bright, tawdy rags heaped on her outstretched arms.

Laure commandeered a corner of the wagon to change clothes in. Her hair and Magda's were too pale to fool anyone in the light, so she tied scarves round their heads and fastened great brass circles in their ears to make up for the lack of free-flowing dark tresses.

"Come on," she commanded. "Up to the castle!"

Their path upward was guided by sounds of merry-making from the castle. When they reached the outer wall, Laure paused for a moment, feeling almost as if she had been thrown back in time some twenty-four hours. Once more the gates were thrown open, a bonfire blazed in the middle of the courtyard; there were Gypsies playing their fiddles and girls swaying like flowers in their full, bright dresses. Several of the soldiers were already the worse for wine and lay snoring with their heads on the stones.

While Laure still peeped in at the gate, the scene changed with dizzying rapidity. A girl sitting on a soldier's knee gave a ringing laugh and slapped at him with something bright and shining in her hand. The soldier's head fell back against the wall and a spreading dark splotch appeared on his tunic.

That blow was the signal for the attack. Knives flashed in the hands of the fiddlers and appeared from the bright skirts of the girls. Within seconds, two more soldiers lay dead on the stones of the courtyard and the remaining men were herded, dazed and sullen, into a corner where the Gypsies swiftly bound and gagged them with strips cut from their own uniforms.

Laure ran into the courtyard and seized the arm of the chief fiddler. "Stephen—the count?"

The juggler pointed with his chin in the direction of the cellar steps. "Up the passage."

Laure lifted her skirts and ran through the great hall to the narrow flight of steps leading to the upper regions of the castle. Quicker this way than through the dark passage. God send the door was not barred!

It was not. She wrenched it open to a scene of desperate struggle. Stephen was lurching across the floor, his fingers buried in the baron's throat. Behind him, Marton and a pale Jansci with a bandage wrapped around his brow stood guard like a pair of executioners.

In their struggle the two men had made a shambles of the bedchamber. The porcelain ewer and stand were in shards on the floor, the hangings had been torn from the bed and one tall bedpost leaned down at a drunken angle across the bed. But the fight was nearly at an end now. Even as Laure watched, Stephen bore the massive figure of the baron to the floor and rested one knee on his chest. The baron's face grew purple and his breath rasped, then stopped as Stephen's long fingers squeezed inexorably tighter around his fat neck.

"Stop them!" Laure appealed to Jansci and Marton. "He'll murder him!"

Marton gave a grin of pure delight that made him look ten years younger, Jansci merely spat on the floor.

"Oh, useless!" Laure looked frantically round the room for something to separate the combatants. The tub of water in which she'd bathed the previous night was still there, half its contents spilled across the floor. She dipped the larger half of the broken ewer into the tub and dashed the cold, scummy water across Stephen's face.

"Isten!" Spluttering, Stephen released one hand from its death hold on the baron's throat to wipe his eyes. Laure followed with another splash of cold water down his back. Stephen's eyes cleared and the lust of killing faded from his face, but a cold determination remained.

"Laure. Go away. I'm not—quite—finished here."

The baron heaved and wallowed under him, and Stephen tightened his fingers round his throat again.

Laure had a stitch in her side from running up the mountain and through the castle. She leaned on the wall and held her side with one hand as she panted through the stabbing pain. "Don't kill him—yet. He's the—robber. Look in—pockets."

Stephen frowned. Laure took advantage of his moment of indecision and her returning breath. "Jansci! Marton! Tie him up. We have to talk. Do you want to see your master hanged?"

To her surprise, Marton came forward and knelt beside Stephen and the baron, followed a scant second later by Jansci.

"Something in what she says," he apologized.

Stephen shook his head till the long tawny hair flew out around his face like a mane. "No. This one is mine!"

Jansci sighed, drew back one brawny fist and hit Stephen squarely in the chin. The shock of the blow rocked Stephen backward and broke his death grip on the baron's throat.

"Apologies, Excellency." Jansci was already busy tying the baron's legs together with a strip from the bed hangings, while Marton worked on his hands. Stephen rolled back and sat up, one hand fondling his chin and a dazed expression on his face. "You can kill him later," Jansci went on apologizing as he worked. "Slowly." His smiled was ugly. "His Excellency the baron had the favor to describe his plans for me in some detail. I'd like to try them out."

Stephen still seemed to have trouble assimilating the fact that he had been struck by one of his own men. While he was sitting, Laure knelt over the baron and dipped her hand into the inside pocket of his coat. What she brought out, in a glittering string, silenced all three men.

"The Bagration diamonds," she announced. "That you are supposed to have stolen, Stephen."

"By God!" His inertia gone, Stephen seized the necklace from her hand and examined it closely. "You're right. Well, well. . . ." His lips curved in a slow smile as he gazed down at the baron. "But how to prove they were on him?"

"If he took these, he took others," Laure said rapidly. She'd had time to think, in that long day of waiting at the hut. "There was a whole rash of jewel robberies this spring, all by a masked man who identified himself as Csikos. That was why Vienna turned against you. The political jokes they could laugh off, but these"—she pointed to the sparkling diamonds dangling from Stephen's hand—"made you a common thief to be hunted down. No one knew where the baron got his money; the Countess Sagan told me his Prussian estates are poor, and everyone knows about his gambling losses. But what if he'd been the robber all along? It wouldn't take many baubles like these to finance a good few seasons in Vienna. And with you as an obvious suspect, no one looked hard for any other explanation." She was pacing about the room now as she made her points. "I'll wager he told no one about his suspicions of you. Don't you see, he had stolen enough jewels now to make him rich. He meant to come into Hungary and kill you, and then all the robberies would stop and he would be rewarded for unmasking the dangerous bandit. But he had to kill you at once. He couldn't risk having you talk. There were too many discrepancies. Someone might have figured out that you couldn't have committed all the robberies at the times they happened. But with you dead and the trouble over, no one would have thought to question him. He'd be safe with his loot." The words were pouring out now, too fast to get her ideas in order. She'd been thinking all day, but only during that last race up the mountainside had it all come together for her. "See, that's why he has so few men. Soldiers! They're no soldiers. Just a gang of bravos he hired in Vienna and dressed up in uniform. He wouldn't dare have the emperor or the secret police in on this—not till you were dead and unable to defend yourself."

Stephen stood, stroking his beard and looking down at the baron on the floor. "You're very clever," he said at last. "But what can we prove? All this was conjecture. If I kill him and take the Bagration diamonds back, they'll say I stole them myself and blamed an innocent man."

"That's why you don't kill him," Laure said. "Leave him here, under guard. We go back to Vienna and search his lodgings. He must keep the other jewels somewhere. And he must have sold some—we can find the men he dealt with. Then you have him brought back for trial."

Stephen nodded slowly. "Good. Only one thing. *We* do not do any of this. I have brought you into enough danger through my folly. You go back to Vienna, now, with an escort, and we keep your name clear. I will settle this matter of von Staunitz myself."

Laure gasped in indignation. "You will? You won't! I never heard anything so mean! After I figured it all out, you want to take all the fun for yourself! You.—"

Stephen seized her by the shoulders and stopped her mouth with a kiss. "No arguing." He released her to glare at Marton and Jansci. "You two, what are you goggling at? Get this filth out of my sight! There must be some place downstairs to keep him."

"I know just the place," Marton said. "Spent some time there myself. Be a pleasure to introduce the exalted baron to his new lodgings." He lifted the baron by the shoulders and dragged his body from the room.

Jansci lingered, a sullen scowl on his face. Laure and Stephen had been speaking in such rapid German that it took him some time to understand what was going on.

"Not kill?"

Stephen shook his head. "Laure had a better idea."

"Sorry I ever helped her." Jansci scowled at Laure. "Thought you meant to let me kill him—slow. That'ud be good. This is stupid!" He spat on the floor again, narrowly missing Laure's skirts.

"Jansci." Stephen was grinning. "You're insolent, and—I owe you this." He swung his fist back and caught Jansci neatly on the point of the chin. Jansci's eyes rolled up and he staggered backward. Stephen caught him as he crumpled and lowered him neatly to the floor.

Chapter Nineteen

THE COACH BOUNCED ALONG A MUDDY, RUTTED LANE. Laure stared disconsolately out the window at the fields of ripening corn. So much had happened to change her life in the few weeks since she had last come this way that it seemed wrong the crops should be only a few inches higher. They should have grown and been harvested, and the fields should have been barren by now.

But it was still summer, and perhaps nothing had changed that much after all. She put a hand to her aching head and tried to concentrate. Had it been only a fevered dream, these last few weeks? Perhaps so. Evidently that was all it had meant for Stephen.

At first she had flatly not believed in his insistence

that she return to Vienna at once, alone, using the story he had concocted to salvage some scraps of her reputation. After all they'd been through together—after his confession of love—how could he send her away at this point?

But all her arguments had been unavailing. He had refused even to discuss the matter with her. At first, to be sure, he had been too busy. Restoring order to the castle and the village had taken all his time. But even when things settled down, it was almost as if he didn't want to talk to her. He simply went ahead with the plans for her return to Vienna as though she were just one more tiresome piece of business that had to be taken care of. When she tried to talk, to argue with him, blank shutters came down over his face and he reiterated his gratitude to her. She had helped him escape from the castle. She had seen through the baron's plot. He owed her more than he could possibly repay.

"But Stephen," Laure pleaded, "that's not the point!" It wasn't gratitude she was looking for, but love—the love that had blazed between them when they were at odds, that seemed to have died now that they were friends. But Stephen only made some courteous, meaningless answer and turned away.

Finally, bruised, unbelieving, she'd come to accept what her intelligence told her must be true. Stephen did not love her and never had. For a brief while, under the stress of the attack, he'd mistaken passion for love. But now that he was on the road to regaining the station and estates he's so nearly lost, he didn't want her. He would want to marry someone of his own class, a daughter of the Esterhazys or Palffys, someone who could add to his own broad acres—not a penniless foreigner. Only his gratitude and the thought of what he owed to her kept him from turning her off as he'd originally planned.

Once she came to accept this, Laure ceased to argue with Stephen's plan. Instead, she passively agreed to whatever he proposed. Would it be convenient for her to leave on such-and-such a day? Yes, certainly. Should she travel with the baggage and servants appropriate to her station? Yes, of course—and she let Magda fuss through the castle furnishings until she had assembled a wardrobe she thought fit for "her" young lady, all to be placed in an ancient leather-bound trunk with a curved lid. She let Magda appoint herself lady's maid for the journey, and accepted the escort of Marton with two lads from the village for outriders. What did it matter? What was the use of fussing about anything?

Then the long ride across country to Poszony, where they rested a night in the flea-bitten luxury of the Duna Inn; and another long day, with two changes of horses, brought them to the outskirts of Vienna. Laure gave listless directions to Josef's house, all the while uncertain as to whether her cousins would still be in residence and what sort of reception she might find there. They might have gone to the mountains for the summer, as so many of the fashionable set did; or there might be so much scandal surrounding her name that they would refuse to receive her. Perhaps, after all, it would be better to go to an inn. Stephen had provided her with enough money to pay for her return to England. But she would have to see Josef and Julie before she left Vienna. There was no point in putting it off.

After all, the meeting was not unpleasant—at least, not in the way she had feared.

Julie must have been waiting at the window, for she

was springing down the steps of the house before the horses had come to a stop, holding out her arms to Laure and babbling happy greetings.

"Oh, Laure, how dull it has been without you! Did you have a nice visit? Ah, but you were naughty to go off on a whim like that! We were so worried! Why didn't you write again? Oh, I suppose you did, only the posts in Hungary are so slow! And you did say in your letter that Count Andrassy's estate is quite isolated." So Julie, at least, had believed the forged letter without question. "But tell me, is he really as rich as they say? Oh, let me look at you! You are so pale, Laure! Has the traveling tired you?"

Julie's chatter continued all the way up the stairs and into the white-frilled room that Laure had had before. Laure pulled off her bonnet and ran shaking fingers through her wind-blown braids while trying to make some sense of Julie's spate of words. Evidently they had been reassured by the forged letter that Stephen had sent. Hadn't they found it strange that she should leave so suddenly?

"Yes, Josef was very angry! But he said no one must know you had been so unmannerly, so I was to put it about that you had gone to visit friends in the country—after all, that is exactly what you did do, so he was right as usual!" Julie perched on the bed in her usual pose, legs tucked up under her skirt. "Tell me, Laure, what really happened? Did you elope with that ravishingly handsome young Count Andrassy? Only it couldn't be an elopement, could it, because you're back?" She giggled and broke off at the signs of distress on Laure's face. "Forgive me, Laure darling. I didn't know—are you unhappy? Never mind! Everyone here thinks it was just an ordinary visit, because Josef claimed we knew all about it. And I must tell you, half the ladies in Vienna are *dying* with jealousy, to think of you having been to Count Andrassy's estates in the country and spending all that time with him! They will be ready to scratch your eyes out now that you are back with us."

And that was all Laure heard on the subject of her so-called visit, from Julie, or later, from Josef. True, Josef avoided speaking to her for the first few days, and there was no resumption of the rather formal courtship which had annoyed her before; but both he and Julie assured Laure that there was no question of her leaving. She was to make their house her home as long as she wished. "In fact," Julie confided, "better if you stay. Then it doesn't look as if you are running away—you see? If it is seen that we all act normally, then people will believe that there is nothing to those other stories—you have been on a visit to the country; that is all. If you leave—well, it would be embarrassing for Josef. He has his position to think of, you know."

There was a touch of conventional propriety in Julie's words that surprised Laure, but she began to understand when Julie revealed that while Laure had been away, she had become receiving the attentions of the Mecklenburgs' oldest son. Young Wilhelm Mecklenburg was already spoken of as a rising force among Metternich's aides, and any family allied with the Mecklenburgs must be in the highest degree respectable.

"Of course, there is no talk of a formal engagement yet," Julie confided, "but it is understood that in the spring, when I am eighteen—oh, and Laure, it will be so nice to have my own house and servants, and everything!" She sprang from the edge of the bed, where she had been perching, and enveloped Laure with one of her swift hugs. "And perhaps you will come and stay with us, seeing that you will not—that is, not since—."

"I understand," Laure said. She disentangled herself from the floating gauze draperies of Julie's shawl and walked to the narrow window overlooking the street. A smartly turned-out hackney coach, all black leather and sparkling metalwork, passed with a great jingling of harness and stamping of hooves. Behind the coach, a broom seller wandered down the street, crying his wares. He rested in the shade of an arched doorway on the other side of the street, where Stephen had stood on the night of his impudent serenade. "I cannot expect to receive an offer myself, is that it?"

Julie's silence was answer enough.

"But I though you said everybody accepted the story of the—visit?" It was unkind to tease Julie in this way. But Laure felt that she must know exactly how bad matters were, before she faced the gossiping, enclosed world of Viennese society.

"They won't question it," she finished in Julie's continued silence. "But—they won't believe, either. . . . Would it not be better if I went back to England, Julie?" There seemed little difference between living with her sister's family and dwindling into Julie's poor relation with the hint of scandal about her. At least in England, people would not be staring and gossiping.

"Oh, not yet!" Julie exclaimed before she thought. "It must not seem as if you are—."

"Being sent home in disgrace," Laure finished for her again. "No, I suppose the Mecklenburgs would not like that, would they? And I must go out in society, too, or the gossips will have even more to speculate over. Well, Julie, how long do we keep up this farce?"

"Josef said—only a few more weeks in the city," Julie faltered. "Then we go to Baden for the rest of the summer. It would seem natural, he said, if you left from Baden to return to your family in England."

Laure nodded and prepared herself to face the pinpricks of society. In some ways it was a relief to know that she need not expect to be courted. It was hard enough to go through the days with a calm face, concealing the despair she felt at Stephen's desertion. She did not think she could have borne to laugh and flirt with the young officers who flocked round Julie like moths drawn to a light.

In the event, it was not so bad as she had expected. Their first public appearance was a discreet Sunday walk in the Prater. After several days cooped inside the house, Laure was longing for exercise and fresh air, and she enjoyed every moment of the carriage ride through the Red Tower Gate and along the broad avenue of the Jager-zeile. And it was an unalloyed pleasure to stroll with Julie and Josef along the broad avenues roofed with the overarching branches of chestnuts and oaks. But occasionally, when a rider dashed by on a strong black horse, she felt a twinge of pain—not for Stephen, she told herself, but for the freedom she had glimpsed in his wild land. "Azt sajnalom, nem a regi szeretomet," she murmured to herself, with a wry smile at her own self-deception.

They encountered few acquaintances on that stroll, and Laure found the delicately pointed questions of Julie's friends amply repaid by the scraps of gossip she heard.

"Just returned from Hungary?" A sylph crowned with masses of black hair fanned herself and pretended faintness at the thought. "So barbarous! . . . Were you not afraid of their bandits? Did you see anything of this so-famous Csikos? He has disappeared from our lives, you know, so completely as if he had never existed. . . . One would think some powerful attraction drew him back to his own land." She smiled under her lashes at Laure.

Laure replied with perfect truth that she had spent her entire visit on the estate of Count Stephen Andrassy and had met very few people in the country, and the conversation moved on to neutral topics. She was left in peace with the reflection that it looked very much as if her guesses about the baron had been exactly right. Why else should the jewel robberies have stopped just when Stephen left the town, unless they were perpetrated by someone who guessed at Csikos's identity and wanted to make sure they could be linked to him?

But that reflection was cold comfort, when it seemed that Stephen had no intention of returning to Vienna and clearing his name. For the thousandth time she raged at the conventions that kept a young unmarried woman virtually a prisoner in her own home. *She* would have settled the matter in a few hours! What was the matter with Stephen! Did he mean to live in self-imposed exile forever?

At the same time, Marton was returning from his journey to Vienna to ask the same question of the young count. He had expected to meet Stephen on the road, and was shocked to find, on his return to the Black Castle, that the boy had evidently spent the days since Laure's departure in a drunken stupor.

"Not quite," Jansci said with a sour look. "He comes out of it long enough to forbid me to torture the baron."

"Once should be enough," said Marton crisply. "Has your generation no respect for His Excellency?"

Jansci made his inevitable gesture. The gob of spittle landed on the near wheel of the traveling coach.

"When he was leading us to start the revolution—there was a man! What's upstairs in that room isn't even a count. No woman's worth getting maudlin over."

"You forget yourself."

But Marton was tempted to repeat Jansci's words when he found Stephen in the upper chamber, slumped over a bottle in a room that was still in shambles from his fight with Baron von Staunitz. The empty bottles littering the room and the reek of liquor were evidence enough of how His Excellency the count had spent his time, while none of his surviving men had dared to breach his isolation.

Marton's efforts to rouse Stephen were unavailing. Stephen lifted his head once or twice, stared blankly about him and then subsided onto the wooden table.

"He'll be like that till he wakes and finds the bottle empty," Jansci confirmed, staring from the doorway. "Then there'll be hell to pay until someone fills him up again."

"No, there won't." Marton lifted his unconscious count half out of the chair by his armpits. "Take his boots, boy!"

"He'll kill me."

"I'll kill you first if you don't do as I say."

Stephen's head lolled back as they struggled down the stairs with their unwieldy burden, and he giggled once or twice but made no protest.

Once out in the courtyard, it was Jansci who protested. "The horse trough? Ah, no, Blessed Mother, you can kill me now, Marton. Better a quick death than rot in the cells like he's left that baron.

"No—no—." He backed away, still stuttering, while Marton, unaided, heaved Stephen's upper body into the greenish waters of the horse trough.

Stephen came up sputtering and swearing, but still drunk. Marton pushed him back under with his foot. The second time, Stephen was spitting bits of weeds out between his teeth. The third time, he was talking coherently.

"Laure? I'll kill that girl." He brushed the hair out of his eyes and looked around the courtyard. "Where is she?"

"In Vienna," Marton said. "Where you should be, too, if you weren't too feeble of heart to face the damage you've done. Are you going to rot here forever while the emperor writes you down a common thief?"

"Laure . . . Vienna." The water was dripping off Stephen's shirt and collecting in rivulets around the stones where he sat. He shook his head and winced in pain. "Nobody else ever had the nerve to throw water at me."

"A lot of people are going to do worse than that to you," Marton said, "if you don't sober up and start acting like the count of these lands."

Stephen leaned back against the horse trough and crossed his ankles with a jaunty air. "Why bother? No Laure, no lands." He waved one hand in the air and tried rephrasing his attempt at an epigram. "No lan's—no Laure. Stupid villagers too craven to fight for me—don't deserve a count. Who wants t'be count anyway? Laure went away." He sniffled. "No Laure. Devil take the lands. Why bother?"

"Because," Marton roared in his best parade-ground bark, "I will personally beat you to a pulp if you don't start acting like the count I took service under, instead of a young fool who starts something he's afraid to finish!"

Stephen rose to his feet, moving awkwardly, like a puppet jointed in sections. He swayed on his feet. "Wha' d'you mean?" he inquired. "Rev'lution—or Laure?"

"The revolution won't start in this generation," Marton said. "You might still have a chance with Laure."

Stephen thought it over. "No. She went away."

"You sent her away, you nincompoop!" Marton shouted. "Damn near broke her heart, too. When I left, you had some notion of going to Vienna to clear your name, then going after her to propose in form. I come back and find you trying to drink up the last season's pressing of wine, single-handed."

"Oh." Stephen's brow cleared. "You want some too!" He placed an arm about Marton's shoulders. "C'mon upstairs. Plenty more. I'll send Jansci to cellars."

Marton raised his arms to the heavens in exasperation. "What am I doing—standing here arguing with a drunken fool!"

"Where?" Stephen looked around the courtyard. "Oh—Jansci. He's a fool, but no drunkard. More shame. Ev'ry good Hungarian boy sh'd learn to drink. Gives y'something to do." He yawned hugely and leaned his full weight on Marton's shoulders. "God, I'm tired. Let's have a little nap." His knees folded under him and he slid down toward the pavement, joint by joint, until he was snoring peacefully with his head on the edge of the horse trough. Marton looked down, snorted in disgust, and stamped off toward the great hall to restore some order there.

But when Stephen awoke, some hours later, he was

both sober and sensible—and, to Jansci's surprise, did not instantly order Marton to the cells for his disrespectful behavior. Instead, they sat together at a bench in the hall, disposing of mounds of sausages and grilled venison, talking earnestly in tones too low for him to overhear.

"It's hopeless," Stephen said. "What if we did find the jewels at von Staunitz's lodgings? That makes him a thief, and me a revolutionary. Which would Metternich rather hang? I've done enough for him to hang me a dozen times over—and for what?" He lashed out with one arm and knocked an empty platter from the table. "For those craven swine in the village, who wouldn't lift a finger to save my life? Will we build a nation out of *that*? I've lost it all for a dream, Marton. Laure, too. Lost Laure before I ever knew her. It was all inevitable. I was already Csikos, you see. How was I to know she'd be—Laure?"

Marton unobtrusively moved the one wine bottle a little farther down the long table and poured clear water into Stephen's goblet.

"With respect, Excellency," he said, "I think you mistake Prince Metternich. I was in Vienna long enough to hear some talk. He's not a vengeful nor a stupid man, and I don't think he is really eager to make trouble by hanging a Hungarian noble. As for the people . . ." He paused.

"Go on, man," Stephen urged him. *"Jaj Istenem!* You're the one man around here who's not afraid of me. If old Marton starts measuring his words"—he gave a bitter laugh—"then I'll know I'm a complete failure as the count. The people would be better off with the old man my father. He was a damned tyrant, but they respected him—and loved him."

"As they do you, Excellency. Those who know you.

What do you expect? The villagers are ignorant. What do they know of you? With respect, what they need is a Count Andrassy who rides the land and watches over them—not one who shoots off pistols in the streets of Vienna and makes noises about political rights they haven't learned to want."

"You sound like Laure. She wanted me to set up village schools and teach them to read!"

"Not a bad idea."

Stephen drained his goblet in one motion and then stared at it with unbelieving distaste. "Water!"

"As you wish, Excellency." Marton pretended to take the exclamation of disgust for a command. He refilled the goblet with clear, cold water.

"I though it was *Egri viz* you were pouring."

"Water's better for a clear head and a good plan."

Stephen laughed and clapped Marton on the shoulders. "Very well, old friend. Show me how to build something out of this pile of rubble I've achieved."

Chapter Twenty

ABOUT TWO WEEKS AFTER LAURE'S RETURN TO VIENNA, society was given a new topic to gossip about. The possible indiscretions of the English girl who had paid such an informal visit to Count Andrassy's estates paled into insignificance beside this new and altogether startling piece of news.

The first Laure heard of it was on a morning visit to Wilhelm Mecklenburg's mother and sister.

"Imagine that stiff-necked Baron von Staunitz being the one after all!" burst out pretty Katya Mecklenburg before Laure and Julie were well inside the drawing room. "I can hardly credit it!"

"I always said there was something sinister about that man," asserted Frau Mecklenburg, who had last season urged Katya to be a little more welcoming when "our dear friend the baron" came to call. "There was something in his eyes I could not quite like." She rocked back and forth, fanning herself in the moist summer air that pervaded even the houses of the rich.

Laure was frustrated by Julie's utter lack of interest in the new scandal and her own fear of asking too many pointed questions, but eventually she was able to gather the broad outlines of the study. The police, acting on a tip from an anonymous informer, had searched the baron's lodgings in Vienna. There they had found a number of the jewels supposed to have been stolen by Csikos that spring, including Princess Bagration's diamond necklace. "They have the man who bought some of the other jewels, too. Of course, they had all been broken up by now, and cannot be recovered. But he described the man who brought them to him, and there can be no doubt it was Baron von Staunitz."

"The Bragration diamonds!" Laure exclaimed. "But that's not possible—I mean—it seems so hard to believe," she ended lamely.

"Is it not?" Katya was too excited to notice the slip. "Only think of the baron's pretending to be a Hungarian bandit. I didn't know he even knew Hungarian."

Laure breathed a sigh of relief. If all Vienna so readily accepted the baron's guilt, Stephen must be safe. Not that it mattered a rush to her, of course. Even if he did return to Vienna, she hoped devoutly that she would not have to see him. . . . She drifted into a daydream in which she met Count Andrassy, quite by accident, in one of the chestnut-lined alleys of the Prater. What cool greeting would serve to crush him with her absolute indifference? No, on second thoughts it would be better if he did not show his face in Vienna until she had gone. Perhaps he might be hoping to renew the flirtation of last spring, and perhaps he might be just a little bit hurt to learn that she had gone back to England without a word or a message for him.

"He hasn't come back to Vienna yet, then?" she interrupted Katya.

The Mecklenburg girl looked surprised. "Yet! I shouldn't suppose he will dare to show his face again. He left quite suddenly last month, you know. He must have known even then that the police were closing in on him. By now I suspect he is safely away to his estates in Prussia."

"Oh . . . I meant Count Andrassy."

Katya looked sorry for her, and forgot to ask what Count Andrassy had to do with the exciting story of Csikos and the Bagration diamonds. "No. . . . They say he usually spends all summer hunting in the Matras."

It must have been Marton or Jansci, then, who slipped into Vienna and planted the Bagration necklace among the baron's other loot, who hinted to the police which jeweler might profitably be questioned about the secret sale of other gems in the past few months.

Laure's hopes of catching a glimpse of Stephen before they left for Baden faded. After all, it was better if she didn't see him again. Not after he had dismissed her with such insulting indifference. . . . Perhaps he had charged Marton or Jansci with a message for her?

For several days she paid unusual attention to every ragged Gypsy with his face concealed under a drooping hat, every beggar whose rags and sores might be a disguise, until Josef was driven to ask in exasperation whether she intended setting up a private charity for the waifs of the city.

"You would do better to spend your time making ready for out trip to Baden," he told her. "We leave in two days."

"Yes." Laure told herself that it could make no difference; if Stephen had wanted to get in touch with her, he had had ample opportunity already. But she counted out every hour of those last two days as if they were golden sovereigns slipping from her purse. Tuesday and Wednesday slipped away in the quiet pattern of visits, needlework, walks in the Prater. On Wednesday night the Mecklenburgs gave a small dance to celebrate Julie's engagement to Wilhelm. That was to be their last social engagement in the city.

The party started late, as was the custom in Vienna. They entered at eleven o'clock. From force of habit, Laure cast one glance round the room, looking for a tawny gold head and a pair of piercing blue eyes. But there was only the usual crowd of extravagantly décolleté society ladies, young girls in demure ruffles and officers whose gold braid and shining medals rivaled the jewels of the ladies. Laure's mouth drooped just a little. But she recovered herself sufficiently to say all that was proper to Frau Mecklenburg, who bustled up with apologies for the thinness of company and a smug smile on her lips that belied all the apologies. She knew it was an achievement to have gathered such a company so late in the season, and clearly expected Laure and Katya to appreciate her efforts in getting a crowd of Wilhelm's young friends to entertain them.

"And Prince Metternich said that he might look in later," she gushed, revealing her social trump card.

"Of course, we must not be too disappointed if he cannot stay for long. He will be working late, as usual. Pressure of affairs. . . ." She waved a plump hand, whose fingers almost disappeared under their weight of flashing rings. "But there, what do you young ladies care for such matters! You are here to dance and have a good time. Wilhelm is eager to open the dance with you, Julie, and Laure, let me introduce you to Fransl Greibacher. . . ."

Laure followed the kindly Frau Mecklenburg to the knot of young officers lounging against the piano, enjoying the irony that she actually had a better idea than Frau Mecklenburg of the affairs of state that occupied Metternich. Why, she could even visualize the study where he would be working. . . . The thought brought a brief smile to her lips, and several of the young officers thought that the sulky *Engländerin* might have some life in her after all and might be worth taking for a spin around the floor. And if those stories about her and Andrassy were true, she might well be amenable to a stroll in the garden as well. . . .

As the hour when Laure was meeting the Mecklenburgs' friends, Prince Metternich was indeed working late in his study. The light from a single lamp shed a golden pool of light over the broad surface of his leather-covered writing desk, now piled high with letters and dispatches from a dozen correspondents. The rest of the room was in deep shadow; only a glimmer of distant stars showed that the curtains were drawn back and the deep French windows thrown open to catch any vagrant cooling breeze.

Metternich worked busily through his pile of correspondence, his pen scratching as he dashed off curt orders to his employees—official and unofficial—in the city of Vienna and elsewhere. A letter to Antoinette von Leykam, the pretty bourgeoise who had recently caught the widower's eye, required more thought. He paused frequently to sharpen his pen, and more than once the ink dried on the tip of the pen while he sat with hand raised, pondering his words. Finally, the brief missive was completed. As he shook fine sand over the paper to dry the ink of his signature, one of the tall shadows by the French windows moved forward, into the circle of light.

Metternich reacted with the reflexes of a much younger man. Even as he spun round in his chair, his hand reached into the desk for the silver-mounted pistol that had been presented to him by the Duchess of Sagan. He faced the unknown intruder with a steady gaze, the pistol resting in his lap and half concealed by the folds of the cloak that he had earlier thrown over the arm of the chair.

Stephen Andrassy opened his arms wide to show that he carried no weapon.

"Not an assassin—this time," he remarked. And then, in the same casual tone, "What is it like, I wonder, to be hated by so many people that one assumes an assassin in every shadow? By the bye, your guards are careless, prince. I had no difficulty in getting past them."

Metternich relaxed, but he kept the pistol trained on his unexpected visitor. "It is not altogether unreasonable to suspect the motives of one who comes creeping through the windows, instead of calling at the door like an honest man," he countered.

Stephen laughed and threw up his hand to admit a hit. He was dressed from head to toe in black. In the half-darkness of the room, his features were indistinct: all that could be seen clearly was the gleam of his hair, strong white teeth showing momentarily when he laughed and the line of silver buttons down the front of his old-fashioned Hungarian tunic. Metternich trained the pistol on the third button from the top and waited.

"You have been something of a nuisance, my young friend," he said when Stephen volunteered no more explanation of his appearance there. "If you continue your somewhat unorthodox political career, you may learn what it is like to expect an assassin in every shadow. You will certainly make enemies enough!"

Stephen seated himself on the corner of the desk. "Yes. I think some of my methods may have been mistaken."

"Very generous acknowledgement," said Metternich. His tone was dry enough to have curled the paper of his letter at the edges.

"That is," Stephen corrected himself, "some of—Csikos's methods. I am not admitting for one minute that there is any connection—you understand me, prince? It might be more comfortable for us all if we agreed that Baron von Staunitz were indeed responsible for all of Csikos's actions."

"Difficult to sustain at a trial," Metternich pointed out.

"There will be no trial," Stephen said. "The baron has discovered urgent business on his estates in Prussia. He feels that the climate of Vienna might possibly be unhealthy for him in future."

"And would it?"

Stephen laughed softly, showing the gleam of white teeth beneath his mustache. "Oh, yes, prince. Most—

unhealthy." His hand dropped to his belt, where he would normally have worn a long, wickedly curved dagger.

Metternich opened a desk drawer behind him and dropped his pistol in without looking. "You begin to interest me. Do I understand that Csikos means to retire from public life?"

"I've a fancy to marry," Stephen answered obliquely. "If the lady will have me, I mean to retire to my estates and devote myself to improving them."

"Giving up the revolution? More wisdom than I expected!"

"Perhaps—pursuing it by other means," Stephen answered. "It might be worth something to you, perhaps, to guarantee the emperor that Csikos would not trouble him again?"

"The emperor has seized with almost indecent haste on Baron von Staunitz as the scapegoat for all his troubles," replied Metternich. "I should not be surprised if he laid the difficulties with the German states at the baron's door, as well as Csikos's actions and that string of jewel robberies. Still—." He stroked his chin. "It would be most unfortunate to trouble him with the news that Csikos had started his activities again. Perhaps Count Andrassy needs something to keep him busy. I shall recommend to the emperor that you be granted a license to import English blood horses for the purpose of establishing Hungarian breeding stables." He turned back to the desk, dipped his pen in the inkwell and scribbled a brief note in his memorandum book. "By the way," he asked without looking up, "do I know the lady?"

"You do," Stephen replied. "Miss Standish."

"Ah. Good. You are a tardy suitor, my friend.

When it was put about that Miss Standish's visit to the country had included a stop at the Andrassy estate, it was expected that Count Andrassy would appear soon afterward to pay his respects in form." Metternich sprinkled sand over the note and looked over his shoulder at Stephen. "Of course, I understand that there might have been a certain—awkwardness— attached to Count Andrassy's reappearance in the city before certain little matters were cleared up."

"There might indeed," Stephen agreed. "One does not make a good proposal from one of the emperor's prisons."

"Precisely." Metternich closed his memorandum book with a snap and leaned back in his chair. "You understand, my rash young friend, that I am moved to help you as much for Miss Standish's *beaux yeux* as for any political considerations. There are other avenues open for dealing with Csikos—avenues that remain open to me, should that irresponsible person cause any more trouble."

Stephen bent his head in acquiescence. "I think we understand one another, prince. Csikos has retired permanently. It is not time for him yet—and when the time comes, there will be no need for him. You and all that you represent will one day be swept away by the tide of freedom."

"I shall live in fear and trembling," Metternich replied. He reached into the enameled box that stood beside his inkstand and riffled through a stack of cards, eventually withdrawing one which he handed to Stephen. "Take this, my friend. You will have more use for it tonight than I."

Stephen looked at the card of invitation to the Mecklenburgs' ball, first with confusion and then with a growing comprehension lighting his face. "I should

304

make haste if I were you," Metternich added. "They leave for Baden tomorrow."

Stephen tossed the card in the air and caught it again as he sprang from the desk. "You are twice generous, prince—and this is the better of your gifts!"

"One word more."

Stephen halted with one boot already resting on the low sill of the window.

Metternich coughed and shuffled his stack of papers. "You are not, of course, to take this as any— concession—to Csikos's outrageous demands," he said. "That is why I tell you now—so that you will understand it as an instance of the emperor's loving care and paternal concern for all his people. You are not to think that he has yielded to political pressure of any sort. I assure you, the arguments of the Archduke Palatine have had far more weight with him than your inconsiderate and annoying games."

Stephen waited, scarcely daring to breathe.

At length, Metternich spoke again. "The Hungarian Diet is to be convened in September of this year."

Stephen gave an exuberant shout and tossed his hat in the air. It fluttered drunkenly on a stray breeze and came down on the head of a Roman statue in the corner. "The beginning!" His face was transformed. "I shall speak at the diet, Prince."

"Somehow," Metternich said dryly, "I felt sure you would."

"And my first speech shall be to offer a year's income from my estates to support education in the Magyar language."

"Before or after you build up the estates?"

But Metternich's question was addressed to the empty air. Stephen had vanished as suddenly as he came.

"Impetuous, these young fools," he murmured to the Roman statue. "Rash, impatient—." He sighed. "I wish I had half his energy!"

He trimmed the wick of the lamp and bent over his papers once again.

Laure made a valiant effort to appear bright and cheerful at Julie's engagement party, but with each hour that passed the effort was greater. The behavior of Wilhelm Mecklenburg's friends did not make her task any easier. At first she was flattered by their attention, but her feelings soon changed as one after another spun her around the room for one dance or even less, only to give her hand a meaningful press and suggest that a stroll in the garden would be delightful on such a warm evening. From dreading the departure to Baden on the morrow, Laure was rapidly coming to look forward to it as her only rescue from an eternity of unwelcome solicitations. The young men of Vienna might not wish to marry an indiscreet English girl, but all too many of them were all too eager to further their acquaintance with her.

Laure turned aside the first few hints tactfully enough, explaining to one young sprig that she was really too fatigued to walk farther than the nearest chair, to a second that she would not dream of missing a moment of this delightful party and sending a third to procure her a glass of the iced claret cup. But by the time she was cornered by Friedrich, Wilhelm Mecklenburg's younger brother, she was fast running out of excuses and tact. Nor was Friedrich the sort to accept a tactful excuse. He had spent the earlier part of the evening drinking with his friends before condescending to grace this insipid engagement party, and he now intended to demonstrate his manhood before those same friends by carrying off the fair English girl with that appealing hint of scandal about her name.

After an energetic galop, Friedrich did not return Laure to the chaperones' corner, but backed her into a corner near the windows, where his actions were somewhat screened by a row of potted plants brought in as decoration for the dance. Laure's laughing protests became sharper as it became evident that Friedrich really did not mean to let her go without some victory to boast about. Her eyes scanned the ballroom. Where was Josef? Nowhere to be seen; and as for Julie, she and her Wilhelm had long since found their own discreet corner. The band was already playing a brisk polka that thoroughly engaged the attention of the dancers, and a scream would only raise the sort of scandal she could not afford.

"Come now, pretty *Engländerin.*" Friedrich leaned one arm against the wall and looked down her low-cut corsage. "One kiss, to show all we're friends, and no hard feelings—eh!"

"I shall certainly not kiss you," Laure said. "You're drunk!"

Friedrich looked hurt. But what might have been passed off at that point became an ugly situation, as his friends, already annoyed by Laure's unjustifiable standoffishness, decided to join in teasing the snappish *Engländerin.*

"Then kiss me—I'm not drunk!" suggested one.

"Or me—or me!" joined in a chorus of voices. They ringed themselves round her in a semicircle, laughing and holding out their hands as if encircling her in a children's game.

"Run, pretty one," one of them teased. "I'd be happy to catch you!"

"A kiss all round, and call it quits," suggested

another. "What the devil right have you to be so standoffish—eh? You were friendly enough with Andrassy. Going to choose a damned Hungarian over an Austrian gentleman?"

Over the noise of the polka, there was the click of bootheels across Frau Mecklenburg's polished dance floor. A black-clad arm broke into the circle and pushed one of the young officers aside so violently that he stumbled into the support of a potted palm. A second fell the other way, pushing his friends into the wall, and a fair-haired figure in black tunic and pantaloons appeared in the gap thus violently made.

He bowed to Laure as if her circle of tormentors did not exist. "My dance, I think." His eyes flashed once across the remaining officers. "I take it that these gentlemen were just leaving?"

The question needed no answer. Stephen had only to look around the circle to dissolve it. None of the young officers was eager to test the courage of Count Andrassy. One by one, stammering excuses, they sidled away.

"Wouldn't have let him get away with it if he was an Austrian," Laure heard Friedrich excusing himself as he slipped away. "But—a damned Hungarian! Probably want to fight me then and there, with his knife. No notion of proper conduct, those fellows."

"Right," his friend agreed. "Fellow's not really a gentleman."

Stephen stood before Laure, a faintly questioning smile on his face, as if waiting for her verdict.

"He was quite right, you know," she said, putting her hand on his arm. "You are no gentleman, but only a common bandit."

Stephen smiled. "No. Csikos is retired. Prince Metternich and I are agreed on that much."

Laure breathed out an almost imperceptible sigh of relief. For all Stephen's bold entrance, she had been half-expecting to see him denounced by an agent of the secret police before he left the ballroom.

"And now," he continued, "I am free to make a certain business proposition to you, which I could not mention before."

"Business!" Laure felt as if her world had turned upside down. Stephen was back, at the last minute, and smiling at her with that tender look in his eyes—and he wanted to talk about business?

"I am to be granted a license to import horses from England," he informed her.

Laure recovered a little of her spirit. "If so, I'm sure it was because it was the only way Metternich could think to keep you out of trouble!"

Stephen laughed. "There were words to that effect. . . . Well? Do you want to hear my proposition?"

Laure tapped her foot in time to the dance music and looked away.

"I shall tell you, anyway. You see, this importing business will require that I make frequent trips to England, in between the months I spend in Hungary. I shall require a partner who speaks English and can help me with my business there. But my partner would also be required to spend time with me on the *puszta* and in the surrounding villages. There is so much work to be done among the peasants!" Stephen pretended to sigh. "It is a long task, to build a nation—a task that could take years. The only way I know to secure such a dedicated partner is—to marry her."

Laure looked up through a mist of tears and saw Stephen's smile broaden. "If she'll have me?" he whispered.

Laure raised her hands to his shoulders. "Oh, Stephen. How could you tease me so?"

"Shh! All your friends are watching."

Laure glanced over her shoulder and encountered the indignant gaze of Frau Mecklenburg.

Stephen gently placed her hand on his arm again. "Perhaps we should take a turn in the garden."

Josef, returning from the cardroom, caught sight of Laure as she was slipping out of the room with her hand in Stephen's. "Shameless!" he said to no one in particular. "That does it. She'll find no more shelter in my house! Let her go and live with this Andrassy, if she's no more sense than to run to him whenever he whistles."

As it happened, the two lovers in the garden, locked in an embrace under the benevolent gaze of a stone cupid, had already come to the same conclusion.

Historical Note

For a story involving the first stirrings of Hungarian nationalism in the nineteenth century, I have borrowed a number of the actions and sayings of a real Hungarian patriot, Stephen Széchenyi, for my hero. Stephen Andrassy's comment about the foolishness of the English king, his proposals to improve Hungarian horse breeding, and his offer of a year's income for the establishment of an institution for cultivating the Hungarian language are all drawn directly from the life of Stephen Széchenyi. The story about Andrassy and the eleven thousand virgins was told of Stephen Széchenyi by his sister.

The checkered career of Stephen Andrassy resembles that of Széchenyi in no other respects than these few borrowings. He is not intended as a thinly disguised portrait of Széchenyi, but rather as what a somewhat younger and more hotheaded man might have become, holding Széchenyi's opinions, in the political climate of the time.

Tapestry

HISTORICAL ROMANCES

Breathtaking New Tales

of love and adventure set against
history's most exciting time and
places. Featuring two novels by the
finest authors in the field of romantic fiction—every month.

Next Month From
Tapestry Romances

DESTINY'S EMBRACE
by Sheryl Flournoy
FIELDS OF PROMISE
by Janet Joyce

POCKET BOOKS

Home delivery from Pocket Books

Here's your opportunity to have fabulous bestsellers delivered right to you. Our free catalog is filled to the brim with the newest titles plus the finest in mysteries, science fiction, westerns, cookbooks, romances, biographies, health, psychology, humor—every subject under the sun. Order this today and a world of pleasure will arrive at your door.

POCKET BOOKS, Department ORD
1230 Avenue of the Americas, New York, N.Y. 10020

Please send me a free Pocket Books catalog for home delivery

NAME _____

ADDRESS _____

CITY _____ STATE/ZIP _____

If you have friends who would like to order books at home, we'll send them a catalog too—

NAME _____

ADDRESS _____

CITY _____ STATE/ZIP _____

NAME _____

ADDRESS _____

CITY _____ STATE/ZIP _____